LAYOVER

LAYOVER

A NOVEL

Lisa Zeidner

RANDOM HOUSE / NEW YORK

RANDOM HOUSE and colophon are registered trademarks of Random House, Inc.

Library of Congress Cataloging-in-Publication Data
Zeidner, Lisa.
Layover / Lisa Zeidner.—1st ed.
p.   cm.
ISBN 0-375-50286-6 (alk. paper)
I. Title.
PS3576.E37L39   1999   813' .54—dc21   98-53463

Random House website address: www.atrandom.com
Printed in the United States of America on acid-free paper
2 4 6 8 9 7 5 3
First Edition

Book design by J. K. Lambert

For Ross Feld

Love is giving something you haven't got
to someone who doesn't exist.

—*Jacques Lacan*

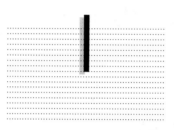

packed for homelessness the way I would pack for a week in Europe—wrinkle-free, in a carry-on. Traveling light is easy in summer. Everything I owned that year seemed to be beige or gray, the palette of Roman tombstones, and airy enough to dry in a breeze, or by fan in a windowless hotel bathroom. The homeless people in cities pushing shopping carts, with their splayfooted, third-trimester walks: I saw no need to be manacled to my past, weighed down by it, when I had so little left. I floated away with no regrets. By then I was a ghost in my own life anyway.

I had no plan. The first time, I simply missed a flight. I'd been traveling for business, and had taken to packing a bathing suit for hotel pools in Scranton, Pittsburgh, Philadelphia. On weekdays, midmorning, the dollhouse-sized pools were always empty, like sets from moody foreign films. No flirting, no kids. I tried to do enough laps to lose count.

People kept telling me to take advantage of the gyms. Even the hotel clerks praised the equipment, always confidential and leering, as if sharing the address of the local S and M joint. I knew exactly the kind of men I could find bench-pressing there, but I didn't want to socialize with them or with anyone else. I just wanted the freedom not to think. The chlorine felt soothingly medicinal. And one day I swam too long, missed a plane.

Only when I was back in my room, in the shower, did I wonder about the time, but I didn't rush. Even when I saw that it was too late to get to the airport, I didn't panic. My trajectory was infinitely adjustable.

This is not the attitude I had been encouraged to cultivate in sales. But for some time I had been silently recalibrating my attitude toward my job. My "career" was old enough, rooted enough, to be allowed to grow or not on its own, as my child would have done if my child hadn't died. I was not less involved with work *because* my child died, though that's what everyone thought—I felt their edgy tolerance, their benevolence and the predictable backlash from their benevolence, their confidence that they were cutting me some slack even when I was performing perfectly well.

So now I told no one who didn't already know. There wasn't anything to say, unless I wanted to discuss theology with strangers in airport lounges, meditate on whether one could find meaning in the statistics of highway fatalities, and I wanted to do this so little that when forced to discuss family status, I lied: I had a grown son in college, and was suffering from a mild case of empty-nest syndrome.

He was at Brown. He didn't know his major yet. If pressed, I would add that he played tennis. If I'd had children at the old-fashioned time, right out of college myself, my son *would* have been college-aged.

Nothing was repressed. My husband, Kenneth, and I had clocked in the requisite hours in therapy, singly and collectively, cupping the coal of grief in burned hands, fanning our grief as it turned to ash. The therapist was a tall man with very bad vision. I could barely see his eyes through his glasses, and their magnified, amniotic softness was oddly comforting. I thought of him, sometimes, while swimming. I could still summon forth his number on my laptop, and had been told I could call him whenever I needed to talk.

But at the time, I felt fine. I called the airline, changed the flight. Still numbly tingling from swim and shower, I lay down, fell asleep.

In retrospect, I understand that my bodily clock must have already been off, the battery low or spring overwound. Since there was no reason to hurry back, to snatch a child from day care, I'd revised how I set up appointments—eliminated some return trips so I could go straight from city to city, make my days less crammed. Avoid airport rushes. Swim in the morning and nap until checkout time, or not even sleep but just drift, waiting to be hungry enough for lunch.

That day, however, I slept past checkout. The maid came in her white uniform, like a nurse. Waking, I took the hotel room for a hospital room, cringed from her tray full of hypodermics and ministrations.

I knew Ignatia from three years of business in that city, that hotel. She knew about my son. We'd actually had a scene—this was earlier, when I would still confess, because I still cried unexpectedly—when I told her about the accident and she held me, smelling of gardenia and ammonia. Then pulled out a snapshot of her grandchildren, identifying each by name and age, which I thought was interesting. Most people will try so hard not to mention their own families, and you can feel their pride to be so restrained in the face of your bad luck, but she seemed to feel it would help me to witness her abundance. "What was boy's name?" she asked. I told her. She repeated it, smiled, and never mentioned him to me again. But she was always cheerful.

I must have looked stricken. "Oh Miss, is okay," she assured me. "Sleepy," I apologized, and she said, "Oh, yes. Work hard," meaning I did, she did, or both. Then she backed herself and her cart out of the room, nodding.

Her wordless concern felt almost psychic, as if she knew about Ken, forgave him for his perfectly understandable little affair as I did, but realized that I needed some extra solicitude.

She must not have alerted the desk that I was still there. Nor did I. When I reached the lobby early that evening, the clerks were busy. I slipped my electronic key card into my purse and left. There was no thought of avoiding the charge for the extra day. But I knew instantly that I wouldn't be charged.

I was a hard-core wage earner of the type hotel ads target. My husband was a cardiothoracic surgeon. My wallet was a garden of credit cards budding possibility, the holographic birds' wings glinting as if poised for flight. No one would ever suspect me of fraud, though I knew enough about the rhythms of that hotel, the staffs' frenzies and downtimes, the secret pockets, to take advantage.

O ver the next week I found myself returning to this idea as I made my appointments and did my rounds, greeting housekeepers and clerks cordially as I had for the years I'd covered this territory selling medical equipment. Across a swath of country, defined as a brewing storm on a weather map, hotel clerks were friendly enough to say, "Ken called to see if you'd gotten in. Said it was urgent." And I could retort, "No pot roast tonight," though Ken had always been the cook in our family; he liked dishes where he got to wantonly chop and toss, as antidote to the precision of surgery. I could wave to the plainclothes detective in the lobby who was reading, just to be inconspicuous, the latest issue of *Security Management,* with revealing articles on methods for controlling "access-related incidents" that result in "guest property loss."

Dollars and frequent-flier miles accrued. I was on the up-and-up, a true friend to "the lodging industry." But more and more often, I seemed to be neglecting to return my card to the desk, until I'd developed quite a collection—pathetic, like people who save restaurant matchbooks.

Meanwhile, I'd begun to sleep later and later, until I was doing appointments in the morning and early afternoon, taking a siesta, and swimming in hotel pools at ten, eleven at night. Then midnight. (The posted signs prohibited this, but at that hour there were no pool police.) Calling room service at 2:00 AM, checking my voice mail at dusk.

Ken: "Where are you?" Ken: "I called Pittsburgh, just for fun." Flirtatious ("I'd send flowers, if you gave me a target state") and weary ("I am not amused"). In each call, hospital pages as background drone, steady as surf. I could imagine his bloody hands emerging from a rib cage as he rushed to answer my page. I'd interrupted surgery when I went into labor, and it was still seductive, romantic, to picture that pried-apart chest being abandoned, Ken storming into Labor and Delivery still sporting his mask and butcher's smock. How much time the both of us have spent in hospitals! The smell of it clung to us, not sanitized at all, but tacky, tumescent: the blood, the piss, the smoke in lobbies and bathrooms.

Every day I left a reassuring message. No need to torture him. But no need to discuss it, either. In fact, there didn't appear to be any need to speak with anyone. Between fax and voice mail, I could go about my rounds invisibly, like the Wizard of Oz. Why board the plane, take the shuttle to the rental car, endure the running totals and ticket lines? Would it be possible to just stay still and concentrate—Tantric sales?

What mainly stopped me was the fact that, after eight days, my husband had thought to trace my itinerary through my credit card use. I'd been leaving my messages on the home answering machine when I knew he'd be on rounds, but he was persistent, and when he dialed at 3:00 AM, hoping I'd just pick up groggily, I did, because I was waiting for a cheeseburger and beer from room service, and it had been a while.

"Hey," Ken said, aiming for breeziness.

"Ken, what's wrong?"

"What's *wrong*? You tell me."

I didn't answer fast enough. "I should never have said anything, okay?" he went on. "But Christ, I was falling apart. It's not like—"

"It's fine, Ken," I said, sincerely.

"In what sense? In what sense is it 'fine'? I called Kramer. This is a stage, remember? He warned us. Like quitting smoking—you think it's done, you think you're safe. You're fuguing out. I mean, what do you need, retaliation? Go for it. But it won't help."

"Sex?" I said, too surprised to get the words out: "Is that what you—?" So Kenneth winced to envision hotel couplings, soothingly anonymous. Maybe that's what he'd sought at his convention of cardiologists, though my impression was that he'd known the woman from his undergraduate days, and that their lighthearted reunion seemed like a promising way to suture past and future, chop out the unpleasant present. I understood that he never intended to bypass me. He just hoped to thrust his way past the accident's impact, the twisted tin. For him it was not a memory. He was not there. Still. The infant in the car seat hardly bloody, but no heartbeat. *Never meant to throw baby out with bathwater* was what I was thinking, what I couldn't work into a sentence, *an unfortunate phrase under the circumstances,* and also, still astonished, *sex?*

The best way I could summarize was "I love you. I'll be home soon."

"When?"

"Get some sleep," I said, and went to open the door.

A college kid doing a summer job nodded to me with the skepticism due a lone woman who orders room service in the middle of the night. (After aerobic sex, I'd presumably deserve to carbo-load.) Someone's son, with huge feet in sneakers like futuristic barges. His white uniform jacket was pointedly small, to stress that the hotel was by no means his real life. He wheeled in the cart and used a Chaplinesque flourish to remove the metal lid from the plate, grinning with a mime's delight at the burger. I smiled back, tipped him.

Fact is, I loved the tin lid with its eye like a porthole, the cloth napkin, the carnation in the bud vase. I loved room service even when the food was tepid, the napkin reeked of ammonia. The failures were almost touching. My encounters with clerks and bellboys made me feel weirdly spiritual, as if we were preparing to rise to the occasion of flood or famine, to transcend the provincial louts we mostly were in daily life.

Especially with the housekeepers. Tips aside, I had a real rapport with them. Like them, I knew how it felt to make other people's beds. And I knew how to use the little Spanish I had—not to insult them with hello or thank you, as if they couldn't recognize those words in English, but if I needed something specific: hand cream, thread. Maybe I credited them with too much insight, but I sensed that many of the housekeepers, even the very young ones, recognized me as a fellow exile, someone on the lam from tragedy, grateful to humbly enter and exit my compartment of the honeycomb.

S o it felt like fate that the next day saw me back at Ignatia's hotel.

At the reception desk, I was greeted by an impressive packet of messages. Multiple, out-of-date inquiries from my husband. One from Kramer, licensed therapist, assigned to case and chase along with my brother, who had already left the phone number of his place in Maine on my pager, which I'd been mostly ignoring, because of Ken. Thus I hadn't gotten word from the day's main client, canceling due to a family emergency.

"Know what?" I said to the clerk processing my check-in. "I don't need to be here."

He laughed. "Stood up?"

"Yup. Footloose and fancy free in Cincinnati."

"You could check out the Air Force Museum in Dayton."

"Thanks for the tip. Why don't I just check out, period."

He laughed as he returned my credit card.

I headed toward the bathroom, and once out of sight of the desk, toward the stairs. Went up one flight, grabbed a couple of towels from a housekeeping cart in the hallway, and took the elevator up. The pool was mine. I draped a towel over my suitcase, briefcase, and laptop case for protection, pulled out my bathing suit (still damp) from its suitcase pocket, and quickly stripped.

Once safely in the bathing suit I folded my skirt, rolled my panty-hose into one shoe and tucked my watch in the other, put the shoes under the chair, and hung the suit jacket over the back, where it looked oddly exhilarating.

I swam until I got company. In a spasm, by spontaneous gener-ation, an extended family—sisters, their brood, in town for a wed-ding. "No splashing!" one mother warned, shooting me the veiled look—part apology, part defiance—that women use to gauge each other's tolerance for children.

As soon as it was polite, I took off, trying to grab my clothes and computer like a carefree person and not a fugitive.

On the fire stair I paused to slip my pumps on bare feet. With my computer case strapped over my shoulder sari-style and my wet bathing suit, I looked like some genetic experiment gone awry, Miss Universe crosshatched with an insurance salesman.

Ignatia was on the fifth floor, nonsmoking. From the end of the hall, I watched her wheel her cart into a room that was often mine. I followed.

"Good morning!" I said, laying my computer down on the desk as if it belonged there.

"Oh, hi, not finished, so sorry," she said, handing me a dry towel from the cart.

"No problem, take your time."

I collapsed on one of the chairs, put my feet on the bed. Ignatia checked the list on her cart. "You here, in this room, you are sure?" she asked.

"No," I said.

"Sorry?"

"I'm nowhere. Not checked in."

She shrugged to indicate that she didn't understand.

The night before, after Ken's call, I'd conducted a database search about hotel security. For all the updated electronic lock systems, it appeared that master keys abounded on the black market and that, furthermore, anyone could walk into any room being cleaned, interrupt and say, "I have to use the bathroom right now." Officially, staff would demand to see the intruder's room key or ID, but most housekeepers didn't feel they were paid enough to be guards. So, technology aside, it was still just like Cary Grant slipping into the imaginary FBI agent's hotel room in *North by Northwest*. You could march right up, rifle through another man's jacket pockets. I wanted no cameras or cash; I just wanted to lie down on Little Bear's bed, like Goldilocks.

"Just need to dry off," I told Ignatia. "Take a nap, then I'm catching a plane. I won't stay."

She gave me an appraising look. "No work?"

"Not today."

"Husband good?"

"Oh, he's fine, Ignatia."

"How long?"

"Just a couple of hours."

"No. Poor little boy."

"Oh, it's not that. I just—"

"Young," she said, pointing to my belly. "Don't worry. Home better. Travel no good—" she made gentle circles in the air, then scattered them, to indicate the pregnancy I was failing to achieve, because frequent travel was throwing off my menstrual cycles.

I laughed. I couldn't help it. She was right, of course. I had the circadian rhythms of a cicada.

"Rest," she said, "but then go home. Airplane, hotel—air no good."

"That's true, Ignatia."

As she swept by me to change the sheets, I stood up to help her. This time she laughed. "No pay is good you help," she said, and we stood on opposite sides of the bed to unfold the blank flag of a sheet together.

I stayed in the Cincinnati hotel for two-and-a-half days, one in that room, which had not been booked again after I changed my mind. The next day I watched a man down the hall leave his room—I'd stayed in that room before too, and just happened to have the key in my collection. The articles forewarned that hotel management sometimes neglects to rekey when a key card is not returned to them, especially in smaller, less computerized establishments. So if the room happens not to have been rented in the interim, you're made in the shade. This man, however, was encumbered by so much luggage that he did not even manage to click the door shut behind him.

I hung the DO NOT DISTURB sign on the doorknob, ate a couple of pieces of toast that my predecessor had left from breakfast and drank the last bit of lukewarm coffee from his personal pot, checked his bed for hair.

Ignatia came in the following morning and shook her head at me with a parent's firm concern. "You clean up and go," she ordered, and I did as she said.

The timing was perfect, as the client who had stood me up earlier in the week was now back at her desk after her father's double bypass, delighted with the variety and vigor of her daily life in the way that only visiting hospitals as a healthy person can make you.

As I walked past the reception desk and waved—the clerk only had time to look momentarily mystified—I thought, as I did more and more often, about Hitchcock, about the scene from *Psycho* where Janet Leigh, moments after stealing from the boss who trusted her, takes a pedestrian crossing and looks up to see the selfsame mystified boss, through the windshield of his car. It occurred to me that I was turning into the kind of woman who could show up dead in a motel or at the bottom of a lake, eyes open, skin translucent as a tadpole's.

But the thought wasn't alarming. Before the accident, I'd worried much more about death. In fact, every time a plane lifted off or landed, I'd had to clench eyes and stomach against the vision of a motherless son, my lovely boy feeling cheated forever because I'd left him rather than letting him decide to leave me, as is every child's right. I could understand the Nazi commanders who shot their wives and children. In the ideal world, all families would die together, in a row, tidy bullet holes in their heads. I understood even then, even without Kramer's gentle help, that much of the fear was guilt, self-punishment, because it felt so good to peel him off me at day care and board that plane, to sit alone in the seat and be allowed to let my thoughts drift, untethered.

After the accident, I had much less to fear. I could walk on nails, eat fire, explode, or be garroted—nothing would ever hurt as much again.

Still, in the tinny, rattling rental cars I drove for work, to and from airports and hospitals, I felt about as safe as I would curled up in a tin can with the lid cut off, the kind children use to make fake telephones. It was on highways, dodging obnoxious drivers in their sport utility vehicles, their Suburbans—all of their fake signs of strength and bounty—that I most often felt really bad.

Airports were easier. I liked the impersonal bustle, the pro-grammed security of gates. Except that air travel, of course, had been getting more difficult. The waits longer, the rows of seats more crammed. More screaming babies.

It had been becoming harder, on planes, to feel serene, buffered. I used to remember to take my vitamins—C against plane flu, E for dry skin—when the flight attendants brought the drink carts, until I had to stop that; it opened up too many con-versations with chirpy-bird seatmates, all of whom wanted to sing Prozac's praises, hold hands with strangers and make a Xanax cir-cle. After almost fifteen years in sales, I could spot, and avoid, the garrulous manic-depressive men with their needy eyes, their onward-and-upward narratives. They were like flat tires, the drugs like those cans of air you're supposed to keep in your trunk. Not even a patch, just a fart's-worth of air to get them a couple of yards down the road.

My technique: I told them early on that my husband was a sur-geon. If I said the word *surgeon* first and then quickly, before they could ask, *cardiothoracic,* they would almost always nod as they vis-ibly deflated, then leave me alone.

This was necessary, I assured myself, but it did make me feel mean. And certainly *unfeminine,* to be so uncaring about a male ego. But I was no longer, in some sense, even a woman. I'd buried myself in work as a man would—it is a good idea, nothing to sneeze at—and rejected everything frilly, decorative. So I was no longer fragile. In fact, I felt almost armor-plated, and that's a shame, because grief at least ought to make you empathetic.

"You're lucky," my neighbor declared—undeterred by my hus-band's status, he'd extracted the empty-nest story. "The boys are much, much better than the girls. Give 'em the car keys and they're out of your life. You just have to worry about AIDS. The girls wanna hang around and torture you. Teenage girls, man. God's scourge. What are they sticking you for tuition?"

Invented son, invented sum. Before I could even utter the amount, he'd added, outraged, *and that's after-tax dollars,* as I could have predicted. To him I had to be aggressively rude. Extracting the laptop wouldn't deter him, since all frequent flyers now have computer come-ons and software bonding; for a female traveler, a laptop is as loud as a red bra spotted sideways through an unbuttoned blouse.

"Truth is," I said, "my son is dead. So I'd rather not discuss him or your kids or your feelings about parenthood, if that's all right with you," which did the trick. He reared back, put both hands up palm forward like a traffic cop, and I did feel a little bad, then, to see his watery eyes in the headlights of the speeding big rig he now saw me as.

On a crisp evening in mid-May, after dinner, I had been just about to take a shower—felt I needed one, after having grilled tuna and cleaned up—when Ken stuck his head into the bathroom and commanded, "Put that dress back on. And come outside."

He had changed into a bathing suit. Did not seem quite warm enough for that. From his urgent tone I assumed there was a problem. Raccoons in the trash. "Not those," he added, pointing to my underpants. He led me out into our fenced backyard and looked for the place where we would not be exposed in the glare of the neighbor's harsh garage floodlights. Chose a tree to lean me up against.

I appreciated this. The dark felt good and so did the air, just the right temperature. The dark, and the air, seemed related to the perfect meal we'd just enjoyed, which I could still taste in his kiss—a Beaujolais at the peak of its short life's curve; the fish precisely pink. His hand went right under the dress with its cheerful floral print to find me wet. This is all a terrible cliché, I am fully aware, but hey, so is spring.

He pushed up the dress so we could get a little chest-on-chest action. Me on tiptoe to reach the tall man's mouth. "Turn around," he instructed. I did, the tree providing a branch at the right height to grasp.

I thought this was all very good of Ken, who had had a particularly arduous day. I tried not to be too alert for the slam of the refrigerator door in the neighbor's kitchen, the high school kids down the block clattering out for some one-on-one on the asphalt. Or too distracted, when I opened my eyes, by the tulips—headless, already goners—in the elaborately terraced bed that Ken had gotten planted, in the spot that had held our son's climbing apparatus, which Ken had gotten taken down and put in a remote corner of the basement, packed up tight as a tent, ready for the new child whom we had thus far failed to conceive.

At the time, I was not thinking these things. Was merely aware, as how could I not be, that he was making an effort to do things my way. "Naturally." As opposed to by the instructions of one of his esteemed colleagues, who had recommended six months of birth-control pills to regulate my irregularities, followed by a six-month "holding pattern" of elaborate record-keeping, then a program of fertility drugs that might, he warned—talking as doctors often do to women, even to doctors' wives—"make you a little nutsy."

Just what I needed.

I had hated birth-control pills when I was young, and dating. They gave me headaches; they made me dry. These were, I understood, minor side effects, especially for a woman who had lost what might well turn out to be her last viable reproductive years to a trance of grief. But the irony felt like the bridge too far: I was supposed to take birth-control pills *now*, in middle age, in order to get pregnant?

So I appreciated what Ken was doing. No calendar. Just trees, stars, and a wife taking it from behind, ass glowing in moonlight.

It would befit the occasion for me to come efficiently, exuberantly. But I could tell that was not going to happen. Ken would certainly do what was required. The man always cottoned to a *project*. Eventually there would be some kind of release. Many of my orgasms, however, had had a distant, thrumming, Novocained quality. Almost not worth the trouble.

I'd basically decided to fake it. Not exactly lie; no prostitutional theatrics. Simply not to have my eyes on that particular prize. Just to enjoy the night, the air, my husband's unexpected ardor. ("It's the thought that counts.")

But Ken surprised me. He stopped, pulled out. Turned me around by my waist and got me draped the way he wanted me on the tree, one hand thoughtfully behind my back to keep the bark from abrading me. Then just began to work on me with his other hand, staring at me almost sternly, the eye contact a challenge: *Concentrate!* I did, best I could. Then surprised myself by coming in a smooth parabola that put me in mind of how perfectly cooked tuna separates when you hit it with a fork, those striated curves.

I was pretty pleased for us. We could have been any old couple, doing the yeoman's work of keeping desire alive—bent over to shovel coal into the damn thing. Marriage like an old-fashioned train. Huffing and puffing, little engines that could.

As Ken finished I said, in gratitude, "Very nice." Then, in the way of the praise any man deserves, especially a middle-aged one, "You been practicing? Bonin' up?"

And he responded, voice cracking, "Only once."

This was the special moment that my husband selected to reveal to me that he had been unfaithful.

Unbelievable, really. I mean, he was still inside me.

I thought I had misheard. But no, he pulled his bathing suit up for a halting confession that was going to include the date and place of the regretted betrayal. "I'm—" he said. "God, I'm so—"

I straightened up. As one would expect. Dress falling back into position. Stared at him. Said, "Thanks for sharing."

At this point he began to yell at me. He was sorry. *But.* My sarcasm typical, etc.

What he said then, and what he revealed in the series of painful conversations we would subsequently have, in which he'd carom from apology to anger, either thanking me profusely for being reasonable or enumerating the occasions on which I had failed to show proper feeling, I could not say. The only accusation that stuck was *fucking zombie.*

Back inside, my work phone was ringing. I heard the answering machine pick up in the den, then the tone that indicated an incoming fax. I stopped in the kitchen to get a Kleenex, to wipe the sperm that had dripped out onto my inner thigh. No Kleenex. Box empty. Used a paper towel. Before I could get to the fax machine, another beep, less familiar. I went in to find the document cut off, incomplete, and a message: "Paper roll empty."

This failure was what made me cry. Or it just hit me then, in a time lag, what Ken had said. Or both.

One of my posttraumatic-stress symptoms had to do with fax machines. Ken knew about it. I did not like to load fax paper. I did not like the oily feel of fax paper, the smell. The car accident that took my son's life had happened on a not-too-busy street less than five miles away, when a housewife—not drunk, not even speeding—turned right on red legally and went into a skid in a light rain. I had just picked up my son from day care and was coming from Staples with a bag full of home office supplies. A box of fine-point felt-tip pens. Post-its. Thermal fax paper—there is a deeply ungratifying purchase.

Ken came in the room and put his arms around me, stroked my hair, murmuring apologies, while the phone fired again, as whoever it was attempted to resend the aborted message. Then tried again.

He led me out of the room and closed the door, so I didn't have to listen.

The next day he managed to find time to leave the hospital and buy me a plain-paper fax machine, so I would never again have to load thermal paper through that guillotinelike aperture. Over dinner told me all about how he had made his consumer choice, the various available features, how much the plain paper copiers had come down in price. This was not an evasion. In our marital tug-of-war, in fact, it represented a gesture of goodwill, that he was not going to be "pushy" about us confronting the issues, parsing out blame.

Still, it was annoying. Ken tended to spend money at emotional junctions. His purchases were often smoke signals. This is not unusual, I suppose. Women get new haircuts; men buy small electronics. Cars and major appliances spell big trouble.

"Well, I am very touched," I told the man who, early in our courtship, had showed up at my doorstep with not roses but pans—he'd found my cooking equipment woefully inadequate. "I guess I should have figured out you were having an affair when you bought the espresso machine."

"If you'd been paying attention," he noted sourly.

I didn't want to even set foot there. We had been down that landmined road already. Up a good part of the night, in fact, numbly going over the timetable. His reasons, my reactions.

"Look, I've already officially forgiven you," I said. Had even made a joke of it, best I could—bad things happening in threes. This ought to do us. Satisfy our little family's quota for taking it up the ass.

" 'Officially,' yes."

"But it's going to take time, Ken."

"As opposed to everything else."

"Exactly like everything else."

"We should go back to Kramer. Help us talk it through."

"We can talk all you want," I said. "But it's still going to take time."

"*More* time."

"More time. Right."

"How much time do you think we've got?"

More than he could spare. Less than I needed. I just let it go. "I'm only saying, upgraded office equipment aside, I don't think we have much of an immediate future in Outdoor Copulation."

Which was a shame. I'd eventually taken my shower the night before, fishy and swollen-eyed from crying, to discover, hosing myself down, that despite the fresh trauma there was all sorts of stray sensation left. If Ken had managed to control the need to confess, he could have joined me there. Backyard, bathtub—Ken had the instincts, if not the follow-through. He had managed to make actual desire well up in me. It had not altogether subsided, even yet, in the bland hotel rooms. It was not, however, exactly attached to Ken. More free-floating.

I was sad about the dress. A cheap little flippy dress, machine-washable, but I'd liked it. I wasn't going to be eating tuna again for a while either. This had all been over two months ago. We were dealing with it now, along with everything else.

In Columbus, I pitched equipment to a dialysis lab, then went straight to my hotel. Took the elevator straight up to the room for which I'd saved a key card. It didn't work. No housekeepers were visible. One floor down, I stopped in front of the parked cart in the hallway. Poked my head in and waved to a young woman twitching a rag at the furniture.

"Hi," I said, wheeling my suitcase toward the closet. "Don't mind me. I'm just going to—"

"Haven't done in there yet," she warned.

"That's fine. I'll be right out. Just going to throw on my bathing suit."

She looked mildly puzzled, but not suspicious. I did my half-second pantomime of sisterly fatigue as I hung up my jacket. She smiled, said she'd come back.

A line you cross, a better sanity test, perhaps, than asking someone to recite the year, month, and current president: whether you will use a hotel soap that someone else has unwrapped, dry your face with a towel still damp and balled-up from use by a stranger. I'm not claiming that I was ready to eat the wrinkled tail ends of hot dogs resurrected from public garbage cans. But I felt no disgust toward the damp bathroom. If anything, I felt the smugness of the ecologically sound: why splatter the planet with that much

Clorox when some poor fellow had rushed out, as I had so often myself, right after his wake-up call?

The pool actually had a guard posted, checking key cards. I'd forgotten mine, but the woman on duty recognized me, and waved me through. "Is your husband up there?" she asked, to my surprise; turns out she was more concerned with my getting back into the room than with my marital status. Good point. I'd pulled the door shut. It seemed risky to pad around the hotel in a wet bathing suit, looking for a trusting housekeeper; risky as well to try the front desk. What was I doing?

I took the elevator straight to the basement, where I was pretty sure I'd find an airless employee lounge with vending machines and smokers on break. I was right. "Can I talk with you for a second?" I asked, poking my head in, to the woman closest to the door. She met me in the hallway. Not only was I locked out, I told her, locking my legs together beneath the towel, but I'd just gotten my period. Didn't really want to parade through the lobby dripping blood on the carpet. She grinned, and marched me right to the freight elevator. "Got what you need now?" she asked as she let me in, and I felt like hugging her.

Room service, obviously, was out of the question. And the door, it was clear, would lock automatically behind me. It took a good half hour of surreptitious fiddling with the mechanism to figure out how to jam it. I went to a place nearby with a newspaper. I hadn't bought it, incidentally. Part and parcel of my homelessness: I got my folded newspapers from the pockets of the airline seats in front of me, from lounges and lobbies. Still not from trash cans, but close. This is very different feeling from that of home delivery, the illusion that the whole world arrives at your doorstep at dawn. What scraps of news felt veiled, coded, as if they were meant for me alone, came to me like messages in bottles.

The article I read over pasta, from the Style section of *The Washington Post,* a stop on someone else's route, was about Tiny Tim of "Tiptoe Through the Tulips" fame. Now an old man, but still quixotically upbeat, he was staging his comeback from a boardinghouse room in Minneapolis, so poor he ate only beans from cans but still faithfully colored his flowing locks with Clairol. I took this as a cautionary tale that whatever I was doing, I would not be able to do it forever. But then that went without saying from the onset. The only question, really, was when it would end, and how.

S omething had begun to happen to me, so subtle that I had not even yet identified it, though I would later carbon-date it to the airport in Pittsburgh. I saw things about people, instantaneously. Especially at airports, where everyone was ripped from context, people's souls would glow phosphorescent, as if X-rayed by the baggage-check machine. Hot spots molten, clearly defined as keys or loose change.

At a gate, awaiting the boarding call, I would sit with my eyes trained on the crowds and watch people pass in suspended animation, frame by frame. In a flash I could tell who loved their wives, who loved their work. Who had gotten laid and who had just spent huge sums of company money in lieu of getting laid. Who was smart as a fox, who dumb as dirt. Who was lonely, empty, afraid. Almost everyone was afraid. Stunning, how much fear was out there. Not fear of anything tangible—danger or death—so much as a fear of being exposed, seen through.

People lurched or glided past like luggage coming down a conveyor belt. Some were threadbare, some spanking new. Many were hard to tell apart. At heart was a hunger to be claimed. To be *met*. By the human beings whose pictures you carry in your wallet. To not spin round the claim carousel, forlorn and unwanted. To not turn out to have missed your life as you'd miss a connecting flight.

Most people, if you yanked them from the throngs and sank your hand into their secrets as you'd search their luggage, you'd find—not much. Deodorant and a change of clothes. Pathetic. But there was, in the pathos, a kind of grim and shining truth. Once you knew, it could make you a misanthrope, or a Christian. You could hate mankind, or love it. But the harder reaction was to not judge them. That required not getting too distracted by the clutter of details. All the bumper stickers of identity, the neckties and hairstyles. All the tiny, useless keys jingling in the tiny, useless locks—all the craving and striving. You had to not be a foreman or general contractor but say: so people's identities are constructed like birds' nests. That frantic and fragile. So what? Most of the time, they manage to hold together.

From my plastic chair at the gate I could, if I chose, connect. I could make a friend, seduce a stranger, even pull out my cell phone and call my mother. My mother loved me! If I died, she'd cry! Occasionally a man passing would seem so startled by me, so drawn to my awareness matching his own, that we might pass, in some drama, as meant for each other. That delicious, complicated shiver of recognition in our click of eye contact. This also happened, occasionally, with older women, widows—a calm acknowledgment of loss, like what I'd shared so sweetly with Ignatia. But most of the time I was invisible. I just sat: a trim, professional woman with a black suitcase on wheels, exactly like all the other black suitcases on wheels. My anonymity was both comforting and suffocating. A sexy veil and an oppressive shroud.

In a *Twilight Zone* episode I'd seen as a kid, a guy flipped a coin to pay for his newspaper as he did every morning, except this time the coin landed on its edge, neither heads nor tails. As a result, this man could now read minds. At first he assumed this would be a useful skill, but it turned out to be a curse. He was almost driven mad by the cacophony of covert thoughts. This episode had haunted me enough that I'd discussed its plausibility with my mother. I must have been eight. I still remember what she'd said. "Only God can read your mind," she'd told me. "And even He would rather not tune in, probably." I must have been in her lap, because this memory trails after it another memory of her stroking my hair in the lazy way she had, separating the strands to run some through the underside of her fingernail. Or reaching out to trace, with one finger, the path of my eyebrows. She touched my face and hair the way, if you were reclining in a canoe, you'd dip your hand into the calm lake. Or, sunbathing, pick up sand, let it slowly go.

At airports I tried to read people in that rhythm. Just notice things, with no point or urgency. But it was difficult. What I understood was a burden. In some sense I was waiting for the coin to once more land on its edge, as finally happened in that *Twilight Zone* episode, and set everything right.

B etter hotels instructed staff to clean the rooms with the doors closed, carts safely inside. But they didn't want to startle any guests returning to their rooms, so they hung MAID WORKING signs on the doors, which rather defeats the purpose of disguising which guests were out. My routines worked perfectly.

In Pittsburgh, a housekeeper named Doris let me into my room on the business floor—too much added danger, I fretted, for free peanuts in the lounge, but I managed to coast in just as the natty concierge was away from his desk, and took the chance. Out the window a huge digital clock, cantilevered on a hill across the river, flashed all night. "So many bridges, so little rust. Coatings from Miles." Paint, presumably. Someone else's product and headache.

If I stayed free of charge in each familiar hotel only once, I had between ten days and a month—nine cities, a day or two, three tops, in each. Obviously, repetition would increase the odds of being caught, although each hotel had shifts of clerks, alternate housemaids, multiple floors; the same routines could be trotted out afresh in different months and/or for slightly different audiences, making for infinite possibilities if, like the bigamist with a wife in every port, I could manage to keep my stories straight.

I started a computer file. Date, city, hotel, room number. Key card functional? A space for comments ("claimed to have period"). At three in the morning in Akron, after a swim, I even developed a macro for sorting this information into columns, with the computer prompting me: *Housekeeper name? Length of stay?* This would join the long list of functions my computer already performed, like alerting me to acknowledge people's birthdays. (It would soon be my brother's. I did manage to find a card in the lobby gift shop and mail it, with a reassuring P.S. about my condition and busyness, thinking, heavyhearted: *birthday cards? I can't do this anymore.*)

Kramer left more voice mail. "Ken is quite concerned," he said evenly. "As am I. Please call." It was difficult for me to hide my exasperation in my answering-machine assurances that I was alive and well on what was, after all, my job, that my days on the road were numbered, but that I'd like to enjoy them in what, I stressed to Kenneth, was solitude.

"If it isn't someone else," Ken demanded, "what is it? Some sort of existential thing? Or do you need me to, what, 'spend more time with you'? Sure love talking to myself. Fuck this. Hey, fuck you, actually," which made me smile.

I'd always liked Ken's straightforwardness. We'd fallen into bed on our first date, which came the day after we met, and while that was hardly unusual protocol in 1980, we'd never needed smoke-and-mirrors, stripteases out of silk, the game theory of seduction. What others might consider Ken's lack of bedside manner I found a refreshing clarity. So his suspicions were frustrating. I almost felt as if he was *prescribing* adultery, for easy diagnosis. Stupid: one night, wet from the pool, I caught myself in front of the mirror, watching my hair drip onto my goosebumped nipples, thinking that sex with someone new might not be a bad idea.

Then I did get my period, or thought I did, which explained it. A curious tic of the human female to crave sex then, the body's last-ditch, kamikaze effort to salvage the egg. Even in grief, I'd always gotten my spasm of premenstrual horniness. That night, idly masturbating, I paused to wonder whether real homeless people ever did this too, late at night, alone on their grates, or whether their sexual urges got as crusted-over as their toenails.

I stopped picking up voice mail, telling clients that the system was unreliable. That complicated my life, since, like Ken, many of my clients couldn't seem to master E-mail, so I had to check in before appointments. Between that and the crime macro, my schedule felt more structured than I would have liked.

My problem, I now realized, was going to be weekends. I would not be inconspicuous at hotels on Saturdays, among the wedding guests and stray vacationers.

I'd started in Cincinnati on a Saturday, but that was Ignatia. I was not as close to Doris in Pittsburgh, which is where I stood naked before the mirror the following Friday night.

Saturday was very hot. I closed the vent on the air conditioner under the window, opened the blinds to the sun, shut off the air in the bathroom as well, put my purse and laptop under the bed as was now my custom, and went to the pool.

By the time I returned, the room was broasting. I opened the vents, then went out in the hall to search for Doris. "Whoo!" I said, bringing her into my room and fanning myself. "Air conditioner's not working!"

She put her hand over the working vent, shrugged her puzzlement.

"I need to change rooms. Who's at the desk, Steve?"

"No, Cindy. Should I call down?"

"No, I'll just talk to Cindy myself."

Whereupon I left Doris to clean the room, headed down the hallway, and ducked into the fire stair in my bathing suit and standard-issue white towel. Sat on the steps for five minutes contemplating the cinder block before I returned to announce that Cindy was moving me to 1502, the room that I knew Doris had just completed cleaning, because they weren't sure when maintenance could get there. I gathered up my things and, with hands full, asked Doris if she could let me in.

This was dangerous. While the business floor would not be jam-packed on a summer weekend in Pittsburgh, there would be upgrades. If caught, I could tell Cindy I'd arranged things with Steve or Steve I'd arranged things with Cindy, shaking my head in surprise that there was no credit-card imprint. I reminded myself that this wasn't pinball, golf, or pool. I was after no unbroken track record, and could always crack out the old card if the situation demanded.

But no one disturbed me.

The only hitch was that they locked the doors to the pool at 9:00 PM.

Doris was on days. I recognized no other housekeeper to bribe or cajole. The freight elevator in the basement, however, was open, and went straight into the locker room of the penthouse pool, where an open closet had been stocked with fresh towels. It was exhilarating to swim alone with moon through the skylights.

When I noticed that what I'd taken for a period was spotting only, the Tampax, with that curious texture they get after swimming, hardly sullied, I decided that my schedule might be messing with my schedule. Was determined not to make too much of it, as I'd tried to swallow the automatic disappointment at getting the period to begin with. If nothing else, to be this out there mentally ought to free me from watching my body for pregnancy as if the train of a long-lost loved one were arriving.

I stayed Saturday and Sunday and on Monday flew to Lexington, Kentucky, where I made a substantial commission on the sale of a new valve that like looked like a $2.98 plumbing part, rented a car, and drove to Louisville. When I finally sludged through the swamp of my voice mail, there was even a congratulatory call from a v.p. in charge of product development at Ohio Chemical and Surgical Equipment, commending my get-up-and-go.

The Louisville hotel, like several others on this part of my route, had no swimming facilities. At home, I belonged to a fine health club with an excellent pool. It was not a YMCA, though I'd once toyed with joining, so I was entitled to the day rates at the local Ys when I traveled. But I was scared off this plan after hearing a story from a colleague, who had come back from his laps to find his locker open and his combination lock gone, along with everything else he'd worn. He'd had to fish through the filthy, forgotten apparel in the lost-and-found bin in order to find something to wear home.

One could, of course, avoid taking valuables to a pool. But not so easily on the road.

Many of the hospitals on my route were university-affiliated, and universities usually have great pools. Sometimes people arranged to get me access. But it was nothing I could count on, or had ever needed to count on. Now I found myself wishing I'd had the foresight to acquire an administrative pass to some of the places on my route, which could probably have been arranged with only minor string-pulling.

I always tried to stay in hotels with real twenty-five-meter lap pools, rather than the fifteen-yard pools—basically very large bath-tubs—standard in so many venues. Alone in a hotel pool, I could swim on a diagonal. That helped some. But even then, one could not do real laps. The exercise was more in the friskiness of the flip turns. And then there were the occasionally inevitable establishments that offered no pool at all, such as the hotel in Louisville.

In Louisville, I remembered my friend returning to his locker. Coat gone, and socks. Credit cards and driver's license—all of identity to be painstakingly reassembled. I thought of him barefoot, in the puddles caused by his dripping bathing suit, in the middle of winter, wondering if he had lost his mind and had simply forgotten which locker he'd used, as you sometimes panic when you cannot find your car in a mall parking lot. Also stolen: an antique watch that had belonged to his father. The insurance company informed him that it was not very valuable after all. For years he had treasured this watch only to discover now that its value was purely sentimental. It would have been better for him not to have known the truth about the heirloom's value, as it would have been better for me never to have heard about my husband's affair. When my friend told me this story, holding up the rubber Swatch he'd gotten as replacement—happy hour, beer at a TGI Friday's near the office—my eyes had fogged up for him.

I shouldn't *need* to swim, was what I told myself. I shouldn't need anything.

Eleven days on the fly. A high point. Without life as a distraction, my work was going great guns. At forty-one, my swimmer's body was in its best shape ever. Everything extraneous was being whittled away, melted down, until only a core self remained. The self would feel vulnerable, like the stub of an uncapped tooth. I accepted that, expected it, even relished the sensation of rawness.

In Ohio, home base, the distances between appointments were shorter, so I had to drive—ostensibly my own car, its mileage tracked for tax purposes. Surely I could rent and avoid the panic that would be precipitated by Ken finding my car gone from the garage. But then my expense reports would alert the office that I wasn't going home at all.

Furthermore, I'd be more traceable. I had not yet even been aware I was hiding. If Ken asked, my secretary would tell him where I was. He was my husband. And clearly he had asked, since I was greeted, at the hotel in Toledo, by an overnight box of mail from back home.

Ken sent everything, indiscriminately. The August issue of *Hospital Development*. A postcard from a colleague vacationing in Rome. Bills, several overdue. He sent no note, but he'd circled the return address on the envelope in red.

What was he thinking? Did he really imagine that a checkup reminder postcard from my dentist was going to make me feel homesick? I had no more lust for the clothes in the catalogues than a nun would. I felt so exasperated at Kenneth's miscalculation that I actually drove to a used-car dealership, with the idea that I might buy a car cash, as people in the movies did, and take on a new identity. But I never got out of the rental car. I was not that far gone.

B y day thirteen, I felt almost cocky as I made my way past the cleaning cart into a just-finished room, and ducked into the bathroom to put on my swimsuit while the girl, back to me, was noisily vacuuming. Waited until she wheeled the cart away before I left, to make sure I could leave the door unlocked. I could do an efficient number with a bobby pin by now, not picking the lock but jamming the mechanism at the base just enough so that the door only looked closed. But it didn't work here. I had to leave the door cracked. I returned from the pool to find that the door had been locked for me, and when I tracked down the housekeeper for my well-seasoned forgot-my-key act, she challenged me, narrow-eyed, to alert the desk.

"I can't go down like this," I objected.

"I'll send someone up then."

"Fine. Let me into the room and we'll call together."

She did. She watched me press 1. "There seems to be some confusion," I told the desk clerk. "Just got back from the pool— let me dress and come right down."

It was bound to happen eventually. I was a little sad that it had to happen in Scranton, where my options for other lodging were so limited.

I didn't have to pack, since I hadn't unpacked. Even then, I felt no particular rush at the prospect of being caught. I am told that shoplifters, who are mostly female, *want* to be caught. I don't think I did. I wanted privacy, not attention. "He seems to have me in another room," I told the housekeeper. "Thanks for checking. I'll go get the right key," and I went downstairs wet-haired and quickly out the exit, as she'd known I would.

The hotel in Wilkes-Barre had no pool. It was downtrodden and demoralizing. I marched past the check-in desk and took the elevator to the third floor, where a maid had unlocked a series of the rooms assigned to her, to see whether there were any nasty surprises in store. I tried a new routine that would only work somewhere with security this lax. In the hallway, the maid's inventory sheet or whatever they call it rested atop her cleaning cart. I could see her in the room in front of me, making a bed languidly, distracted by a talk show on the TV. With her stub of a pencil I checked off a room two doors down as already cleaned. Then took the room. This would give her pause, but not for long. The rooms all looked the same, after all.

The room could have benefited from her services. There was pubic hair on the bathroom tile and wedged into the grout. The air from the fan was sour, brackish, lifting an almost doggy smell off the humid carpet.

I brought in dinner from McDonald's. Actually I had acquired the food earlier in the day, coming back from my appointment at the hospital, so I would not have to go out again. Congealed burger, fries hard as if lacquered—that food is not terribly pleasant to eat cold. Despite throwing the bag out down the hall, near the ice machines, I couldn't clear the oily scent of the fries out of the room.

I slept very badly.

When I awoke, a man was standing at the foot of my bed. I was naked, and he was centered between my legs, looking down at me as an obstetrician would.

"I'm sorry," he said. "There must be some mistake." He held up his key card, as if to prove that it had admitted him to the room, and shrugged his bafflement.

I was too startled to pull up the sheets. I lifted myself on my elbows and focused. A chubby, chinless man in his fifties with lots of hair—kin of the pubic hair. But where was his luggage, if he'd been checked into this room before I took it? Or, if just checking in now, why had the room not been cleaned?

"They must have—made a mistake," he repeated. Then smiled.

I didn't smile back at him, but I didn't move, either. He appeared to be paralyzed too—by embarrassment, or by the automatic lust of a male presented with a naked female. Five seconds, maybe, we stayed like this. I managed to focus enough to compute that he was going to read my behavior here as an invitation. And he must have, because now he looked around the room. Actually bent backward a bit, to position himself for a full view of the empty bathroom, as if to ascertain that I was alone. (Stupid of him—my bruiser-boyfriend could have been out fetching coffee.)

I managed to say, evenly, "Gotta go."

"You don't have to," he offered.

I watched him walk slowly around the side of the bed. With equal deliberation, he reached out a hand and, with thumb and forefinger, squeezed one of my nipples, maintaining eye contact. "We could share," he said, thick-voiced.

Both of us were now looking down at the breast, the big hand with the wedding band, flesh puffed around it, the black hair on the knuckles.

I processed the following thoughts: that my response time here was inadequate. That some woman could actually enjoy this. That I probably wouldn't, although I felt a strange lack of animosity toward the man. Even, oddly, sympathy: this was the only time in his life he was going to behave this way. *I don't know what came over me,* he would tell himself for years, with mingled horror and pride.

Then, from his extended pressure on the nipple, a trace-memory of breastfeeding so powerful that I gasped, and recoiled.

"Sorry," he said immediately, rearing back himself.

"No," I said, reaching only now for the sheet. "I'm—you know, I lost a child a while back."

"Oh, I'm sorry," he said. "How terrible."

I didn't argue.

"I'll go," he said.

"No. Just let me dress. I'm leaving anyhow. Do you have kids?"

"Two boys," he admitted.

"My boy was getting ready for college," I said. I don't know why I told this lie at this point, but it did seem to calm me, immediately. "I'll just go in the bathroom here."

He turned his back politely as I grabbed my clothes.

When I came out, dressed, he was gone.

I was surprised to find myself surprised. I'd expected him to stick around for apologies, condolences. Maybe offer lunch. I'd refuse, of course, but—as I followed this train of thought, I decided that after two weeks, a respectable vacation, I was approaching the end of the line.

My business in Wilkes-Barre was done. After Philadelphia, I

could fly home. I sat in the room watching CNN, the half-hour spin cycle of victims and refugees, and tried to feel like a normal traveling salesman, whose home is a nest brightly shining over the next hill. I was in the room long enough to be caught, was numbly resigned to a stern knock. But no one showed up or even called.

At The Children's Hospital in Philadelphia, I thought, churlishly: why am I here? Seeing children in wheelchairs, children with IVs, is not something that should be expected of me.

Inside, I walked fast, head down, as if dodging snipers.

"Is everything all right?" asked the purchasing officer's secretary, when I arrived.

"Sure," I said. "Why?"

"Your husband called Bill. He said—well, hold on." She buzzed my contact, who opened his office door and shook my hand with pointed warmth, except that he didn't actually step out of his office. He stuck out one hand and anchored the other inside somewhere, on a desk or doorknob, to avoid getting dragged off.

"Bill," I said lightly. "What's up?"

He closed the door, gestured for me to sit. I did, while he leaned against his desk—a bad sign. "I spoke to Ken," he said, "and I know what's happening."

"What do you mean?"

"I understand. After the—after, no one expected you to continue in this line of work. Isn't it torture, really? Like you're afraid of flying, and have to work as a stewardess?"

"Bill, what are you talking about?"

"Or you hate cockroaches, and you're an exterminator."

He smiled, pleased with the analogy, then reeled himself back.

"We're all burned out," he admitted, subdued now. "It happens. How could it not? But you. I mean, you don't need to be doing this."

I stood.

"No offense. Nothing sexist. Hey, if my wife were a surgeon, do you think I'd be here?"

"Look, I don't know what Ken said, but I can't imagine what it has to do with anything. Don't we"—I looked at my watch, for emphasis—"have an appointment?"

"Not today. Go home, hon."

Furious isn't a nearby galaxy. Behind my back, my husband had threatened my working relationship with one of my biggest clients, maybe threatened my job itself, since he would have had to sketch out the situation to my office to track down the appointment. Was this even legal? Bill opened the door for me, and I flew past his secretary—"Hon? Hon?" she called (a conspiracy of condescension!) talking aloud to myself, like an actual streetperson. *What is this, the fucking fifties? What's he gonna do next, commit me?*

People don't behave this way in children's hospitals. It's heartbreaking, really, how soldierly people manage to be, like John-John, Jr., saluting his father's coffin. As I got to the lobby, a security guard sprang to alertness; I watched the arc of his hand reaching for what I feared was a gun, then saw was a walkie-talkie. Lobby to parking garage? I changed course, left my car where it was, took the main doors into an invisible fence of heat and humidity, took a cab that was moving before the door was closed.

My usual hotel was out of the question, obviously, as an unpaid or paying guest. For all I knew Ken was there already, waiting. I could leave Philadelphia immediately, except that Ken might be skulking around the airport.

I directed the cab to the Four Seasons and was almost there before I realized that my luggage was still in my car, in the hospital garage, so I took the cab back, had the driver wait while I fetched my things from the trunk. The meter, obviously tampered with, pinwheeled crazily.

The Four Seasons had rooms. Rooms were not a problem. Nor did I expect to sneak in. I fully planned to pay in the ordinary fashion. So thirstily did I want to submerge in the pool that I could almost taste the click my credit card would make as it got imprinted on the little machine.

But my credit card was declined.

"Happens all the time," the clerk reassured me. "Bureaucratic screwups. Want to try another plate?"

I reached for another credit card to discover that I didn't have one. Only now did I remember that, in a recent spasm of efficiency, I had gone through my wallet, removed all the plates I did not regularly use: not only the Visas with bad interest rates but the library card, the stamp card that would entitle me to a free sandwich after I bought another dozen at a restaurant I no longer frequented. This act had been inspired, partially, by the colleague who had gotten his belongings stolen from the locker at the YMCA. Now I would have less to fret about and reconstruct, in case of theft. How pure and light, productive and organized I'd felt doing this, for all of ten minutes. The pleasures of middle-class life: the orderly sock drawer! The change not scattered on the dresser but sorted by type, brought to the bank! I'd actually hefted the cleaned-out wallet, as if the purge represented a major human accomplishment and life improvement. But this meant I had no other credit-card plate to offer the hotel. And in a flash I knew what Ken had done.

"Give me a sec," I told the clerk.

In stepping aside and dialing on the cell phone, I provided my mother's maiden name to a voice in an unidentified state, and learned that yes indeed, the card had been reported stolen. A new one, with a new number, had already been issued this morning to my home address. How did Kenneth, who was not listed as a coholder on this or any other of my credit-card accounts, have it canceled? His secretary, no doubt. His secretary given my dead mother's maiden name. I could certainly give the new number to the hotel, the operator offered. What was the point? By now my husband was probably calling hourly, to track the card's use.

But I outwitted him. Asked the location of the nearest ATM machine, pushed past panhandlers with their medieval smell, withdrew $300 in cash, the maximum, and paid for the room with bills so stiff and fresh—made right there in Philadelphia, at the Federal Reserve—that I had to lick my thumb to pry them apart. Paid with what my tailor called "cash money," as an adulteress would, or a prostitute.

No doubt Ken felt very clever about the credit cards, but he had no experience with banks or cash. He didn't go to grocery stores; he didn't pick up dry cleaning; he ate in the hospital cafeteria, on a monthly account. He probably hadn't entered a bank in a decade, every transaction that wasn't automatic done for him, by me or his secretary; it would be days before cash occurred to him, if it ever did. And he couldn't freeze the bank accounts. They were joint. He would need my signature, which he couldn't forge—he wrote like a surgeon, and his secretary wrote like a Catholic school eighth-grader.

The pathetic thing, I planned to tell my home answering machine, was that I was coming home. I told you I was. You should have believed me, because now you have made it impossible.

But I didn't make the call, because I realized he was probably tracking my cell-phone calls, too. Looked toward the phone booth, but even if I remembered my phone-card number from pre–cell-phone days, he might be on that trail as well, and I felt no urge to reassure the man who had forced me to need fistfuls of coins.

W hen I returned to the desk, my luggage, computer, and briefase were gone.

I had just left them there, unguarded.

After a power surge of panic, I calmed myself. Either I would reconstruct all the records at the office, when and if I ever got back, or I wouldn't. Just quit. Underwear, toothbrush—so little was necessary, really. Taking loss lightly was the point, after all, of this sojourn. I could buy a bathing suit in Philadelphia.

This being the Four Seasons, however, it turned out the octogenarian valet had discreetly moved my belongings to a luggage rack, and once the clerk and I had finished our transaction (if I'd known I'd be paying cash, I could have used a pseudonym) I was being led to my room at a pace both efficient and stately, like a rajah in a carriage.

Trembling slightly, the valet opened my drapes, cracked the closet door, flipped on the lights in the bathroom. How I loved these hollow rituals, the turned-down sheets, the tinseled chocolates. I tipped the valet a ten, for return of my worldly goods.

Although it was rush hour, no traffic was audible. At the window I watched the eerie mime of cars lurching forward in spasms. The pool was what I wanted, but I wanted to be there alone, and first I wanted to drain the day out of me. On the bed, with the blinds closed, I zoomed in on an image of my wheeled suitcase adrift on a sea of carpeting, twisted the axis so the bag soared away like a spaceship, hardware glinting, rode the ship's tail fin into sleep.

When I woke up I went straight to the pool, to find it had closed for the night.

No way around it. Doors were locked everywhere. I couldn't even get near the freight elevator. I had to eat room service, go back to sleep, and wait until late morning, when the businessmen cleared out.

N ot only did the Four Seasons have a guard at the pool at all hours of operation, it had a waiver form. Guests signed to assure the Organization that accidental death will not be its fault. Everyone everywhere covering their asses. A guard, a waiver form, and then, of all things, surveillance cameras, as if at a bank or convenience store. Security cameras at the door, in the locker room, and aimed straight at the pool itself, documenting all horseplay, anemic crawl, or drowning incident.

There were no other guests. But the laconic guard, and the camera's eye, made me self-conscious. My stroke felt military. I couldn't relax the muscles in my mouth.

I kept going, not looking up and pointedly not changing my pace, as another guest dove into the pool. You are not supposed to dive, of course, into three-and-a-half feet of water, unless you want to crack your head open. Signs everywhere reminded that it was prohibited. The guard barked, "No diving." But the guy, crash-landing, didn't hear her. He had already gone into the butterfly, the stroke of assholes.

Anyone doing butterfly anywhere is an obnoxious idiot, but to do it in a small hotel pool is beyond endurance. Arrogant, preening, beady-eyed little pricks in muscle shirts do butterfly. Marines and state troopers, premature ejaculators. The kind of men who clap between push-ups.

He plunged right into a showy intramural-style routine—a lap of butterfly with a flip turn into backstroke, with a flip-turn into breaststroke, then a flip turn into freestyle. Given the size of the pool, this was ludicrous, a cartoon of swimming. Who was he performing for? The guard was reading a book. I stayed in the lap lane I'd already been occupying, refusing to acknowledge him, persevering through the batter he made of the water.

He was quite bothered that I wouldn't admire him. He kept edging closer to me. He couldn't bump me out, unless he came under the rope, but he had managed to get our progress across the pool almost parallel, and on the breaststroke part of his routine he was almost swiping me with the overreaching arc of his powerful arm.

Did I need this, after the pig in Wilkes-Barre? Were all business travelers these days just right of certifiable—auditioning to be rapists? I started to come out of the water with my mouth in a rictus, ready to tell him off, but then stopped, shocked, because, now that I regained my balance, I saw his face, turned my way for his gulp of air.

He was a child. Seventeen, eighteen tops, almost hairless chin, his height and heft so new that he hadn't grown into them: his butterfly not a mating dance as I'd assumed but a celebration of his body's new power. He just wanted to play, like a puppy. But he'd been fooled by my slimness and stroke. Now that he saw me face-up, he looked embarrassed. Even with goggles on, I could not pass for a teenager.

"Slow and steady wins the race," he offered.

"No race," I said sternly. "Just trying to do some laps."

We had both stopped now, at one end of the pool.

"In the Soviet Republic of the Four Seasons," he said, jerking his head toward the guard, still immersed in her trashy paperback.

"It's like a high-school gym here," he added. "I don't know. The Four Seasons. I expected—"

I couldn't help but smile.

He was still breathing heavily. He took his hair out of its pony-tail, regathered it, smoothed it back from his forehead, on which I could see a touching spray of acne. An unconscious gesture, not a seductive one, and strangely not effeminate, though the hair was long, still that shade of childhood summer—cornsilk on top, darkening to brass underneath—that no hairdresser can duplicate. The softness of children's hair and skin! It had been a while since I'd remembered the pleasure of stroking and smelling a baby, holding a child's foot, the sole still completely smooth: not smooth as silk or butter, not comparable to any other substance or sensation; just the essential *footness* of it. At almost four, Evan still had those relaxed baby feet, the toes with an almost dewy plump-ness.

The boy heaved himself out of the water, went for his towel. I found myself propping myself up by my elbows on the concrete edge of the pool, hands tucked under my chin, flirtatious as a girl, watching his back.

And I thought, *Evan!* Allowed my brain waves to ebb around the smooth wet surf-rock of my son's name.

The boy turned around in a T-shirt: *Brown University.*

No transcendental coincidence, I fully recognize. But given the direction of my thoughts at that moment, it was hard not to exclaim "God!"

He looked uneasy.

"Swim team?" I asked.

Now he smiled. "I start in the fall."

"My son, too!"

I was still wearing my goggles and bathing cap. Found myself wanting to look, to him, bold, Amelia Earhartish. Whipped off the goggles, so he could see me.

"Really?" he said. "You don't look that old."

"Well, thanks, I guess. My alma mater. What's your major?"

"Premed."

"I'm an MD."

"Yeah?" he said, sitting down by the side of the pool. "What's your field?"

He expected internist, pediatrician. By eighteen they're already sexists. They can't help it. So I surprised him, whipping off the cap and freeing my hair as I announced: "Cardiothoracic surgery."

"Cool," he said, pronouncing it *coo* with an ironic teenage head-bob like a dashboard accessory, but clearly he was impressed.

How far was I willing to go with this? In the shudder or shutter of that instant, I decided, pretty far.

W omen did this. I personally knew a couple of them, had listened to their breathless confessions over white-wine lunches. As story, tryst with younger man was already codified. Professor and student, movie star and personal trainer. Always, unless it was wartime—the grown men all out of town, all relevant parties orphaned or widowed—the older woman had to be in a position of power; unlikely the twosome would meet in a bar or swimming pool.

The boy who introduced himself as Zachary, I decided, was too young to think of the poster for *The Graduate,* the innocent boy framed behind the woman's leg, the leg raised and threatening, like a nutcracker. We chatted about medicine. Now I had done my residency where Kenneth did his residency—in North Carolina, in tobacco country, where people guzzled Jack Daniel's and gorged on pure lard, every single adult a potential client. I rattled off some of Ken's more dramatic stories as if they were my own, with a mounting desire to—the phrase was in my head like an army sergeant's shouted command—jump his bones.

Describing a procedure, I caught his eye, pointed to the relevant place on my own chest, let my fingernail trace an arc near my nipple, its outline visible through the wet suit. Traced the path again as if to plant an idea of roundness, entering, hypnotize him into the dizzy middle of some kind of Stonehenge circle.

The selfsame breast had just seen service, in the Wilkes-Barre hotel room, and I realized that, like the dark-haired man there, I was not registering the target of my seduction. My lust was impersonal in the purest sense. As I talked, I focused on the double-image of his shoulders. They were clearly a man's shoulders, but underexposed, still bearing a ghost of the way he would have carried himself as a child. The shoulders, the back, the back of the neck: it's the sweetest place on a little boy. Despite the muscles, the irony, and the zits, the smooth vulnerability of the boy was still there. Sex with him, I felt, would be like a long exposure, mounting slow and steady as a time-lapse. *How absurd!* I also thought, not being a moron. For that kind of sex—selfless sex, like Buddhist meditation—I'd do better with my husband, or with some other middle-aged male who knew my terrain. Not an eighteen-year-old boy who would hump like a monkey. Yet that felt like part of the experience, part of the double-exposure: tenderness, joy, and wonder hidden behind the haste and thrust of the butterfly. As opposed to the boor in Wilkes-Barre, who was only crude.

But like that man, I didn't want to have to ask. I should be able to do what all mating people everywhere have always done, and many species of birds as well: a quick, shy glance away, followed by a frontal gaze that says *come with me.* Your room or mine.

Amazingly, it worked. After the obligatory discussion of the rigors of medical school, it became clear that unlike his, my room had a view toward the park. As well as being a swimmer, Zachary had been a high-school track talent, and the idea of a jog around the park, with company, appealed to him. We only needed to stop at my room, to get my running shoes. That I didn't have running shoes was something I figured we'd deal with later.

T he room had not yet been cleaned. As he headed to my windows, and my view, I slipped the DO NOT DISTURB sign into position. By the time he turned around, I was in position to be in his arms. We were in bathing suits, so the journey to bed shouldn't take long. I was aware of trying to be perfectly clear about the invitation, while at the same time hanging back enough so that I didn't scare him, or repulse him—I feared that with *Let me be perfectly clear* I could seem, coming at him for the kiss, like Richard Nixon through a fish-eye lens, old and hairy, tremulous. Though he was probably too young to have any picture whatsoever of Richard Nixon: the fabled problem of communicating with a younger mate, over the long haul. Though the long haul, I reminded myself, was not what I had in mind.

"Oh, man," he said.

In the split second before he zoomed in for the kiss, my lust drained away completely.

It was amazing. The mere thought of Richard Nixon had apparently done it in.

But why was I thinking about anything, I asked myself, no less Nixon, in this situation?

Now he was kissing me. The kiss was exactly the combination of aggression and tentativeness that I had anticipated. The smell, however, was a surprise: some childish combination of July dusk and broken-in sneakers.

This was my idea, after all. If I backed out now, I'd be sending a message that grown women were addled and two-faced, no different from the teenaged girls he'd tried to seduce in cars and parental rec rooms. Though it was possible that the girls in his high school had been pretty willing, for he was an expert kisser, modulating the activity of his hands in my hair to the pressure of his lips and managing to be intense without getting my lips too wet—*coloring in the lines,* I thought, my body the outline he was following, as a diligent child would, with a fat crayon. Though maybe an attentive boy could learn all this from the movies.

Though, though, though, I thought. *Chill!*

Despite the flurry of brain activity, meaningless as static, the rest of me was responding on cue. I heard my own moan as he guided me toward the bed and maneuvered me backward while still locked into the kiss, a move right off the cover of a romance paperback. He pushed down the damp bathing suit, swooped. My eyes jerked open to see him watching the breast he was licking, completely alert, his nose so close it was immense. I got another nursing flashback then, as powerful as the one in Wilkes-Barre: Evan looking up, glassy-eyed, his fist relaxing in my palm.

Once more I gasped. But my lover took it as pleasure, increased the pressure.

What was this? It wasn't as if I hadn't had sex for three years. Granted, not much—and too much of it in a campaign at ovulation—but from now on was I going to have to raise my son from the dead each time I made love?

I was trying to calm myself. But then my milk came in.

It happened as it always had. That solid click, substantial and precise as a lock correctly dialed. You don't really perceive the flow of the milk once it gets going so much as the release, not like a river undammed—nothing that pastoral—but more like a safe door swung open. Oddly *metallic*.

As I felt the rush, Zachary screamed something like *ack!* Reared back in slow motion, arms flailing, action-adventure style, as if he'd just fallen off the wing of the plane he'd been clinging to. Then wiped his mouth with the back of his hand, grimacing. "What the fuck was *that*."

My nipple appeared to have excreted something. I pinched, got a drop more. It was clearer than the milk I remembered. Last time I'd seen my OB-GYN, he'd given my nipples a squeeze that would have struck the easily offended as sexual harassment, but he was checking, he'd explained, for galactorrhea. I remembered the term now because he and I had discussed it, laughing— sounds, I'd said, like a *Star Trek* sequel.

"Hormonal misfiring," I explained to Zach. "It happens, when you get older. I assume it's all perfectly normal."

"You've *got* to be kidding." He kneeled now, his expression still horrified. "Your tits leak? Like sperm before you come?"

I smiled.

"Tastes like shit," he said. "Tastes like yak milk."

"It's yellow and it's thin," I said. "But babies like it. I hear it's pretty sweet. Try again," I suggested, thumbing the glistening nipple with its ragged opening.

"No *way*. I wasn't breast-fed," he added, as if that explained something, and maybe it did.

"None of us were," I agreed. "It was taken to be unsanitary and savage for a while there, back in—when were you born? Seventy-seven? Seventy-eight?" I nodded in disbelief and shock as people always did, at the idea of someone being born while they themselves were in college.

"Maybe that explains everything. All these grown men with their family values, desperate to have their cocks sucked. Maybe they want to just curl up at the altar of devoted moms, of the type they missed. Suck or be sucked, what's the difference, so long as the woman is harnessed into service? As if sperm tastes so divine."

He was inching off the bed, I noticed, while I talked. Still on his knees but trying to escape, unblinking, as if from a mad-woman on the street, in his tight, shiny little bathing suit like a codpiece. I felt in a rush how I must seem to him, and I was sorry, because I had brought him here, and I would seem crazy with my incontinent breasts, blathering away, whereas before I had been desirable, and what kind of lesson was that to teach a boy who had never drunk from his mother's breasts, who was already doing the butterfly, already calcifying into the wrong kind of man? So I sat, reached, slowly pulled down his bathing suit, made soothing noises as he cringed, then steadied the now-limp penis, brought my head to the edge of the bed, took the penis in my mouth, aware even as I did so that the better thing to do was let him go. And I swear there was a comfort in the steadiness of the sucking and the simplicity—no tricks; nothing fancy or older-womanish was required; and as long as he didn't look at me, as long as he was focused on the sensation, we were fine. And it wouldn't be long.

By this point my head was clear. I pulled him up and inside. Sensing that too much sound would unnerve him, I turned my head sideways, buried my mouth in the bedspread with its paisley pattern, so that sensation began to follow paisley paths, curling into tails, then opening again to roundness. By the time he came I had no thoughts. I was wonderfully empty of thought, except for the pattern of the pleasure, those baroque paisley curlicues.

As I came, I thought: birth control.

I thought: *none.*

Delighted: *I am pregnant.*

Except that I suspect I'm supplying these words in retrospect, because at the time the knowledge was as wordless, as almost graphic, as the paisleys. A conception of conception.

t was as if my body, all on its own, in its waning days of (uneven) procreative functioning, had chosen its moment, then produced this specimen of manhood to further the master race. Deemed that my personal problems were no impediment. Goaded me into action, and I'd complied, single-minded as a ghoul or Stepford wife.

What to do, though, with the knowledge that flooded me? It was a joke. Though I'd gotten pregnant relatively easily with Evan, there had hardly been a ringing bell or pinball *bing* when sperm met egg. It's true that before the grind of fertility problems, trying to conceive had lent a pleasing gravity to the proceedings, a ceremonial quality. But that was hardly the case here.

Zachary, in fact, was smiling, pleased with himself. An expression for semifinal team triumph. Whatever sex education he'd been offered had failed: AIDS had not even yet occurred to him. I almost said, indignant, "For all you know I could be a hooker," but then realized that he assumed I'd taken care of things, because I was a trustworthy adult. I was as certain to be clean, and without risk of pregnancy, as his parents were certain not to let him drive the Honda without insurance.

"Now how about that run," he said.

"Confession," I said. "No running shoes, in point of fact."

"You got me up here on false pretenses, you evil wench?"

I tried to strike an expression somewhere between proud and sheepish.

"What size do you wear?" he asked.

"Eight. Why?"

"Put on some thick socks, and borrow my mother's."

His *mother!* She had not occurred to me, until that moment. Nor had it occurred to me to wonder why he was at a hotel, with whom he was staying. As he gloated I did some math, somewhat desperately.

"She's eight and a half," he said, "and she won't be back for hours. Throw on some shorts and we'll—"

"Nothing to jog in. Just work clothes," I said. "Power suits," though he would know this for a lie: I came and left the pool in a T-shirt and shorts. But I felt a need to be rid of him, to contemplate my feelings about my first-ever infidelity on the possible scale from deep shame to bemusement. I had sat up. Zachary stood above me, smiling and bobbing, hyped-up as a kid on Halloween candy. "Too tired anyhow," I added, collapsing backward on the bed. Aware of myself collapsing, and aware of my awareness; aware, too, that I seemed to have developed a habit of telegraphing all of my comments to this child with a gesture, as if he were a waiter in a foreign country. *Gracias! Ciao!* But once I was backward, my toes left the floor, where they'd been rather skittishly working the carpet's pile, and I lifted my legs, knees to my stomach in the classic jogger's stretch.

To hold the sperm in. Instinctively, that's what I was doing. Two or three minutes you're supposed to give the buggers. Hard not to think of them as cartoons crouched on their starting blocks, me watching from the bleachers.

Zach, however, misread my posture as another semaphore.

Wide-eyed, idiotically grinning, and hard again, he dove on top of me.

Teenaged boys. No surprises there. But it is astonishing, really, the curve of the adult male's performance, the very narrow ledge when they're at the peak of the curve, between instant ejaculation and sex so slow that they can slog semihard in you for hours, so you feel like a talk show they're not quite committed to. Women, meanwhile, coming ever faster, more efficiently. That makes sense: once the children are on the scene, no time to waste; pack those lunches, wipe those asses; diminished expectations as we work around our mates' herniated disks and cosmic fatigue. Of course, we would do better to fuck the young bucks, and let our husbands take their gentle time with the fillies. And so they do, if they're inclined, whereas we rarely tempt the younger fellas. The human race is fixed to give maximum options to the men, who are lucky to be having sex at all; in most of the animal kingdom they would have long ago slunk off, having acceded to the biggest baboon, the horniest and hugest-horned.

I'd always been a sucker for the nature shows that explain why the zebra has its stripes, why the flounder's eyes migrate, and found myself, as I often do, thinking of them then. Thinking what a remarkable luxury human sexuality is, how emblematic of our aspirations, our need to be a self in the world. Animals, presumably, don't have identity crises. Most animals can't even compute a mirror image and yet there human babies are, from almost the very beginning, cooing at their own reflections.

In the time it took Zach to finish, I had time to think those vague thoughts, and feel a spasm of nostalgia for Kenneth. In bed in pajamas, The Learning Channel on, both of us shaking our heads as the lions tore apart their fast-food prey or the Chinese acupuncturist performed the C-section, the woman awake and chatting away to the nurses as the doctors sliced her open. Ken has ideas about evolution. He has ideas about the body's mind—he's shockingly New Age, for a surgeon. When Evan was a baby and colicky, had a hard time falling asleep, Kenneth examined the problem. Developed a method for turning him three times in the bassinet with his head like a compass butted against one bumper one way for three minutes, then another thirty-degree adjustment, then in three minutes another adjustment. Three was the charm. Evan was always asleep within ten minutes, head at north-northeast, where Ken had discovered his progeny enjoyed the strongest trace of womb memory.

As usual, the thought of Evan as an infant made my eyes burn. And the heartbeat-blip of grief headed off any possibility of my own orgasm. And then Zach groaned, rolled off.

If I were with Ken, I could finish the job myself, with a little help if he was inclined, or he could just watch, or not.

I could push Zach's head down, continue his education. Leg around his back, toes pointed. *Taste yourself oh yes,* all corny and porny, but as I looked at him carefully studying my reaction, I thought no, I felt actually bashful, exposed. I crawled toward the head of the bed so I could reach for the sheets, pulled them over me, gave him what would have to pass for a sated smile.

But for some reason—a mind reader?—he dove under and there was the tongue, and I didn't have a single thought for how-ever long until I breathed, "Christ, Zachary, your mother really lets you watch too much cable TV," and he laughed, giving me that break (for his style here was, like his breaststroke, overzealous) to mash myself back into his still-bared teeth.

Thereafter, guilt. Immediately I felt dizzy and sick, as from MSG in Chinese food. What a childish thing to do to my husband. On cue I'd fulfilled worse than his worst-case scenario of penny-ante retribution.

"It's true," Zach said cheerfully. He rolled over on one elbow to study me. He wiped his mouth with the back of his hand, then sniffed the hand, did a skit with pinkie out, an oenophile rejecting a vintage. I couldn't look anymore. I turned my face toward the pillow.

"My father has quite the collection," he continued. "Couple hundred of 'em right out there in the open on the custom book-shelves. He jacks off I guess after he finishes with depositions."

"And your mother allows that?" I asked, surprised. "Do you have any younger siblings in the house?"

"Divorced. This would be in Counselor's bachelor pad. Pretty close to here, actually, if you want to sneak over and check 'em out."

"No thanks," I said. "My husband says I'm a prude, but I just hate how stuff's always done in exactly the same order. The gardener comes to the door. Drinks are poured. He kisses her, kisses each tit. Kiss, kiss, kiss, a little mouth-tit trinity. Rubs 'em together, *boing boing boing*. Then he goes down on her. Close-up of her with her bad shag haircut, whimpering. When he unleashes the banana, the camera does a reverent low-angle shot like it's the monolith in *2001: A Space Odyssey,* she oohs and aahs, then the camera records his blow job at considerably more length and with considerably more interest to the tune of music from an airport bar. Orgasm always from intercourse, orgasm always mutual. As far as I'm concerned, cooking shows are more erotic, though I suppose they do get one going. If that's all one needs. But sexy? About as sexy as a Water Pik fighting plaque. Might as well stick your finger in a light socket."

He just stared at me.

"Just making conversation," I said.

"What's 2010 a space odyssey?"

I laughed.

"Actually, my father likes the kind with a couple of girls. So they're a tad more, shall we say, atmospheric."

"Yeah, until the guy comes in at the end to bestow ecstasy like Santa Claus with his big banana."

"So you're married?" he asked.

"Sure," I said. "Have a girlfriend?"

"Sure."

"What's her name?"

"Guess."

"Kimberly," I said. "Heather."

"Wrong. Wrong."

"Jennifer."

"Nuh-uh. Petra and I—weird, huh? Sounds like diesel fuel— are attending different universities in the fall, and have mutually agreed to 'see other people' for the nonce."

"Are you from Philadelphia?"

"Burbs, but my mother and I jumped ship after the divorce."

"Was that hard on you?"

"Piece o' cake. Loved every minute of it, actually. So what about that run? You ready, or you still wanna get to know me better first?"

He must have learned this particular style of sarcasm from the loathed, revered father. It didn't quite fit. Odd that it should be his fake-urbane speech, and not the sex, that made him seem most painfully young. That and the short attention span: he was now gazing longingly toward the window, anticipating the workout in the park, I guessed, but really it was my open laptop, set up on the desk.

"You on-line?" he asked. " 'Cause I really need to check some stuff," and before I had time to respond he had lunged for the machine, unplugged my phone, plugged in the modem, commandeered the mouse, found a local access number. "Give me your password," he demanded.

Given that I'd just let him fuck me, you'd think I could tell him my password. I could always change it afterward. Instead I got up and punched it in for him, quickly, so he couldn't read it. Then galumphed back to the bed. It amazed me that he could be this relaxed, naked, with his back to me.

"No smutty chat rooms now," I warned.

"Yes, Mom."

"Oh please."

"America Online is shit," my mini-man informed me. From the bed I watched him log on to check baseball stats, then stock quotes. Stock quotes! He sat as if on a bar stool, knees up and out, his toes, which for some reason I expected to be longer, thinner, hooked on the rungs. He was bopping to the graphics. My shame was turning into a low-grade burn, like the onset of a yeast infection. I checked my watch showily—pointless, since he wasn't looking.

"It's late," I prompted. "I assume your mother will be missing you."

"Nah. Shopping. Won't be back for hours. Days maybe. Down memory lane, past the old haunts with her wallet open. She'll come back like those bad movies, so many packages in her arms she can barely see over the top."

"How old is she?"

"Your age, I guess. Little older."

"You don't know how old she is?"

I must have sounded petulant. He turned to study me. How could he be this cavalier at eighteen? I swear the wary expression was exactly that of a long-time bachelor, calculating how to squirm away from the grasping intentions of the chick he'd just bedded. This couldn't be, I told myself. I had to be imagining it. Either that, or I was projecting my own morally questionable use of him, my own intense, almost physical desire to have him gone.

"Sure," he said. "Forty-five."

"I'd like to meet her."

His trigger-finger stopped itching on the mouse. "What for?"

"Maybe we could all have dinner together or something, after our run."

Now his gaze was curious. "I don't get it."

I don't either, I thought, but then I said, "I don't have a son starting college. That's just what I tell people. My son's dead. It's still painful. My marriage is shaky. *I'm* shaky. So it would do me good, I guess, to see a woman my age with a boy the age my son is supposed to be. And it might diffuse some of the awkwardness, no? Of what we've done. Because though you're being very cool here—shockingly, almost pathologically laid-back and cool—I just can't accept that this is all in a day's work for you. If it is, that's very sad, Zach."

He contemplated his response to this for a minute. "Man," he finally said. "You're weird."

We both laughed.

The laugh was surprisingly tension-dispelling. My physical embarrassment seemed to bottom out, so that I felt perfectly comfortable sloppily sheeted, while Zachary sat naked at the hotel desk. Actually, I felt somewhat maternal, in all of the full and complicated senses of the word.

At the laugh's tail end, a commanding knock on the door, like a policeman with a warrant. The door swung open immediately—the key must have already been in position—and a huge, furious-looking woman stormed in. "Clean!" she barked.

The maid had diamond-encrusted fingernails so long they curled under, and one of those Nefertiti coifs, hair swept up and sculpted high on the head with decorative things caught in it like debris in a fishing net. She looked from me to Zachary with unmitigated contempt. "*Clean* I said," she almost spat.

"Are you new here?" I asked.

When she made no response, I continued.

"Because I sincerely doubt that this is Four Seasons protocol. Try 'So sorry, I'll come back later.' "

"Fuck you," she said, and violently shot me the finger, in case I had failed to understand the words themselves, whereupon she spun the cart around and thrust it out ahead of her, leaving the door to the room open.

When I looked up at Zachary, he was recoiling, slack-jawed, from the hurricane-strength force of her.

I got up to close the door, sidling along the walls, since I was naked.

"I don't think she even noticed anything out of the ordinary here," I observed. "Too caught up in her own anger."

"What was her *problem*?"

"How should I know? Resents the Republican Congress? Needs some exercise? Speaking of which. Come on, Zach. Let's get your mother's running shoes and do that run."

He grinned agreement, threw on his bathing suit, threw his towel over his neck. His neck, shoulders, and back, I noticed only now as I put on my shorts and T-shirt, had a serious acne problem—weight lifting? I remembered to stick my automated teller machine card in my shorts pocket: time for another cash infusion. When Zach got to the door, he made a point of going low to peer out cartoonishly, looking left and right as if there were a sound track for his escape.

I did the same, sneaking up to him to press my breasts into his back, mold my chin into his chlorine-smelling hair. What can I say? The boy pleased me.

Because of the Marx Brothersy, *Room Service* way we were positioned, both Zachary and I saw the same thing at the same time. Down the length of the long, long hallway, in the middle of the day, an impossible number of illicit couples were entering or exiting hotel rooms. Rushing in or rushing out with a rustle. Except for one tired fat man hefting a crushed and woeful garment bag, every guest here was an empty-handed participant in the same classic drama of lust and satiation, and they all seemed to be acting it out at the same moment.

Zach turned backward with eyebrows raised, to see if I'd seen. I beamed my amusement.

We took the stairs up two flights and on his floor, too—right next to his room, in fact, the room which, it turns out, he was sharing with his mother, he in one double bed, she in the other—the same thing. Manic sexual activity. Giggling and spooning as people came from the gym or lunch. A veritable *Ziegfeld Follies* of broad-daylight copulation. It was surreal, positively Roman—there were so many writhing bodies I was almost expecting togas, vomitoriums.

I can say that in all the time I have been a hotel guest, I have never seen so much syncopated in-and-out. Usually the hallways are almost threateningly empty.

"Is this the place that had the Legionnaires' disease?" I asked Zachary. "There must be something new in the air ducts here. We oughtta can it, sell it."

He had no idea what I meant.

He cocked his head. Through the wall, behind the dresser, a squeal, then a grunt, then a moan—two moans, comically operatic. As the moans escalated Zachary bopped to their rhythm, then puffed out his lips Jagger-style and did some kind of Egyptian or Madonna posing routine with his hands at a funny angle, like the one you'd use to do shadow puppets of ducks. Then went over to the closet and threw open the doors, still in rhythm, thrust out his hands like a game-show hostess to reveal the bounty within. I watched him with mounting uneasiness as I realized that everything he did—everything I observed, in fact—was being translated through this scrim of reference. Even the moans themselves: I had been about to say "How *Animal Farm*!" to Zachary before his little dance began and I remembered how inappropriate and useless literary allusion was as a mode of communication with this particular human.

And now he was handing me his mother's running shoes, one shoe resting in the Cinderella pillow of each of his upturned palms. Then, as an afterthought, some socks.

The running shoes looked brand-new, barely worn. As far as I could tell, they had never even been completely laced up. They had that deeply satisfying new-running-shoe smell, enticing as the smell of a new car. I put them on, flexed my toes. The fit was perfect—he must have gotten her size wrong.

"Wow," I said, glancing up at the contents of the closet. "How long are you in town for?"

The mother had enough clothes for a couple of weeks. Six or seven pairs of shoes. Business suits, evening gowns, multiple choices for snappy casual.

"Couple of days," he answered, with what seemed to be fond contempt. "But it's always a costume drama for Mom."

"Don't you think she'd mind, about the shoes? It's not like she won't be able to tell."

"She'd mind. If she noticed. But she won't. Anyhow, she wouldn't mind as much as she'd mind the other stuff." He laughed. "We just have to beat her back."

He watched as I lined up my sandals at the end of her soldier-row of footwear. My shoes looked dog-eared and unprofessional, frank impostors. "Ready?" he said.

I was. In the elevator, where we were alone, we both limbered up, actually took turns getting down on the carpeting to do tendon stretches. We exited the hotel, caught the crossing light, and sprinted into the square of green surrounding the fountain in the park, where we fell into a companionable pace. Whatever competitiveness he had brought to his swimming was gone now; he was almost chivalrous as he ran beside me on the outside of the pavement, closer to the traffic. I hadn't run in years—had never liked it all that much, in fact, though I'd done it to keep Ken company, before his knees got too bad for it, early in our courtship. Ken had a lovely, loping stride. Zach's was creakier, more lumbering. I wasn't really looking at him so much as feeling him beside me, feeling the tension he was trying to keep in check. It touched me, how he didn't quite inhabit his own body. Imagine having a son this age, imagine having a boy this age bend to hug you. It must be so strange. There must be a kind of grief in that too, if you get there. I was really eager to meet his mother, to watch them together.

"Boring," he announced, after four or five rounds. "Thisaways?" I nodded assent and let him lead me onto the city streets, where we panted and sweated through the tendrils and thickets of the workers of the world, mostly tired and defeated, or distracted, but some leaving work early with boxed cakes and flowers and the secret smiles of actual lives passing behind their eyes.

At some point I stopped to catch my breath. Stupid: it had been too long, too far, for an inexperienced runner. I would have shin splints at least. Zachary kept on for a while, as if he wasn't aware that he'd lost me, then circled back to me, charged as a boxer. I just shook my head no, not ready. He did the same puppyish loop, back and away, back and away.

Strangely, I wasn't sweating that much. But my lungs hurt. I felt as if I'd just swilled down fiberglass.

"Why don't you just go on," I managed to get out, "and I'll meet you back at the hotel."

"You sure? I can wait."

I waved for him to go on.

He saluted me and took off. I was frozen in place, trying to breathe. Men in suits eddied around me, curious; secretaries, overdressed as for junior proms, contemptuous. I was dizzy, bent slightly, hands on my thighs. My eyes were squeezed shut and my breath came in trios of short bursts, followed by gasps—breathing for labor, I realized. Lamaze breathing.

At that moment, on the Philadelphia streets, something subtle scattered or congealed in me. It was as if I'd breathed sharply enough to make all the physical sensations of the last hours converge: the pleasure of the sex, the grief, the longing for Ken and the anger at him and, at the base of it all, the promise of pregnancy that was a bath of light, amorphous as endorphins. It was a sudden clarity so complete and unexpected that it felt religious—then, immediately, close to crazy. Because I swear I could locate that sperm in my body, felt its homunculus personality like Zachary himself, guileless as a golden retriever with a Frisbee in its mouth, as it panted and slobbered its way toward its destiny. I was sticky, and it was sticking, that sperm. I could feel it. I was pregnant!

And then, still panting, I scolded myself. *Don't even think about it. Get a grip!*

I opened my eyes. I existed, almost naked in another woman's shoes, on a city street full of shops: the bright, impersonal promise of commerce. On my left, a money machine. On my right, Victoria's Secret.

T here was no one in line at the machine. I got $300 in cash. "Would you like another transaction?" the machine asked. "Yes or no." Sure, I said, and tried to get another $300.

I'm sorry, the machine informed me, but you have reached your limit for cash withdrawal.

Well, why did you offer then?

Three hundred dollars in twenty-dollar bills makes quite a pile. I was standing on a street corner with this roll of cash, large as something relay racers would hand to each other, with nowhere to put it but in the pocket of the nylon gym shorts. I tried to accomplish this without looking around too anxiously. To my amazement, no one seemed to have seen. Usually, in cities, the ATMs are fairly heavily patrolled by panhandlers, but this one had been left alone. The cash weighed the shorts down so much that I looked lopsided, deranged, like an outpatient, but it seemed like an even worse idea to spread out cash here to divide it up evenly, between two pockets.

Then I went into Victoria's Secret.

My thought at first was only to kill some time, in case anyone had been surreptitiously watching, and acquire some kind of box or bag to help me get back safely to the hotel. The second I entered the store, I grabbed a satiny pastel bathrobe off a rack, as if I'd fallen in love with it upon sight, and held the hanger up on my shoulder so that the garment covered my hip and the wad of bills. Then I strolled around: just taking a little jog, thought I'd duck in and see if I needed anything. This working-girl posture seemed perfectly reasonable to the salesclerks, who nodded, fake-chipper, as I meandered through racks and racks of push-up bras in jewel-toned laces, satins, and velvets appropriate for a grade-school play about royalty. It occurred to me, I *could* use some clean underwear. I was going into my third week on the clothes in my suitcase. Who knew how much longer I would be away? So I found some reasonable bras in beige and white, gathered up matching underwear (*panties* is not a word I will use voluntarily, even in such a place), took them into a dressing room.

By this point I had finally stopped hyperventilating. I looked calm: a grown woman with a good if somewhat disarrayed hair-cut, in need of undergarments. I stripped out of the T-shirt, took off my bra. Then the shorts and my underwear too, which of course was not part of the program. Stood naked there, skin slick and tingling, pubic hair slightly matted (I had not showered, after all, after Zachary), nipples hard for no reason other than the change in temperature: a woman who had enjoyed a couple of vigorous bouts of sex and run a couple of miles and was now just going to see how some bras fit.

But I was excited. Unquestionably. Titillated in idiotic Victoria's Secret with its classical music pumped in to bestow an aura of class on all that trampy, blue-collar lust among the cleavage, thongs, and garter belts. Well, why not. Why not. Who cared. I tried on the bras, which fit nicely. Brushed the shadow of my nip-ples through the translucent material, turned sideways as the catalogue models would to admire the firm curve of my hip and the swimmer's hollow of my gluteus maximus. Not bad for an old lady.

It occurred to me that I could masturbate, right here in the fitting booth. Or just think about masturbating, which, given the new, improved responsiveness of my body, amounted to almost the same thing. Though certainly, for official moral or legal purposes, there must be a difference. I flattened my hands on my hips with fingers spread as a lover would, sucked in whatever the vaginal muscles are called in a slow roll that fluttered up my neck to my face, closing my eyes; then sent the roll back the other way, slow and stately, like a red carpet slinking down the steps of a presidential plane.

I do recognize that this is not normal behavior, although I also suspect I'm not the first woman in the history of retail to have done this in a fitting room or contemplated doing this in a fitting room. Maybe the same characters who, once they find lovers, like to take possession of them in public rest rooms or elevators. I'd like to know, actually. I'd like to know if the overweight women— I'm assuming they're women, as I'm assuming they're overweight, sedentary at their desks with their sodas and corn chips, soap operas blaring on tiny, tinny TVs in the background—whose job it is to scan these fitting booths have any feelings about what they see. My guess is not much, mere flickers of contempt. It was three o'clock. I imagined the guard with her feet on the desk, calling home to make sure her children had gotten back from school. "Whatcha doin'?"

I shook my head at myself in the mirror, got dressed. Divided up the bills between the pockets, leaving out enough for my haul.

Paid for the merchandise with my beautiful new bills, requesting a box, of course, for the robe. Watched the salesgirl daintily fold the garments into the rustle of tissue paper, as if even too lingering a touch on the luscious fabrics was somehow naughty. I slipped the cash into the box as I left the store—the guard on duty, who was in the middle of an extended sports conversation with a male patron, didn't notice.

I did make one other stop before I returned, at an athletic-equipment store providentially placed in my path, where I held up my foot, pointed at the running shoe, and asked if they had them in my size, for Zachary's mother. They did. The salesclerk plopped himself on the bench and opened the box, ready to help me try them on. Ready to help me decide. I shook my head as I peered into the box. I'm sure they're fine, I said. He looked amazed, either because this was such an easy sale, or because I was foolish enough to buy two pairs of the identical overpriced running shoes. The woman who rang me up looked equally impressed or suspicious about the cash.

I walked back to the hotel jauntily swinging my bags, like any consumer.

According to the Four Seasons' elegant clock, it was almost four, which means that I'd met Zachary less than five hours ago. It felt like far longer. In fact, when I hit the air of the lobby, a gnawing fatigue overcame me, which was fine. I was in a hotel, with a bed. Except that only then did I remember I'd blown off the afternoon's appointments—not even called to explain, or reschedule, but simply failed to show up.

I went into the room braced for the phone's message light to be frantically, accusatorially blinking. I could hardly imagine how I would cope. But there were no messages. No one in the world knew I was here, except the Four Seasons management, and they didn't even feel the need to ask if I planned to stay on, so clear was it that I did. Why would anyone voluntarily leave? I kicked off the shoes, wadded the cash on the end table, lay down clothed on the bed, and slept.

A word about the tools of my trade. Many modes of communication were available to me. I carried a cell phone in my briefcase, and a pager. E-mail could be fired at me both through my port at work and through a commercial server. I had voice mail at work and an answering machine at home, fax machines at both home and office, and a secretary at a tastefully decorated work station answering an 800 number, should anyone crave the sound of a live human voice—not exclusive use of her, but use of her. Perhaps because we expected blessedly little of each other, she included my productivity, the smooth, orderly hum of my schedule, as part of her reason for being. She knew the system. She could check orders, run interference, if it was required.

As a backup I had a husband who was always, if not asleep, in the shower, watching TV, or talking to me, easy to locate at the office, in his car, or at the hospital. He had a secretary, a beeper, and a paging system ready to summon him from any location at the hospital, from the surgical theater to the urinal. How dare people call doctors arrogant? Kenneth is so shackled to his work he might as well be wearing a prisoner's monitoring device on his ankle. Once or twice a month we had dinner or a movie out alone or with another couple. Once or twice a year he went to a medical convention. At one of these, after several of the worst years that can be wished on a person, he had one lousy indiscretion. But I could have gotten in touch with him, I am convinced, even at the moment of orgasm.

And for what? Aside from keeping hearts beating in patients on gurneys, what is the payoff for all of this instant communication? In major metropolises, women now saunter into restaurants in their tight little black dresses, holding not pocketbooks but remarkably tiny, slim phones. What do they really need to hear over dinner? Offers for new gold credit cards? Charity solicitors? These are single women with tight hips and pursed lips—not the mothers who, in cell-phone ads, are always stranded on the side of the road, in dangerous thunderstorms. "Sorry," I always imagine the restaurant ladies hearing as they rush to answer, dainty dandelion greens stuck to their teeth. "Wrong number."

Once a week, I had a maid. She particularly enjoyed causing deep, random grooves on carpeting with a vacuum cleaner. Like the secretary, she loved me because, since Ken and I were rarely there, we made only mouse-size messes. We didn't splatter the oven. Most of our laundry went out, as dry cleaning. When she was in the house she picked up the phone if it rang, and could recite from the magnetized list on the refrigerator door, in English, all of the most likely places for a message to me to be expeditiously intercepted. On the days when she was there she gathered the mail off the floor, where it scattered from the slot in the door, and arranged it in an artful fan on the kitchen table. Like everyone, I got mostly bills. Who writes, with cell phones, answering machines, faxes, and E-mail?

Hardly anyone ever called me at home. My mother called two or three times a month for her frail, melodic "How are you, dear?" My father had been dead for long enough that my mother had been forced to start over, before it was too late, in Florida, where she had a circle of chipper, supportive cronies and even a boyfriend. Like my secretary, she required almost nothing from me. Neither did my brother, whom I'd never been close to anyway: a big blond hearty accountant, who golfed and fooled around with a boat.

As far as friends: I had them. But it had been a while since anyone I knew was mired in any urgent business. No one was getting married, pregnant, madly in love, or contemplating divorce, going bankrupt, or awaiting biopsy results. Except for the odd dyslexia or food allergy, the children were all in good health, skipping through that breezy bower between difficult toddlerhood and difficult adolescence. Even if my friends had troubles, they probably would not confide in me, since my relatively recent woes still officially eclipsed everyone else's. I could not convince them that I asked for no prizes for suffering or endurance. There had been an accident. It had changed things, inevitably. That it was simple did not make it painless. Nevertheless, I understood that all of our feet were pretty much glued to the same wet bed of domestic arrangements.

For confirmation that we had selves—that we existed as people someone might seek out, for advice or diversion—we all had our own Rolodexes, Filofaxes, and computer address lists, numbers automatically programmed to dial from our cordless phones. Jogging buddies, spicy food buddies. Friends from college. Those who felt ennobled by ballet subscriptions, those willing to get soused at ball games. I had a girlfriend with shapely feet— high-arched and reliably pedicured, with toe polishes in unexpected colors, who wore nice sandals in summer and swung her crossed, tanned legs and made me feel good to drink in the sun beside at an outdoor café. If I called her, she would be sympathetic. I could wake her up in the middle of the night; she would speak to me. I had coworkers with whom I could engage in serious conversations about product development or the future of health care.

I did not have, it is true, friends who were parents of my kid's friends. Women to gab with near swing sets. But as someone who made not a single friend in childbirth class, I had never much warmed to those kinds of alliances. Maybe when my son had gotten older they would have become more indispensable. As it was, I hardly had to give any up.

I was no one's mother. A mother might be the only person ever called out for, in the middle of the night, in a way that matters. "You need to feel connected," Kramer had admonished me, repeatedly. Well, sure! Who didn't? Still, I contend that my loss only highlighted the inevitable loneliness that everyone feels, even my friends with children sleeping across the hall, faces haloed by night-lights.

It would not help to volunteer in the preemie ward or join a grievers' group. And just because I was rational did not mean I was without emotion. I simply could not be, could never be the kind of person who either looked milkily skyward and said, "My son is with God now," or hurled myself down to wail and beat the soil with my fists. I might not be a creative person, a sculptor or philosopher or curer of cancer, but I could still live with energetic, clear-eyed purpose; I could try hard to be airily grounded, a woman with both heart and brain.

Right now, I realize, I was just floating. Trying to float. Skimming over my life, letting life tickle my feet. I had no plans to glide off entirely. Soon I would dip a toe in, test the temperature.

Was that so bad? Why did I not have that right? Why did I need so many distractions, disruptions, tugs, and knots?

And I was a salesman. That was my "living." My "livelihood" depended on generating "contacts." I was good at it. I was serious yet fun. Eager, yet never pushy. Competent but no automaton—I could drink at lunch, laugh at a joke, generate lighthearted E-mail messages. Bestow that "personal touch" essential to selling medical equipment so dull, ugly, and without personality that anyone would feel a chasm of churning emptiness open beneath them to have to deal with it on a daily basis, however much we proudly remind ourselves that such goods "matter" (as opposed to, say, push-up bras at Victoria's Secret).

As far as I was concerned, my job itself was reason enough to feel suicidal. My job itself was reason enough to lie on a bed at a hotel in a strange city, refusing to pick up my messages. If I arose from that bed and double-clicked the mouse on the tracking system for my current orders in progress, no less the problematic back orders or the lists of clients with whom I was in the process of developing relationships, I could probably get myself into a frame of mind appropriate to hurling myself through the sound-insulated, double-plated glass of the window onto the steamy pavement far below. As far as I am concerned, knowing that it was *not* the time to call clients or check orders represented sanity, self-control.

This is not, Kramer, "dissociation." Let's use more positive language, a more optimistic mind-set. This is "getting some distance," "giving yourself a break."

But I did it. It had to be done. After a short nap I got up, gritted my teeth, and checked my messages.

Thirty-one of them. It took almost a half hour just to record them all. They were pretty much what you'd expect, except for four notable things.

First, the multiple pleas, pardons, and updates from Kenneth I'd anticipated did not exist. He'd left one message only, on work voice mail, clipped and emotionless as an Rx on a prescription pad: "I will leave no more messages." Good for you, Ken! At last! The second was from the secretary at the office, asking how I would like her to deal with a call that had come in, from my husband, and another, subsequent phone call from him, retracting the first and saying never mind, he and I had merely missed each other, everything was fine; and a call from the purchasing officer at Children's Hospital in Philadelphia, asking to talk to my supervisor. She thought she should check with me first. Since it all seemed kind of strange. Before she passed the message on to Jack, who was not only my supervisor but the executive vice president, and she could easily hold off on doing so because, truth be told, he wasn't in town anyway. She hadn't seen me in a while. "Well, have a nice day, wherever you may be!"

Then, Dr. Kramer, whom I called Dan to his face as I'd been encouraged to do—I'm not sure why, in my mind, he existed so curtly as Kramer—but whose message had a halting formality I wasn't used to from him.

"Dan Kramer here. I am in a bit of an awkward position, Claire, and could use some guidance. I am leaving this somewhat elliptical message on your voice mail rather than on your home answering machine for the obvious reasons, and trust that your messages are listened to by you exclusively. I am sure you can understand why your husband is concerned. I have no way of knowing if his version of events is an accurate one, and in any case I cannot, will not, ethically, intervene on his behalf, as I have explained to him.

On the other hand, it is my impression that your husband may be behaving or contemplating behaving in ways that could have unpleasant repercussions for you. So if you are okay—and I trust you are, did my best to assure him that you were, in all likelihood, fine—you should probably make that clear to him. Meanwhile, I assume you know that you're welcome to call me."

Lastly, Zachary, on the hotel's voice mail. He did not leave his name, but of course I recognized him.

"Yo!" he said. "Doctor! Gotta problem. The shoes. She called fucking security. I'm down at the house phone, 'getting a Mars Bar.' So. Want to, like, ring once, hang up, meet me at the pool? Then how the fuck do I get them back into the room? I should of just told her I loaned them to somebody but by the time I got back she had three dicks up here. *Your* shoes are in evidence. Better just write 'em off. Sorry. So anyway. It's almost five. Bye."

brought both pairs of running shoes to the pool. Zachary brought the candy bar that was providing our cover. The scenario made me feel giddy. I could have worn sunglasses and a raincoat, as a joke, but the latter item was not currently available to me. I got there first. When he came in I nodded to him spy-fashion across the couple of stray splashers. In his baggy shorts and T-shirt, sockless in sneakers, he looked his age. But my shame seemed to be gone, I was interested to note, replaced with curiosity. It was refreshing to see him. I felt braced by the cognitive dissonance of his zitty face, his brash movements, and the grown-up sex I knew we'd had.

"Do you want brand-new shoes or hers?" I asked.

"You bought more?" he asked, surprised. "That was stupid. Hers. While she's in the shower I'll put them under the bed or something. Pretty lame when she had three security guards in the room with notepads and flashlights. Three! They were trying to look concerned, but you could imagine what they'd be saying the minute they left. Can you believe it? Storms in from her facial and marches right for her running shoes. Because she's in the same city as my dad, right? All of a sudden she has to be Linda Hamilton in *Terminator 2*. Now she's lining all the jewelry up on the bed. 'Let me think. Did I bring? . . .' I mean, *fuck*. Her fucking Hermès scarf from Paris that has pictures of fucking bicycles on it. Right.

Very hot item. They're just dying to get their hands on her fucking Hermès scarf. Maybe we ought to wash these off or something," he said, turning the shoes over to inspect the dirt ground into the treads. "But maybe that's worse. I mean, maybe she forgot she doesn't run."

For punctuation, he opened the candy bar with exaggerated force, as if he were doing a Greco-Roman wrestling hold on the plastic, ate most of it in one bite. "Gonna ruin my *app*-etite," he added mincingly, in Mom's voice.

"Are we having dinner together?"

"I told her I met a lady cardiothoracic surgeon at the pool," he reported, mouth full. "She said there were no women in that field. They're all big, dumb jocks, she said. Frat brothers. Guys who enjoy crushing beer cans in their bare hands."

"Well, she's basically right."

"So what about you?"

I did a classic bodybuilder's pose to show off my swimmer's shoulders.

"There's something wrong with you," he observed, holding his hands out for the shoes.

That was true, of course. But I did manage to extract the time of their dinner reservation, and the site: Le Bec Fin, a lavish French restaurant utterly inappropriate for a teenager. She would have had to make the reservation months in advance.

"You looking forward to that?"

His face twitched, then went blank. Shorted out. He was watchful behind that blankness, though, surreptitiously trying to process who I was. And it didn't look as if he was having much luck. Who could blame him? Clearly I didn't compute.

He did, though. And this is when my airport X-ray vision

shifted into gear, shifted into overdrive. I felt as if I were scanning him, not only who he was now but who he would be—the outlines of his adult self shifting into focus, shadowy but present, as you'd read a sonogram. His acne-scarred adult face leaner but also more open, more forgiving. I could see him exchanging confidences with a woman huddled in the crook of his arm. He'd just made love to her. Eventually he would marry her. Tickling her back in the aimless way men will sometimes, after sex, he was telling her about this marginal lady surgeon he'd bedded at the Four Seasons Hotel in Philadelphia, Pennsylvania, in the weeks before his freshman year at college, by no means his first fuck but a formative one. How so? she asks. (Just then I notice she's Asian. Vietnamese, actually, her darkly lustrous hair an oil slick. Won't his mother be surprised!) You know, the Older Woman, he says. But because this girl is important to him and he knows it without yet knowing it, he softens, adds, "I don't know. She was nuts. She had a dead kid. She hadn't really gotten over it. I guess I was part of her cure."

And the girl whispers, "How sad." Those two plangent words. He answers, "Not really."

"Well *that's* good," she says, and they both laugh.

Then I swear to God I was imagining their children, the hybrid curve of their eyes, their dark but imperfectly straight hair, their thin, elegant, dusky hands. The wife is so fine-boned. Their son will not be Zach's size, will not be athletic, but Zach won't mind; it will surprise him that he doesn't mind. And won't he be surprised when their daughter turns out to be the athletic one, pushing right past ballet to karate and gymnastics, a tumbling powerhouse with a pert ponytail and black belt, and I could see them in bed again, discussing how to handle her, because as much as they love to imagine themselves in slow motion, cheering her at the Olympics, their eyes wet with pride, they don't want her to have that kind of life, who would wish that on a child?

This all came to me in several seconds, with the force of prophecy. Then dispelled. Nothing similar had ever happened to me before. I liked it. Thereafter I would feel less disdain toward the detectives who call in psychics to aid in murder investigations.

When I came to, the teenaged Zachary was staring at me, concerned. "What's with you, anyhow?" he asked. "Can't you take a pill?"

"You're my pill, Zachary. Didn't you know that?"

"Don't fuck with me," he said coldly.

"A little late," I observed. "I just want some company on the road, in a strange city. What's the big deal? Besides, my son's at Brown too. Isn't that reason enough?"

He sighed. He didn't seem to remember, or care, that I'd already blown my own cover on the lie of the son at Brown. "You won't like my mother," he said, but I told him I was sure he was wrong. I was immensely curious about her, about why she had an opinion on surgeons, on (and I realize this sounds stupid) how she would look, how she would look at her boy.

The first thing I noticed about her were her feet in sandals. I saw her feet first because as we'd agreed (oddly, since we were all coming from the same place), I was already at the bar, seated, so as they approached her feet were closer than the feet of strangers usually are. Plus they glittered. The impeccable toenail polish, thick as car paint—I tend to notice such things because I've never indulged in a pedicure, am about as likely to do so as I am to learn to bungee jump or speak Japanese—sparkled, as did the shoes, which were in some kind of spangly pewter. They were *confident* feet.

They needed to be, because every inch that your eye traveled upward from the feet, past the exquisite armor of her clothes to her face, you watched her lose the smooth élan. Her face was pure, naked anxiety. Please, please, please, this face said. Don't hurt me.

Zach's Mom, Marjorie. Who went by the more dignified, Continental, hopeful Margot. ("As in *escargot*," Zachary would later offer.) *Mar* to her friends.

Marred, unmarried Mar.

"Very pleased to meet you," she said, proffering a tiny, nervous hand.

I gave her a certain salesman's handshake—fast motion, but incongruously light pressure—to register respectful curiosity.

She would never get over the divorce.

All those years ago but she was right, there was no cure, nothing would work: she would never recover.

Because I found myself nonplussed by the force of my own knowledge (this was the second time in a day, after all, that I'd felt almost omniscient), I reminded myself that I was, probably, not clairvoyant. Just a salesman. A salesman can speed-read not only the walk, the voice, the clothes, and gestures—all of the loudspeaker announcements of identity and aspiration—but the aura of a customer's need. No one can hide from a good salesman. It's less true in pushing medical equipment than it is for cars or face creams, but it is the same principle. Although this is not the conventional wisdom, I believe that the salesman's instinct is kind. Even altruistic. Like priests, we find the ache and aim for solace.

Zachary in a tie and jacket. How cute!

His ponytail, still damp from the shower, pulled back smooth as a ballerina's.

He'd tacked on an expression of patrician Swiss neutrality. He looked almost as formal as the maître d' who seated us.

Two middle-aged women and a teenaged boy. The maître d' tried to look noncommittal but he'd already taken our measure, dismissed us, ushered us to a table against the wall with "We have no bad tables" defensiveness, and within minutes the efficient waiter ("Ladies? Gentleman?") had taken our drink orders, dismissed us as well. If salesmen read the soul, waiters scan right through you—their eyes like the cameras airports use to X-ray luggage—right to the contents of your wallet.

Which reminded me of my cash-flow problem.

Why it hadn't occurred to me before I agreed to meet people at the most expensive restaurant in town is not quite clear.

(On hotel voice mail, when I returned from the pool to dress for this rendezvous: the Four Seasons desk, politely noting that they'd need my credit card now, if I was planning to stay on. How long, if they might ask, was I planning to stay on?)

The waiter had given Zach the wine list. Zach was reading it the way you'd read the back of a cereal box, because it was there.

"Shall I do the honors?" I asked.

Zach slipped the wine list to me low. Locked eyes with me over his domestic beer as his mother fluttered at the menu. Beamed me a "Don't Tread on Me" glare, tight-jawed. I returned an ingenue smile.

"Oh everything looks so *yummy*," Mar said. "So where's your boy now? I hear he's on the swim team too."

So he hadn't told her. Or hadn't heard me. Or had simply forgotten. I looked at him, trying to determine which, but he was now surveying the room, diligently avoiding eye contact. "Red or white?" I asked brightly.

Mother: "White."

Son: "Red."

They laughed the same volcanic, barking laugh. I'd assumed his laugh was the father's, but it came out of her like she was belching up a poltergeist. It made me feel a rush of warmth toward her.

Even before the compromise rosé arrived (the sommelier opening it with the grave ceremony of a bomb defuser), the starched tablecloths, the flowers glinting in candlelight, were beginning to work on me. Why pay this kind of money for dinner otherwise? To see your own flushed face in a mirror across the room. To see yourself register in a stranger's eyes, or register anew in your spouse's.

Ken and I hadn't gone out much. Without discussion, it had been clear to both of us that it was pointless, too trashy a consolation. Nothing like grief to turn to dust the dry, weightless world of things. Vases, cars, clothes? All husks. Exotic fish and game in ambrosial sauces, baby greens and out-of-season fruit flown in with the kind of care reserved for donated organs? Who cares. Who cares.

For almost three years I had eaten mechanically, for survival only, like people in the cafeterias of hospitals. I'd gone out; I'd drunk with clients. Even good wine tasted like NyQuil.

But it was lifting. It was lifting and it was somehow because of Zach, and his mother. I felt protected and protective at once—a golden mean, like the rosé. As the waiter recited the epic poem of the specials, I breathed in food from the tables around me and realized, no question, I was getting excited; I felt animated, inhabited.

I felt like a baby bird, neck raised, mouth open.

Which is interesting because there was something avian about Marjorie's pinched, pointy face, her flittery movements. (Zach got her mouth. But that appeared to be it. Face shape, skin color, eyes, body—all from absent Dad.)

"As I told Zach, I was very surprised by your specialty," she said, ordering accomplished. "In all my years I've never heard of a single woman in cardiothoracic surgery."

"There are a couple of us. Have you spent a lot of time around physicians?"

"Oh, I've done my time. Is your boy premed too?"

"Yup. Leaning toward orthopedic. Sports medicine."

"They sure do warm to the idea of breaking those bones. I keep telling Zachary, forget surgery. Do something that requires a brain, like endocrinology."

She didn't seem to realize that this could be construed as a derogatory comment. "Endocrinology's good," I agreed.

"Right," Zach said, sighing. "Diabetes is a blast."

"It's true you got diabetes and thyroid as your bread-and-butter," I said. (Convenient if random, almost certainly inaccurate memories from double dates during Ken's residency.) "But most of your diseases are interesting. You get weird things: Dwarfs. Sex hormones. Theochromocytoma!"

Mother and son both looked at me, impressed.

"Then again, you need endurance for surgery," I merrily prattled. "Which I guess is why so many of us swim."

This was the perfect moment to 'fess up. *I should tell you, my husband's the surgeon. And my boy*—but why would I be here with them, if it weren't for Brown and swimming and medicine? To expose the lie now would be to expose the hotel sex to Zach's mother. Although why would they think I'd choose their company, a physician in town for a convention, was a question, too.

"I dated a pediatrician once," Mar offered, and before we knew it, just like that, we were back to her central sadness and subject: how singlehood was hurled like a massive boulder on her road to happiness. How she could never trust anyone again. How men were all alike. How badly she wanted to be held by any one of them, even bald or potbellied or poor if only kind, with a mind.

She didn't say any of this directly, but over her salad (of course salad: she had to keep thin for the man who didn't exist), she made it clear to me by implication that it was hopeless, and she still couldn't help but hope. Zachary, who knew this tape loop, concentrated on his ridiculously rich crab cakes, tried to stifle his contempt. I admired him for that. She didn't need his contempt as well. It occurred to me that he was unusually mature, to not give his mother the grief that any mother should expect from a teenaged boy—playing loud music in his room and staying out late with his chums. Instead he was in the world, acting out with his cock, like an adult male. The thing is, he'd chosen *me*. Or allowed himself to be chosen by me. Or who he thought I was. Not only an MD, but a confident, strong MD in a male-dominated field. He wanted me to know, too, that he knew the difference between me and his mother.

So when Mom launched into a mini-tirade about doctors and lawyers ("Yes, they're selfish, but at least it's up front"), he allowed our eyes to meet in a way that said, *Let's ditch her here and meet in the alley.*

Not that he wanted to, really.

But I did appreciate the thought.

"Are you sure you really want to mix wine and beer?" Mar interrupted herself to ask her son. He was gulping it, Gatorade-style. Any male would feel parched listening to her, even a fledgling one.

" 'Mix'?" he scoffed. "Wine, beer, and tequila—that's mixing, Mom. Wine, beer, tequila, and Black Russians."

"I certainly hope you have more sense than to drive under such combinations," she said, with what I'm sure she considered restrained concern.

" 'Drive'?" he said.

"Drugs, too, probably," she pointed out to me, complicitly.

" 'Drugs'?" he said.

What was he doing? He sounded eleven.

At this point she got off Man-as-Beast, onto The Trials of the Single Mother. Which was, I guess, the very point of his behavior. Unsticking her. Fast-forwarding the tape. "Don't get the wrong idea. Compared to most, Zachary's a good kid," she informed me. He batted his eyelashes, mock-appreciatively. And we both let her go on, rearing back so the busboy could remove our appetizer plates, rearing back again for the flourish of the entrées.

"Oh my! How lovely! How many gazillion calories do you think this sauce has? Pure cellulite! On me it goes straight to my hips. *Straight.* How do *you* keep so slim, Claire?"

A competitive weight conversation. Right in time for dinner.

I managed to get out a sentence or two about the relaxing, centering properties of swimming laps.

"Of course," Mar said, "at our age you can't win. If you manage to stay thin you get *these.*" She jabbed with her fork near her crow's feet, her mouth. The one advantage of being fat, she remarked: smooth, flushed skin. Have you noticed how beautiful fat women's hands are?

We might have been able to drift on to how hard chlorine is on the hair, but I had been with this woman less than an hour and I hated her. *Hated* her.

I didn't manage to suppress a look to Zachary that meant, Is there any way to turn her *off*?

The look he shot me back said, laconically, I told you so.

We had this exchange fairly openly, since she didn't seem to be paying any attention. But she noticed immediately. It is always surprising how quick oblivious narcissists can be to catch a slight. Mar sighed, hurt. Even this nice dinner, the sigh said. I can't even have one nice dinner with my son. What I said next surprised even me.

"Mar. May I offer a piece of advice? As a still-married woman? If what you want, more than anything in the world, is to be tenderly held, I can tell you that you're going about it the wrong way. Entirely the wrong way."

She audibly gasped.

How easy it still is to shock people with the truth. Any truth. Well, she asked to be hurt. Here was her self-fulfilling prophecy.

"Certainly you must know that," I went on. "Talking so much is one thing—Christ, read *Cosmo*. But the neediness! It's stultifying! Where do you expect to get, presenting yourself like this? If you think the problem is your body—your thighs, your wrinkles—then work on your body. Lift weights. Do some low-rep sets two, three times a week. Build bone density. Build confidence. Exercise is good. But come on! Your gestures! They're anti-sexy! Start with *stillness*. Stillness and concentration. Yoga— that's what I recommend for you. Not weights. You don't need to become a grand master. Just learn the basics. Lie down, close your eyes, and feel the muscles in your body that are tensed, which on you is just about every single one of the available six hundred. Learn to untense them. Your eyelids, your neck, your knees. Learn how to be slack. Then maybe you can start to uncoil your mind, which is so knotted-up you can't hope to feel love, or peace, or just about anything else but futile anxiety."

"Who are you to—" she stammered as I began, but then she just listened, helpless. As did Zach. Neither of them was eating. I was, though. Thoughtfully, talking in between, so this speech took a fairly long time to deliver.

"I'm not trying to be unkind," I went on. "I'm trying to help, really. Stillness is the key. What are you rushing on to? Death? *Stop.* Let's have a lesson. Look around. If you could fuck anyone here, who would it be?"

Zach pointed a cocked finger toward the cleavage of a babe in a push-up bra.

"Not you." I smiled. He shrugged, enjoying this despite himself.

"I—" she said. "I—"

"Not 'you.' That's the point. Just look around and try to be open. Try to pretend that anything can happen to you, at any moment."

"They're all married," she objected. "Married or with their mistresses. They're all *with* someone. It's easy for you to talk. You don't have—"

"Watch," I said. "Say I like that man over there—no! For God's sake, guys, subtlety please!"

(They'd both swiveled so violently to stare that the prosperous-looking fellow in question, though halfway across the restaurant, looked up sharply.)

"Okay. Let's start over. I won't tell you which one this time. Watch."

I admit I was tipsy. I folded my hands under my chin and fixed my gaze on a middle distance in which Margot and Zachary didn't exist, just the flowers and the candles, the restaurant's lavish haze. Let my eyes go out of focus. When I zoomed in again I was staring at the profile of our waiter, bent slightly at the table beside us and stacking someone else's used plates up his arm. He was a career waiter in his early thirties, sculpturally handsome enough that I'd taken him for gay. He returned my gaze. His posture shifted, so the plates seemed to be better balanced, almost floating on the arm, and he moved toward me, lips slightly parted.

"Do you—need something?" he almost whispered.

"Oh," I said. Giving each word a little smoothness, a little burn, like a bite from a crème brûlée. "No. Thanks. It was—great."

"I'll be right back," he said. "To take your plates."

And he was, too, beelining.

"Thank you!" I said.

"See?" I asked Mar, when he'd left.

"Cool party trick," Zach said. "Can you make glasses rattle too, like in *Carrie*?"

"What's the big deal?" Mar said roughly. "You flirted with a waiter."

"No. Not at all. I just acknowledged him as an actual human being. If you give attention, you might get some back."

"Are you suggesting that the best I can do is to pick up waiters?"

She hadn't heard a word I'd said. I tried to proceed without rancor or condescension.

"Well, you just delivered a speech about how much you hated mercenary doctors and lawyers. Maybe you should give waiters a chance. Writers, actors. Car mechanics. Carpenters. Just think, Mar, if you'd married Harrison Ford while he was a humble carpenter, you'd be married to Harrison Ford now."

She couldn't help but smile. Now *that's* what she had in mind, in a man pushing sixty years old. Her eyes softened for long enough to imagine them on their Montana ranch.

"How long have you been alone now?" I asked. "Well, alone with this charming boy." (Zachary mock-bowed, accepting the compliment.) "All that time treating your singlehood like a prison sentence for a bum rap, rattling the bars, carving knives out of soap. So he left you! So what! You must have had some therapy after the divorce, but even if you didn't, come on, this is standard pop-psych shit. The only prison is self. Self itself. All that time, but you can't act like it was time wasted, you can't act like it's too late. Because here is your boy, all grown up, and here is your life."

When I finished she was fighting back tears. The look she gave me meant I was right, of course I was right, but it was hopeless; she not only couldn't change her attitude, she couldn't even keep herself from openly weeping at Le Bec Fin.

"Hey Mom!" Zachary said.

She looked at him, trembling.

"*Mom!* Gimme a hand!"

She moved the hand toward him. He picked it up by the wrist and shook it vigorously, as a wet dog would shake itself off. Then let it go, tossed her arm in the air, caught it. Worked the hand into some kind of elaborate locker-room high five, thumbs battling.

"Remember this?" he asked, still working her palm and thumb.

> "Margot, Margot,
> Eating escargot!
> Throwing the shells
> Straight into hell,
> Be you friend or foe
> Your garlic farts
> I will forgo!"

Mother and son jointly laughed their Vesuvius laugh. She grabbed her hand back from him and clutched her stomach.

She did cry now, but they were socially acceptable tears of deep hilarity.

"Back, Zach!" she said.

> "Don't gimme any flak
> Don't get me off track
> Or I'll have a heart attack!
> Alas, alack, fair Zach!"

Astonishing. He had cured her. "Oh, my," she said.

"There aren't really any rhymes for Zachary," he explained to me.

" 'He explained to me,' " I suggested. " 'Rosary. Had to be. Set me free.' "

"Hey! Not bad. Next time, you can play too."

Margot wiped mascara off with the back of her hand. Then she looked at her boy, happy. She hadn't *totally* thrown away her life, and here was the proof. For a moment she looked at her boy the way I'd seen other mothers look at other sons, a look so imperceptible that maybe only someone who has mourned the death of a child, or someone who couldn't have children and desperately wanted to, might register. Others could dismiss it as ordinary pride. But it's more complicated. Head pushed slightly back on their necks, as if they're trying to get the proper distance, to view whole what they have made. As if they're feeling, "Here is a life not flashing before my eyes but staying there, continuing to unfold and surprise, if I can only continue to observe this subtly, without being noticed." Very specifically a mother-son thing, because of the cheerful detachment. The most decided asexuality: a woman viewing a man she loves, but will not make love to.

(With women and their daughters, there's pride and pleasure too, but also the wistful sense of the grown woman being shoved aside, replaced by the nubile and new.)

"Well!" Mar said, cheerful now. "I guess I'll go fix myself up before dessert!"

For a longer-than-usual time after she left, Zachary and I did not speak. We just looked at each other, enjoying the undemanding silence. His gaze was disconcertingly adult. Didn't therapists have a word for the kids made into divorcées' confidants and comforters? I hoped the precipitous sophistication would not hurt him too much, turn him into a misogynist or gigolo.

"You were so good with her," I said. "I'm really impressed."

"And you were—kind of rough."

"Sorry."

"You can't imagine the progress she's made. I mean, she got through almost the whole dinner without talking about my dad once."

"I'm sorry, Zach."

"You, anyhow, no offense, do not seem like any Michael Jordan of Mental Health, to go lecturing someone else on their game."

"True. Sorry."

He shook his head at me, in imitation of a stern headmaster.

Why had I been so mean? Out of protectiveness for him, of course. Out of indignation for him, that she didn't even *pretend* to take more consolation from being his mother. Why do awful parents always get such sensitive, self-sufficient kids? It doesn't seem fair. And because every so often I couldn't help playing Nobody

Knows the Trouble I Seen. I was supposed to think she had problems, over a *divorce*? Still. I felt so bad for turning the woman's special night out into *Lord of the Flies* that I thought I might cry myself.

As if reading my mind, he said, "Hey! Forget about it! It was *fun*! Good clean fun to beat up on my mom! She can take it. Believe me, when she comes back from the bathroom with her new lipstick on she'll be fine. You, I'm not so sure about."

"Me," I agreed.

"Yes. You. As in 'you.' "

The *you* hung there, like a reproach.

But Margot had returned, bright-lipped as Zachary had predicted, led by the shiny feet in a runway-model swagger, full of high spirits and forgiveness.

"I haven't missed the famous Le Bec Fin dessert tray, have I?" she asked. "Have you ever been here? What does your husband do, Claire, incidentally? You didn't say. Waiter?"

"Surgeon," I sighed. "Cardiothoracic."

"How romantic! Did you meet in school? Do you practice together?"

Here was my chance to set the record straight. There was no excuse not to. So I did. Just blurted out the microfiche-condensed version: accident, troubled marriage, unfaithful husband, fictitious kid at Brown.

"I apologize to you both. And to you especially, Mar, because I have no right . . ."

Zach was craning his neck desperately. Hoping for the arrival of the dessert tray to forestall further revelations. But Mar's eyes were filling again, with sympathy. "Horrible," she said. "So hard." And: "Do you love your husband?"

I nodded to indicate that I did, very much.

"Then let me give *you* some advice," she said. "Hold on. Even if you're not sure what you're holding on to."

Our waiter then appeared wheeling twenty or thirty desserts on a cart. He gave us time to rapturously ogle. He explained, caressingly, the identity of each item. We could have whatever we wanted, even a bite of everything. Made much of composing the plates to each of our kid-in-a-candy-shop liking.

We smiled, and ate, and moaned. The waiter put the bill on the middle of the table and Zachary swooped for it. He mimicked all the gestures of an adult man approaching a check—crossing his legs, reading the check sideways in its black folder in his lap, withdrawing a credit card and slipping it in with the folder in one move like a man picking a lock—so well that he would have seemed just like an adult male, until he said:

"Let's test out this card, Mom. See if it works."

"Well, thanks!" I said. "To you both!"

Hey, I was entitled to the dinner for services rendered. Sex. Psychotherapy.

But I paid for the cab back to the hotel.

The dessert had stunned us all. We didn't really talk about anything but our joint satiation.

In the lobby Mar and I shook hands. There was so little between us now we really could have just met at a medical convention. Like me, she was somewhere to the side of inebriated. Zachary seemed to be the only one able to hold his drink. More practice, probably.

Was it me, was it the alcohol, or did every move this kid make have a kind of ironic shadow, a ventriloquized sarcasm? As if he were sitting behind himself making faces at himself, like that old

Chevy Chase *Saturday Night Live* skit. Which he wouldn't have
even seen. Too young. *"Doctor,"* he said, moving the arm toward
me in a slow-motion arc, as if it was part of a tai chi move. "Very
nice. To make your acquaintance."

"To Brown," I said. "To swimming."

I was trying to imply I could meet him at the pool, but I
couldn't—I knew that, even if he didn't—and anyway the invitation swam right by him.

"And remember," Mar said, "if you ever need to chat—"

"Thanks!"

"—just call! Call right up!"

"I will! And good luck to you!"

If I knew what state she lived in, to which state she fled after
the divorce, I had already forgotten. But Zachary, I knew, I could
find. He would soon have a PO box at his dorm, an E-mail
address.

I also knew I would never see or speak to him again.

Except in the elevator, which we had to share. Nothing like
exchanging totally shallow good-byes twice.

My room was too cold and smelled vaguely foul, like ice cubes that hold the odor of the freezer where they're stored, the bad tap water from which they're made. My bed had been turned down. My message light blinked spastically.

I turned down the air-conditioning and stood beside the window, rubbing my goose-bumped arms. Tried to take in the city's twinkling lights as comfortingly impersonal—a big wide world that I was a part of. But there was no solace in the thought. I wasn't a speck of sand in the desert that God made for some seagull to peck at, part of a grand, melodic plan. I was just a speck. No more momentous than a runway light.

How dramatic, I thought and also, *You really can't drink.*

Shortly thereafter I found myself before the toilet, retching. Wretched.

No offense to the famous chef and his touch with butterfat in all of its glorious manifestations.

There's nothing like puking in a strange bathroom to make you long for the comforts of home.

I returned the phone call to the desk. The clerk said that if I was planning to stay on, they would need an imprint of my card. My card had been stolen, I reminded him. I had paid him cash. But only for the first night, he noted, and that would not necessarily cover incidentals. I said I would call back with the number (which I had not thought to transcribe, on the phone with the bank).

"I'm not sure that'll work," he said.

"And why on earth is that?" I inquired, roughly.

"Once you're here, we require an imprint of the card. Anyone, you know, could pull one of your credit-card receipts from the trash and pretend to be you, use your number."

"So you want to see my driver's license? It's got my picture on it. Anyhow, wouldn't that be equally true for the deposit you give over the phone, in advance?"

"I'm afraid that's our policy, but I'll check with our manager," he said, with strained patience.

This is the treatment one can expect when one *pays*? Hotel staffs had been more accommodating to me when I was a squatter. Even if I managed to get back to an ATM, the hotel might not accept a cash payment, just as you can't rent a car without a credit card to prove you are financially solvent.

I told him I would take care of it, soon. Then I lay down fully clothed on the bed with the thought that, yes, expired: Ken could come now. Ken could come and get me.

Didn't even brush my teeth. Just crossed my arms like a mummy and waited for Ken.

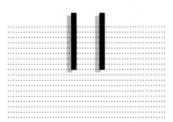

E xcept he didn't come, of course.

It was—Wednesday? Thursday? Day sixteen, seventeen of my walkabout? On my watch, the day and date had become stuck; at noon they would creep halfway to the next stop and stay there, trembling, like a house cat frozen in the middle of an intersection, until midnight, at which point they'd leap a day or a day and a half. Decidedly not a weekend, in any case, and Dr. Kenneth Leithauser would be at his office, seeing patients, any one of whom could, unlike me, actually up and die at any moment.

Easy enough to stand, turn on the computer, check the date and time. Flick on the stock-market channel, check the date and time scrolling along the bottom along with the quotes. Easier still: twist my neck, look at the clock. Digital. No need, even, to process the meaning of hands along a dial. But it was pleasant somehow, or necessary, to not know.

Leithauser. I lay in bed, cesspool-mouthed, trying to conjure my husband. Trying to think about him. He was a brainteaser, as his name was a mouthful. I wanted to mentally embrace him with a wife's easy fondness but I kept getting ensnared in some intangible tangle. *Leithauser:* I tried saying his name out loud to myself, caressingly. Tried to follow *lighthouse* through the obvious metaphorical connotations—the comforting beam of light leading me home—but the lighthouse kept turning phallic, the sea below dark and matted as pubic hair, and then it would be, as I tried to draw eye and brain upward, not even Ken's lighthouse but Zachary's. Pinker. Sex itself a computer-animated game of ring-toss where I was the life buoy bobbing nearby, being shot upward toward the mammoth head, but I couldn't reach that high and I would never fit anyway, then sinking back into the undertow. Wailing, in Betty Boop squeak, *Save me!*

Zachary also did not come.

Not that he was expected. But maybe a phone call. A good-bye, nice-to-meet-you phone call would have been gallant. I kept semi-waiting for it; when he calls, I thought, I will wake up, get on with things.

Hitchcock again. The climax of *Notorious*: Ingrid Bergman, steadily and insidiously poisoned by her Nazi hubby, quite fetching on her deathbed, hair combed and lipstick on, pale in her opaque nightgown, groggy and foggy, so that Cary Grant, when he arrives, has to swoop her up and carry her down the long, long stairway. Where was Ken?

Cary Grant, cardiothoracic surgeon. *This won't hurt a bit.* How beautifully the lab coat drapes on him. Pulling the bulky stethoscope from his pants as suavely as a pocket watch.

I tried to get out of the operating room by imagining my myopic husband taking off his glasses to kiss me. He always took his glasses off before we kissed, so why was I imagining—why could I only imagine—the first time he did so? It had been obvious we would make love, we both knew we would, when we arranged the date. I sat on his couch after the movie, expectant. He sat not next to me, but across from me, on the ottoman from the matching chair. Stood up solemnly to move the ottoman closer. Here's the part I kept replaying, how all of these things happened at once: he swooped the glasses off by grabbing the bridge piece and reached beside him to put the glasses down (he wouldn't have had time to fold them); he emitted the tiniest of moans, not excitement so much as an exhalation of surrender, defeat; and then I was locked blindly into his hard kiss. No romantic farting-about with Ken, not even at the start. He's not a tickler or licker, no maestro of escalating series of exploratory anythings. He is as functional and forthright as the rented, Scotchgarded living-room furniture he had then as a medical student, which sexually, at its best, translates into a blunt urgency straight out of TV shows about emergency rooms. And at its worst is marriage. Managed care.

But that first time his eyes were open. He couldn't see, because he's blind, and when my eyes fluttered open he was watching me. Trying to watch me. More than first seeing his veiny cock emerging like a bald eagle from its bird's nest of black (now graying) hair—erect it looked angry and put me in mind sometimes, cartoonishly, of the Black Panther power fist—seeing his naked bluegray eyes felt like being trusted with a secret.

When I think about falling in love with my husband I feel that moan and the vulnerability of his eyes. It is cumbersome to describe but in memory it happens in less than a heartbeat and is etched in me permanently, the strength of the memory in direct contrast to the moment's delicacy, like a fossil-print of a fern. The intensity because it is a moment only, unrepeatable. As opposed to marriage (washing and meticulously drying his glasses, dropping his glasses, "where the hell are my glasses"). I had had sex with Zachary only the day before and already the memory had less force than my first time with my husband, but that is because you need history—time itself—to give the moment weight. Which is why all the seventies rhetoric about "living for the moment" was such a crock. But then, we were eighteen. Everything was a crock.

Crock, cock, and here is the bleed, the blood: the birth of my son. Another moment, preserved trembling not in aspic but in fetal cheese. The final push and the fact of the flesh of my flesh. During the hospital tours I had been obsessed with the procedures for labeling the newborns. Didn't want someone else's. Wanted my own. But I recognized him immediately. Smashed and bloody, splotchy, wrinkled and ragged-nailed, wary, indignant, resigned: mine.

This I cannot describe, even at length. How I *knew*. Alien as he looked, he had not been sent from outer space, he had just exploded from inside me, and I felt the first second the doctor held him up that you could throw him naked at night into a field of babies, babies multiplying like ears of corn—all crying, a racket like crickets in summer—and I could still pick him out, still hear his cry. Zoom right to him.

BOY NEWBOLD, the wrist tag announced; I never changed my name, and my son's name hadn't been definitive for the first day or so. I loved the sound of it. "Boy Newbold": valiant, King Arthury. We'd wanted a name that swaggered, not the weight lifters or car repairmen of Wayne or Guy, just masculine and decisive without being silly. Those one-syllable Hun/Viking/biblical names: Ned, Luke, Matt, Jake. But then we saw him and we couldn't do it. Saw his softness—even breast-feeding, purposeful, there was something gentle in him. Courteous. Almost formal. Ken's parents found it pretentious (and WASPy, of course). "What is he," Ken's mother tssked, "a law firm?" But what did they know. "Evan" wasn't even the top contender until we met him, and it was his name.

"Love at first sight?" Any woman who believes she has felt this about a man is a liar. Not this. You really have to start from scratch, from birth. From the namelessness of creation, before language, before even sex.

And isn't what makes the love of an infant so profound that it puts you back to the most bedrock layers of yourself, when you barely existed but needed to be loved. Don't all of us replay, individually, the history of mankind, the evolution from tadpole to mammal. And all of us need to be loved not as accomplished, attractive adults, but as we are when we were born. Ugly as moles. Needy. Blind, open mouths.

If my son had lived, he wouldn't have remembered a thing that had happened to him so far. Not a single thing. But his life as an infant would have been there, fossilized, in his most secret places. He would have felt it when he kissed a woman, when he held his own newborn.

The head of a penis is not like the head of an infant. It is more like the head of a leprechaun or elf, bald and shiny, cheerful. But the penis has an infant's eye, that blind and swollen slit.

Speaking of slits. These are the kinds of things I thought about and did, locked in the Four Seasons hotel room, fuguing out as Ken would say. Semi-sleeping, I would follow the circuit of these thoughts and then, at *slit*, see it as a entry in an old-fashioned, wooden-drawered library card catalogue. SLIT, SPEAKING OF. Typed on an old-fashioned manual typewriter, the kind where the periods struck with such force they'd punch holes through the paper. As illustration of the force I would reach down and simply yank on my underwear—wasn't there a word for this as a fraternity hazing ritual, cold-cocking, cold-cunting?—until the edge of the cotton was shoved in the crack. Would attempt to make myself come this way, simply by concentrating on the misplaced edge of lace and elastic, on words like *cold* and *crack,* their sharp simplicity. Couldn't. Would realize I had to pee. Would contemplate getting up. SEE ALSO: HOLE. Wet. Would contemplate getting up, taking a shower, going to the pool. Would envision myself going back and forth, back and forth. *You should make yourself come, it'd make you feel better.* But I had to pee. Not enough energy, even, to get up and do that, no less swim laps. Not enough energy to get up and make sure that the DO NOT DISTURB sign was in position, so that I couldn't masturbate because I would be interrupted, momentarily, by someone trying to clean the room. I was in terror that it would be Nefertiti, from yesterday. This time she would be armed. Well let her see, I would think, rousing myself enough to throw off the covers, take off my underwear, openly masturbate. But a stroke or two would remind me I couldn't. I had to pee. And it was too cold. Not enough energy, even, to get up and adjust the thermostat.

But eventually I would, and go to the bathroom, in time for it to get too hot, and I'd need to start the process over again.

Through all of this a persistent image: the rental car in the parking garage at The Children's Hospital. Just parked there.

Where, even, was the stamped receipt. I hadn't seen it. Should go through my purse. Wasn't even sure I remembered what car it was. Was not sure when I returned to the lot I could find it. Red? Gray? Buick? Camry? I had no idea. None. The rental car had fled from my head.

B.F.D. I would say to myself, you can call Enterprise, they will look it up in the computer, like they care that you are a ditz. That is all you are, you are a ditz. But I knew I was far worse than a ditz and also far better because the connections I was making—the long ribbon of sex, self, procreation—were real and true, even if I had to go a bit crazy to string them together, let myself go out of focus enough to see the faceted beads of these thoughts glinting.

The question was how crazy. The question was how deep into myself I could bear to go. HOLE, SEE ALSO: I was like one of those cave scuba divers without a tank, plunging straight down. How long could I hold my breath, how far could I get from the surface. I was like one of those math problems on the SAT that I used to be so good at, could do so effortlessly—if X is traveling at Y speed, and going so far, how long will it take them to reach wherever.

But I wasn't going anywhere if I couldn't stand up, couldn't pee, couldn't shower and dress, check out, get to my rental car.

If I called Ken, I could say come and get me. I'm sorry but could you please come to Philadelphia and get me. He would not be angry. I am at the Four Seasons. He could come, immediately. Although it was August I saw him wrapping me tenderly in a coat, leading me to the elevator. Saw myself in the safety of our silver Legend, engine running, the leather seats cool against the backs of my legs, waiting for him to take care of the rental car. Heard him talking to the parking attendant in his imperious physician's voice. No we do not have the ticket, fine charge us the maximum, do I look like I care what you charge me for parking just get on with it.

But he would fly not drive. But how would I wait for his car, how would I recognize it. Who cared what kind of car he rented at the airport, let it be a Cavalier for all I cared, just get me out of here. Maybe we wouldn't even have to return the other rental car to the airport. Let Enterprise figure out what was missing and come and fetch it the way they claimed they'd do so joyfully in their TV spots.

As such I would be lost, for hours at a time, in the logistics of disentangling myself from the hotel.

Clearly I was not capable of getting to the airport alone.

However, I was not so far gone that I was going to call Ken in this state. Nor did I imagine, given the way I'd acted for the past two weeks, that Ken should somehow sense I'd changed my mind, know to come as Cary Grant had intuited the moment had arrived though he had been told he was not welcome at Ingrid Bergman's house. I had asked for space and now I'd gotten it, big time. This is not the Milky Way, I chided myself, this is a hotel room, you have not even left the capsule and even if you did you are wearing your space suit, you have cut no ties.

What I needed to do was call Dan Kramer.

Dan Kramer needed to get me a dose of Zoloft or something.

That might necessitate my getting dressed and leaving the hotel room to pick up the prescription, but maybe not. Maybe the Four Seasons had people to run errands.

I saw the ancient bellboy at my door. I would have to get dressed and answer. I would have to find my purse, calculate a tip. If they would even bring me room service, before I had settled up with The Desk. If I had to do all that I might as well pick up the prescription myself.

Thus I would get exhausted again.

This went on for two-and-a-half days. Then I sat up and called Kramer.

A re you able to eat?" Dr. Kramer asked.

I called him at ten of the hour, when he was between patients. He actually picked up on the first ring, and I explained to him that I needed his help since I was suffering some failure of will, some kind of temporary paralysis, in a hotel in a city where I didn't live, and needed a small amount of the appropriate drug that would get me home.

"Well, I was eating."

"So your appetite is normal."

"It was. Then I threw up."

"Intentionally?"

"The food was just too rich. World-famous French place. Plus I'd been drinking."

"How much?"

I sighed. I guess he had to go through all this. "A small amount of white wine." Eating? Come to think of it, I was getting hungry. (Best not to even start thinking about room-service menus, calls to room service.) It had been, maybe, almost three days. My eye went to the still-locked mini-bar. Honey-roasted peanuts? Probably not a good idea.

"Claire? Are you sleeping at all? Are you able to sleep?"

"It's one of those not-quite-sleep sleeps. Sort of—hypnagogic.

But yes, I guess. Not that I feel particularly rested but who would, under the circumstances."

"Are you thinking of hurting yourself?"

"Of course not," I said crossly. "Not exactly *thinking* about it but I rather am, don't you think?"

"You are not, I assume, able to work from there? You've suspended your appointments?"

I exhaled loudly and squeezed my eyes shut, trying not to visualize the thirty-one unreturned phone calls as thirty-one crooked tombstones in snow. More calls now. Many more now. I didn't respond. Somewhat cruel of him, I thought, to bring this up. When I opened my eyes I noticed that the message light on the phone was doing its spastic dance: how had I managed to dial Kramer without noticing this? How had I managed to dial Kramer at all?

"Claire, do you think you want to call your office, say you are seriously under the weather, just to take the heat off?"

"Yes. But can't."

"Or have me do it, if it'd be easier, as your physician, unless you feel that would alarm them? Maybe Ken would be better—"

"No, you. Say flu. Thank you."

"Have you called Ken?"

"No. I was kind of waiting for him to bust down the door here, on a horse."

"You did tell him to lay off."

"Be kind of hard to get a horse in the hotel elevator anyhow."

"I see you haven't lost your sense of humor. That's good."

"Actually I'm not joking. I'm literally seeing him on the horse, charging into the lobby. White horse, white lab coat. Horse's mane aflowing."

Ken pushed his glasses up on his nose, which sort of ruined the picture. I didn't say this out loud, I guess. Also didn't mention that the horse was—well, hard.

"Another symptom I should maybe mention to you. I'm just— I'm horny."

"How so."

"How *so?* In the normal way, except more of it. I've been masturbating a lot, wanting to even more. Also I seduced this eighteen-year-old boy I met at the hotel swimming pool. It was strange, but kind of lovely. Then went to dinner with him and his mother and toyed with the idea of having sex with her too. It's something I've never done, sex with a woman."

Why was I saying this? It wasn't even true. I hadn't considered such a thing at all. But now I got lost in wondering why not.

"Claire." He called me back by using my name, it seemed, too insistently, trying to stretch the *a* out into a steadying caress. "Are your cycles pretty regular?"

"Pardon me?"

"Your menstrual cycles."

"Not very. Why?"

"The overflow of sexual feelings could be hormonal. Obviously there are lots of psychological reasons we could explore, and the link between sexuality and grief is less unusual than you might think—I assure you, you are hardly a freak—but when were you last at your OB-GYN?"

"I don't need a Pap smear, Dan. I need Prozac."

"Claire, you know very well I can't just prescribe medication to you over the phone in the state you're in. In a different state to boot. What if something went wrong? Getting the right dosage of the right drug is a complicated business. Anyway I'd never prescribe without—listen, could you hold on for one second?"

I did, while he poked his head out the door to put on hold, I assume, the patient in the lobby.

"Thanks. Are you still there? Sorry. Where were we? No responsible doctor would prescribe that kind of drug without first eliminating the physical causes. Hormonal. Thyroid."

"Plus you aren't licensed to prescribe, having evaded the rigors of medical school, and you wouldn't have the foggiest idea what to prescribe, would you?"

He didn't take the bait. He remained calm. "Claire, if you needed medication I would be the very first to get you to an MD who could work with you. Don't you recall how eager Ken was to put you in touch with someone? It was you who chose not to go that route, and I happened to agree with you. You are not depressed. You do not need antidepressants. You are a strong, smart woman who had a very tragic loss which for the most part you've handled remarkably well. Then there was this business with Ken and—the business with Ken, but I think the two of you can work that through. The question here seems more to be about the nature of your cry for help. Do you or do you not want Ken to come and get you and take you home? I am fully confident that if you wanted him to, he would do so. You do not have to be committed to a mental hospital in Philadelphia, Pennsylvania, in order to get that degree of attention from your husband, although I understand that his frustration about your remoteness has been hard for you, especially given the extra difficulties introduced by your schedules, and your anger with your husband is something we'll want to focus on once you get back here."

"I'm not angry at Ken."

"I see. You're not angry. You love your husband and you love men in general. You just want to become a lesbian, right?"

He said this jovially. Was this the proper tone for him to use to talk to me? I did not reply.

"Can't imagine," he continued, "what problems that'd solve for you, although you must admit it is interesting that you should have that fantasy now. And certainly we should talk about the boy at the pool. There are issues. Obviously. If you honestly believe that you are incapable of checking out of the hotel, getting to the airport, maybe the best thing to do is to call Ken and have him come. Or let me call him. Is that what you want?"

"No."

"Okay. Then let's try to put all your energy into getting back here. What do you think that would take?"

"Dunno."

"Don't you think that maybe if you took a shower, had something to eat, you'd feel a lot more—centered? Capable?"

I imagined bacon and eggs. Pancakes. The dumb garnish: a strawberry and melon, like a clown's nose and smile. The personal pot of coffee, black. The tinny click of the silverware. He was right, surely. But it just felt too hard. My mind was as cluttered and inadequate as the too-small table on which breakfast would be served.

"Would you mind terribly calling room service for me?" I said.

"Dan," I said. "Please. If you wouldn't mind."

Then I started to cry.

He let me. I don't know for how long. Asked me my room number. What was the phone number there, was it printed on the phone? What did I want to eat. Breakfast stuff, I said. He said gently that he had a patient now but he would have some breakfast sent up to me and did I have any Valium in my travel bag? No? I had taken Valium before, though? Did they tend to calm me down? Yes, I said, chortling now but still sobbing hard, although they also tended to make me incredibly horny. Well we would cross that bridge when we came to it he said but listen, he would investigate whether it was possible to get a couple of Valium to me, just to help me get home.

"Thank you," I said.

He told me, very gently, the exact time at which he would call me back. He said he wasn't sure exactly when he'd be able to get through to whatever physician was on call at the hotel, but he would call me back, in any case, when he was done with his patient.

"Ring once and hang up," I said, "so I know it's you."

"Are you expecting someone else?"

"The desk." I looked at the blinking phone light. "I'm not supposed to be here, actually. Ken stopped my credit card, believe it or not, so they don't have an imprint of my new plate. Could you call the front desk? Could you deal with that? Tell them I'm crazy but going as fast as I can?"

"You're not crazy. You're not crazy, Claire. You're hungry."

"What are you, a therapist or a nutritionist?"

He laughed. "You're fine," he said. "Let's just concentrate on getting you home."

W ould a Four Seasons valet, greeted by a naked lady, drop the tray or carry on, unperturbed, with the fierce professional grace of a stevedore? "Just put it there, please." *Yes ma'am and where* [unzipping his pants] *should I put this?* Out comes— what you'd expect. Or a bouquet of daisies. Or a large frying pan. The options felt surprisingly circumscribed, depending on what kind of movie you tuned in: Buñuel, The Playboy Channel.

This is what I thought about, while brushing my teeth. My sense of scale had been damaged. Both the head of the toothbrush and my scummy tongue felt gargantuan, like some kind of rusty scupper scouring the bottom of a river. On the other hand, my entire naked body felt tiny, containable. *Cute as a button* I thought, because, were I to trill "come on in" and lie down naked to greet the valet, my "private parts" would look so much like the garnish my mind kept anticipating on the breakfast plate: pert pink nipples as eyes, and then, below, the lettuce-ruffle of the nose-bush from which poked, as lone berry, the cherry. *Boop-boop-eee-doop:* a mouth dainty and succulent as a doll's.

I was not delusional (here I found myself taking notes, as if anticipating further questions from Kramer), could still easily distinguish events in the real world—the clatter of the pipes as my neighbor's toilet flushed; the blinking message indicating the hotel desk and not Castro, the CIA, the Son of Sam—from the boundary-defiance that my brain, spinning off its axis, seemed to be engaging in. I did not really want to greet the valet naked. There was no percentage in getting him or hotel management all riled up.

While pulling on my shorts, I remembered a lunatic I had seen on a commuter train once, talking to himself in sign language. I don't speak it, but when he made a doughnut of the thumb and forefinger of one hand and stuck the third finger from the other hand through the doughnut, repeatedly, violently, I understood that he had in mind for someone to go fuck themselves. He saw me watching, glowered, lowered his hands, managed to keep still for a moment, but then his shoulders and neck began to shake as he returned to talking to himself in his lap.

I was not that far gone. Not off my meds; not, as Kramer reassured me, even a candidate for them.

Just hungry.

How hungry I had not realized until the food arrived. I couldn't wait for the delivery person to leave so I could eat. But he moved very slowly and deliberately.

He couldn't really look at me. Couldn't meet my eyes, was just staring at me chest-level as I thanked him and gathered up his tip. I found this disconcerting enough that I lowered my chin to look down, to see what he was seeing.

Merely that I was braless in my lightweight T-shirt. No *Sports Illustrated* swimsuit issue here—the outline of my nipples not even really visible, my breasts just swaying slightly—but enough to throw the young man off balance.

My Lord, was I going to have to fuck him too (I imagined myself inquiring, dramatically, of Kramer). The whole world, not just me, totally obsessed.

"Um, someone left something for you," he said. He bent outside of my room and produced, from the rug, one of the plastic
bags the hotel provides in the closet—for laundry presumably,
though it would have to be small laundry since it's exactly the size
of an airplane's barf bag—which someone had written across, in
ballpoint pen that snagged on the plastic, FOR CLARE.

"Thanks," I said.

"Huh?" he said, sticking his head out the door as a maid, down
the hall, rattled to him in Spanish. "Oh. Uh. She wants to know
when she can clean the room."

"Soon. Not now, though."

"She wants to know are you checking out or staying."

Don't we all. "Soon."

I had to almost push him out the door.

Didn't look in the bag right away, because I was too ravenous.
A bomb, a million bucks in counterfeit cash, Van Gogh's ear—it
would just have to wait.

Tore the lid off the food. Cheese omelette, wheat toast, fruit
salad. God bless Daniel Kramer, Ph.D. The grape jelly, cheerful in
its cozy cabin; the festive paper hat over the glass of orange juice;
the stray flop of parsley atop the omelette, sole purpose of which
is to need to be removed, ceremonially: all of these familiar sem-
aphores induce in me a deep feeling of safety. I freed the cutlery
from the straitjacket of the napkin and, almost moaning with
appreciation, I snorfed, chipmunked my cheeks full. Then forced
myself to rest. To slow down. Butter, cantaloupe, salty egg: all
celestial.

In the bag (sated, I could now investigate), my shitty sandals,
and a note from Zachary.

The sandals looked like something excavated from days of yore that should be in the Bata Shoe Museum in Toronto, artfully displayed along with the embroidered shoes in which they sacrificed Peruvian girls, the slippers for bound Chinese feet. I needed new sandals. Leaned them against the empty juice glass, though, and propped Zach's note against them, so I could read it as I continued to eat.

Dear Clare/ire/[Last name—keep thinking DOGOODER?!??]

You'll always be DOCTOR to me.
Saved yr shoes.
Thanks for the mammarys
        (bet U dont think thats funny)
                Stop by/Say Hi
                    if your ever in R.I.
                                X
                             XX
                    X
                    Z.

Jeez, computer literacy hasn't done much for normal old-fashioned literacy, I noted, but then I just felt touched. Poured myself some coffee from the silver pot and let my eye linger on the curves of my man-child's writing. The note began printed, loped into cursive, and had this strange shape, concrete poem or mere sloppiness it was impossible to say. The X's trailed off in a way that looked like a hoof at the end of a bull's back-kicking leg. I pictured a satyr, Zach's head perched atop a beast's furry bod.

At *furry* I spat my first gulp of coffee back in the cup.

Vile. I opened the pot to see if a dead mouse was curled inside, but it appeared to be unpolluted coffee, steaming. Took a more tentative sip, as repulsive as the last.

Then mentally gasped: I *am* pregnant!

Could not stomach coffee when I was pregnant.

Ripped off my T-shirt and went to stand in front of the mirror, to inspect my breasts. Put my fingertips to them tenderly, to check for soreness, swelling.

If I was pregnant, I was only seventy-two hours pregnant. And I'd done my unintentional purge'n'fast, so I hardly looked fat. Who could tell anyhow with my kerflooey cycles, since I was usually some version of pre- or postmenstrual, spotting or clotting, at the mercy of my perimenopausally creaky plumbing.

Yet again, after a nutritious breakfast, energy temporarily restored, playing with myself: the slightest Braille of fingerprint to nipple, trying to will into being that nimbus of early pregnancy, not even a quickening but the promise of it.

Was in that posture when Kramer called, let the phone ring once and called back, as arranged. What a peach.

By the time I raised the phone to my face, the energy was gone. Sank right through a trapdoor in the bottom of me. When did pregnancy's exhaustion set in? Couldn't remember. Certainly not three days, though. I flopped on the bed, thinking Kramer was right. A blood workup was in order.

I thanked him for breakfast and told him I was feeling better, if alarmed by my fatigue. Realized, hearing his voice, that I was very much looking forward to seeing the five-milligram Valium with its scored lugnut hole in the center, tasting its bitterness on my tongue.

But he said in order to get a prescription for even several of them, I'd have to have a little chat with the hotel's physician. My call. The physician would come to the room, or I could go to him. Kramer had spoken to him, but for liability reasons—

"Yeah, right," I said. Given the restrictions at the swimming pool, I could imagine the waivers you'd need to sign to get even a Tylenol with codeine if your arm was dangling off. "Forget it."

Perhaps Ken could do something, he suggested. Ken would not have a license to prescribe in Pennsylvania, but maybe there was someone he could call.

He'd like that, would our Ken. He could get right on it, calling the classmate of some classmate, or sweet-talking the (female) resident on call at the closest ER.

"That's okay," I said. "I'm pulling out of it, really. But did I mention to you I might be pregnant?"

"Really!"

"Wouldn't be Ken's. Would be the kid at the pool."

I appeared to have rendered him speechless.

"Not that I'm sure," I added. "Need to check the computer, see when my last period was. Not that that would be conclusive either. Anyhow it would only be a couple of days. But I have a feeling."

"Are you happy about this?"

Pregnancy itself one of those travel-distance math problems, a thorny calculation of space-time coordinates. "If it's true," I said, "it's like—God, I sound sixteen. 'Meant to be.' "

"Do you think Ken would be pleased?"

I let that one go. Yes, it seemed mighty likely that Kenneth Leithauser, MD, would be tickled pink to raise a child who wasn't his own, born of sex his wife had in a spasm of grief, revenge, mental instability, iron-poor blood, or all of the above. The very threat of the conversation I'd have to have with Ken was a major setback.

"We sure have a lot to discuss when you get back here," Kramer said, heartily.

I could see what he was trying to do. He was mirroring my own tone of zesty detachment. My life like a great book you missed in both high school and college, but could now, in the fullness of middle age, discuss with your book club. My life as bad art, not quite Elvis on black velvet but the kind of pastoral scene you buy at hotel expos. Maybe, though, that wasn't his tone at all. I was in no position to evaluate his tone. Already, breakfast aside, I was ready to surrender to another half-life of sleep. *I'm melting!* I wanted to croak, like the Wicked Witch of the West. But it seemed like too much trouble to say. And if I couldn't get that out I wasn't going to be able to explain to my therapist this other symptom, beginning to grow more troublesome: how for these couple of weeks I'd kept translating my own distress into pop-cult references, Hitchcock and *The Wizard of Oz,* so that my own life had been clouded by a gluey layer of allusion. It reminded me of the coat of anonymous white paint that they slap over the walls of rental apartments when new tenants move in, without even priming.

And what was going to be there when I stripped all that goop away? "My husband is a jerk?" "I still miss my baby?" "I want a family?"

"Oh, Dan," was all I could say.

"How 'bout we work on a game plan," he said.

Sure. Let's get busy.

We walked together through the necessary steps to departure, gingerly as father and daughter at a wedding rehearsal. There was a shower, packing the suitcase. There was the call to work (he had not yet had a chance to make it), the call to the airlines. There was the matter of the rental car in the garage of Children's Hospital, which he let me go on about. Lastly, and most anxiously, there was the mounting mountain of unreturned phone calls and E-mail, the ribbon of numbers on my pager. I would need the equivalent of an air traffic controller to figure out where my life was, where I was supposed to be.

"Is there anything so urgent," he asked, "that it couldn't wait until Monday?"

"How would I know? I don't even know what's out there. But I could march straight into the ocean and never come out and I'm sure it wouldn't make a ripple in the great wide universe if that's your point, although a couple of people would be inconvenienced."

"That wasn't my point, actually. My point was just that it's Thursday, heading toward lunchtime. I'm just trying to determine how efficient you really have to be, under the circumstances."

"I happen to know you can wax existential as well as the next fella. But I guess you're trying to get me to stick to the point, whatever it may be."

"Right. 'The point.' "

For a second, parroting, he sounded just like Zachary. Impatience surged: shouldn't my therapist be more profound than a college freshman? Shouldn't he be willing to engage me more fully? I had chosen a down-to-earth, warm kind of guy, quite against the advice of my husband, who of course considered them all charlatans and would prefer to treat grief with a CAT scan and a controlled dosage, and if there were side effects well then he could treat the side effects. (Not that he'd take psychotropic drugs himself. Like a hairdresser with an atrocious haircut, he considered himself above his own ministrations.) Even the term "grief work," which Dan had perhaps overused during our couples sessions, made Ken twitch—it had kind of endeared him to me, actually. His long, lean legs crossed, his posture studiously calm—the ideal patient, displaying patience—one leg would jump, as if his knee had just been bopped with the rubber reflex hammer.

"The point," Dan continued, "is to sort out which exigencies need to be attended to there, and which are better left until you return. I know it has been enormously important to you to have your work, and I respect that. It's also fairly self-evident that you're not unambivalently looking forward to 'the comforts of home.' To be blunt: you've run away."

"Not really."

"Exactly. 'Not really.' Just sort of."

"Exactly sort of," I agreed.

"So why don't you sort of come back, where you and I can at least really talk. If it turns out that you find you need some kind of buffer zone, you could always stay in a hotel here."

"Now there's an appealing idea. Hide in a charming Holiday Inn three miles from my house."

"My trouble, Claire, is that from this distance it's hard for me to sort through all your layers. You're clearly being sarcastic, but you also sound kind of energized by the idea. The one thing I can tell is that you're genuinely distressed."

He was right. Of course he was right. "All right," I said.

Together, Dan Kramer and I assembled a list. We discussed each item and I wrote them down, in order, on a piece of Four Seasons stationery. Shower first, pack second, and so forth. I found myself attacking this process with gusto, trying to do it like an outline for a "process" paper in college—

> I. Shower
>> A. Remove Clothes
>> B. Turn On Water
>>> 1. Get It To Right Temperature
>>> 2. Test With Back of Hand
>> C. Close Shower Curtain—

—could see myself, in the outline, tipping my head back into the spray. "Take it," Dan was saying, "not even day by day but just action by action, thinking, 'What is necessary.' " Was it necessary to tip your head back? Was it necessary to rub the shampoo in? Was it necessary to rinse it out?

Yes. The answer was yes, or I'd end up here forever, a four-star-hotel bag lady, compatriot of Howard Hughes, checking coffee-pots for water bugs.

C lean, dressed, lipstick applied even, I felt emboldened to study my punchlist, off which I could now cross "shower." *Pack* was next, but that amounted to only several garments, and I felt up to something more challenging. Surveyed the game plan: call the desk. Call the office (sick). Then the optionals, extra credit for degree of difficulty:

—Check messages [check only—what's desperate] (!)
—Swim????

Swimming made no sense; I'd just showered. So I girded my loins and retrieved messages.

On hotel voice mail, three different people, on different shifts, at the Four Seasons desk, threatening me with eviction for nonpayment of room charges. Evidently I had slept straight through all of these phone calls, as well as some frantic knocks at the door. Had they entered, proven unable to rouse me, gotten worried? Perhaps, because the last message said silkily—even apologetically—that everything had been taken care of. I paused only briefly to wonder how (had Dan gotten the credit-card number from Ken?), decided I did not care. Then called my voice mail at work.

Not bad. Only thirteen, fourteen additional messages, some superseding or merely confirming requests or questions already left in previous last calls. It was, I remembered, late August. Hospitals were still open for business, ready to embrace the dying and dead, but in general people took vacation. (Why was my therapist working?) They endured horrific traffic to reach the beach. They ended work early on Fridays and just hung out in their backyards—too hot for urgency.

What if my whole slow-mo dive off the deep end could fall under the perfectly respectable American heading of *need a vacation*?

So braced did I feel by this thought that I decided I'd return a call or two, and I began with the one I assumed would bring me the most potential pleasure: the clean slate of a new customer. Couldn't quite make out the name—"Hill Cataract," sounded like, in the secretary's harried voice; but it was a clear phone number from New York City, and the geography, outside my usual referral route, made me curious.

This small decision, it would turn out, was a big mistake, unless you happen to believe that there are no mistakes. (I, however, having studied probability as a math major in college, happen to believe in accident. In the accidental nature of accident.) Breakfast and a shower had not made me feel strong enough to deal with my husband's lover, and that, not a new customer, was the person behind the phone call.

"You're in luck," a woman said, chewing, when the secretary put me through, as she had apparently been instructed to do. "I'm eating. I can talk."

In luck was not what I felt. "I am the woman your husband screwed once in Puerto Vallarta": someone else might have managed to hang up, but I was so stunned I just listened in cowed silence. My *hus*band, she said, who had refused ever to speak to her again after they made love the one time, who had rejected her efforts at normalizing collegial communication, had just last night called her out of the blue, ranting. At home! Had called her not at her office but at home and, without even inquiring about the whereabouts of her husband or children, proceeded, paranoid, to blame her for deeds she did not commit, including, evidently, the threatened dissolution of our (Ken and my) marriage. Luckily, the husband was out, the children at camp. But Kenneth, she said, was insane. "And I said," she said, " '*whoah*.' What are you *talking* about. At which point he told me you had left him, and this, it seems, is my fault. 'Excuse me,' I said. 'Did you *tell* her? Did I ask you to tell her?' To which he replied that he was not a snake like his esteemed colleagues, that he and you had a committed life together with full disclosure (as if my husband and I do not) and who did I think he was? Didn't I realize there were real issues here? As if—excuse me a minute."

I actually waited, paralyzed, while she took another call.

"Okay. So. Anyway. Look. I don't know what's going on. Obviously. But I thought it might be helpful if we talked. Because I realized that I was—because Ken—"

Whereupon my husband's lover's voice choked. As if she was fighting back tears. Or merely gagging on her lunch. Horrible hospital-cafeteria "chef's salad."

"To be honest: he messed with my head. My feelings for him were completely unexpected, and likewise I think, and it was very, very interesting, and I will say—if you want me to, if it helps— 'I'm sorry.' "

"That's quite all right," I said cheerfully.

These might have been the very first words I got out.

"*Is* it?" she said. "How could it be?"

Fair question. I rooted around for an answer. Dug past the mental topsoil of the obvious answers, which were—I noticed that the Four Seasons ballpoint pen was poised over my list, as if this exchange were about to become part of it—(1) It wasn't all right; and (2) It was not the time to discuss whether or not it was all right. In either case detachment had risen in me again, for protection—a detachment that felt almost wet, slippery, like the fluid protecting an eyeball.

"I'm sorry about your son," she said (did I imagine this?) roughly. "I do not, believe me, begrudge you going the saint route. But I've seen it often enough in my line of work, and it's a problem. Because alas other people have lives and emotions too, you know. Life goes on, as they say."

She punched out each word with ghastly flatness. Bitch! At that moment I knew she was a surgeon. She had a surgeon's cruelty. "Life. Goes. On. As. They. Say": I saw each word as a musical note on a scale, her voice as the bouncing ball that, in old movies, helped you to sing along. Then the black note got flipped on its side, until it was a cartoon ant, flipped on its back, its antennae wildly waving. Archy and Mehitabel. *Alas.*

A mistake. I was losing it again. I was speechless. No choice: I just listened to her.

My husband's lover's name was Hillary Katzenbach. I imagined her solid, feisty, and short, but that's not really fair. That's just Mrs. Clinton with her dolorous piano legs, claiming the name. Bessie, Eleanor—First Lady names. I imagined a kind, firm nurse.

But that's not fair either, because Hillary Katzenbach was an MD. Not just an MD but a surgeon. Not just a surgeon but a pediatric cardiothoracic surgeon, one of maybe a hundred in the country and, it appeared, the cream even of that select crop. Sought after for difficult surgeries. Of course they would all be difficult, if they were pediatric.

She had a surgeon's voice. I had met enough of them to know the voice. "Cool," "hard" are polite understatement. Frozen steel more like it. Petroleum by-products for blood: "Alien," the big mamma. You would think the women would be gentler, but having survived not only medical school, where they still get treated like the only female cadet at an all-boys military academy, but particularly grueling residencies, they tend to overcompensate. They're even worse than the men. Don't fuck with me and here are the facts. I had never met a female pediatric cardiothoracic surgeon, but I had met the men and they were the worst. The very worst of the already bad lot that are surgeons. They watch children die every day. How could it not harden them, if they are to go on?

Imagine the flash of hope a parent would feel when Hillary Katzenbach entered a hospital room, thrust out her hand. Meticulously manicured nails—female physicians, I'd noticed, are often fetishistic about their nails. Imagine how fast the hope would fade, the second they heard her say her name, her voice as hard as those consonants. *Here's the procedure. Here are the risks.*

I knew that Ken met her at a medical convention. Remet her—in fact he had already slept with her a couple of times, a quarter century ago, as an undergraduate at Michigan. I knew that she was an MD. But I had not, when he confessed the affair to me in the spring, asked for further detail. Did not ask her name, marital status, medical specialty. I was much more interested in what it meant that he'd felt the need to tell me then, since it was my conviction, then and now, that he shouldn't have told me, certainly not almost a full year after the fact, when it was, he claimed, a totally done deal. I was not on a need-to-know basis on the matter of why he threw someone against the wall of an elevator at a medical convention.

(That is what I saw, if forced to contemplate it. I watched them leaving whatever seminar together. They are alone in the elevator as he begins to kiss her. There is nothing tentative in the kiss, it being Ken. She collapses backward onto the wall. In my home movie he takes both of her hands, low, and as she tries to raise them, to hold him, to hold his back in the conventional fashion, he grips her more tightly, she's pushing against the pressure of his hands, so by the end they are twin crucifixes against the wall of the elevator, or sucking starfish. This is not a movie I enjoyed replaying and I hardly needed to get sharper focus by asking him her height or the height of her heels, her hair color or her place of residence.)

So I knew she was a doctor. But a pediatric cardiothoracic surgeon: this I did not know. Why would Ken choose, as someone to fuck at a hotel, a woman who was smarter than he was? More respected? In the pecking order of medicine, a pediatric cardiothoracic surgeon—no less one at a world-renowned Manhattan teaching hospital—would be alpha-wolf to my husband's scrawny mutt. While she was saving the life of a newborn, working with superhuman efficiency and precision in that tiny chest cavity, he'd be doing a bypass on a crude, ungrateful sixty-two-year-old insurance executive. Ken wouldn't even know the man's name, he'd just enter and do the procedure, working against his own best time like any repairman, while the family of that newborn would be gazing up at Hillary Katzenbach as if she were God Herself. She was a wizard, a savior. My husband was a plumber, cranking out cardiological Jiffy Lubes.

So what did she want with him? Were their immigrant grandparents from the same town in Russia or Poland? Did they recall to each other the bloom of their youth, their hashish and tie-dye halcyon days? Granted, cardiothoracic surgeons are pretty distasteful: imperious, territorial, and ferociously competitive not only at work but at play, as they ski and jog, sail and golf, grunt at the gym, and whack tennis balls at each other. Real Don Juans too, which is sort of a joke. Most of them are hunched-over, balding guys, of below-average height, in unflattering glasses. Duck-toed walks. Hair in their huge nostrils, hair in their ears, hair poking out between the holes of their surgical gowns, beepers bulging out of the pockets of pants that ride too low on their waists, and they still think all the nurses and receptionists should swoon.

Believe me, a couple of hundred arrogant cardiothoracic surgeons at a convention is not a pretty sight.

Compared to most of them, Ken would seem dignified, sensitive, suave. Ken is a man who enjoyed his OB-GYN rotation. He would tower over his colleagues, literally and figuratively. He is soft-spoken. He is clean-shaven, with a full head of hair.

So maybe, simply, that's what Hillary Katzenbach was doing with him: "I may be a surgeon, but I'm still a girl." And what he was doing with her. If he'd been more disciplined, he could have done pediatric cardiothoracic surgery himself. Or he should have just been a cardiologist, plain and simple; the work was much more interesting, and if he hadn't been so painfully, neurotically in love with the sound of *surgeon* he would have recognized that. But now it was too late. Now he was boxed into this practice in Ohio, always arguing with his partners, his take dipping up or down but always in the vicinity of three, four hundred grand a year.

Poor, poor Ken.

"The problem with Ken," Hillary Katzenbach informed me, "is that he has a heart. He's just not entirely sure what to do with it."

Speaking of heart, what did Hillary Katzenbach's husband do? Neurosurgeon? Civil rights attorney? Mergers and Acquisitions? No. Hillary Katzenbach's husband was—a poet.

A poet!

She told me his name with a well-trod irony, knowing that I wouldn't have heard of him, but implying that I would have, if I were literate. There was a hint of apology for her own implication, an acknowledgment that she was tired of having to dutifully express disdain toward people who had not heard of him, because let's face it, no one had heard of him and no one ever would.

Because he was a poet. (And for the record who had heard of her, outside of her field? Who had heard of anyone?)

Well, this was very interesting. If you figure that, of the hundred pediatric cardiothoracic surgeons practicing in the country, twenty, thirty of them are women, then how many of them could be married to poets? She would be the breadwinner, then. Her poet would cook, and clean, and occasionally teach, and do much more than the usual male share of taking care of the kids.

A boy and a girl: Allison (thirteen) and Daniel (eleven). Right sexes, right age spread. Hillary Katzenbach somehow managed to get through medical school and establish a prestigious practice and deliver two children, no doubt without an epidural. (The OB-GYN probably a school chum of hers, another straight-talking woman who brooks no guff, but they would hug each other, warmly laughing, afterward.) "I'm very sorry, but we did all we could," she would tell the parents of a child she didn't save, and then go home to find her kids already bathed, duck in to kiss them good night and smooth the sheets that a maid washes and changes, and tell her strong-yet-soft poet-husband about the sadness of her job over the dinner he will now reheat for her. He pours her wine. Expertly massages her back, lifts up her hair, kisses her neck. A poet, as opposed to a cardiothoracic surgeon, would kiss necks. Then he writes a poem about it, about the beautiful tension of his wife's back. *For H. as ever.*

Thus, the official version of their blessed life.

But. The facts. What is the finely wrought poem celebrating: her back or his own exquisite perception of its beauty? Lovely language about his lips grazing the tender flesh, but the truth is they barely touch. The tediousness of the marital dialogue: he points out that she is never home. When she does pop in she looks at her children as if they ring a bell, from a previous incarnation. So much money, but vacations are an impossibility. When she goes off to medical conventions—her husband never accompanies her, even to the ones in Hawaii in February, because what male poet could bear being emasculated by the hairy surgeons—he would know what to pack for lunch, know whom to call for play dates. Most of the time he would do it gracefully and most of the time she would remember to be grateful. But now and again he would feel resentful, try to, say, fuck her at two in the morning, in some of the postures of domination suggested by bad pornography, as a way of taming the educated women who really want it like that, will beg for it once you strip them of their intimidating credentials. What are you doing? she says. I'm tired. I'm saving lives all day, whereas you are—*writing poems.*

To which he would reply, You cunt. That's the long and short of it then you do not respect me.

"Let's review what I actually said. All I said—"

"I heard what you said. I do understand the English language. I am not one of your *patients.*"

"Don't you think I get tired of you implying I have no imagination?"

"Well, do you? Any imagination, or sense of play, or empathy, or even simple human kindness?"

And so on until she would marvel, What was I thinking? *I should have married a surgeon.*

Someone who understands.

Enter Kenneth Leithauser, stainless-steel eyes glinting.

For what has Ken been walking around the house squeezing a rubber ball in his fists, if not to make those hands strong enough to heft a woman up against the wall of an elevator and cup her ass.

How proud they must have been, they of the steady nerves and the stellar hand-eye coordination, the long workdays and the tedious decisions about billing and staff, arms scrubbed germ-free right up to the elbow, to be so overtaken with passion.

I'd already tried not to begrudge Ken the elevator scene. Intellectually it made sense. A human being sometimes wants to feel open, wants to glimpse the possibility of transcendence. Sex is one option. It is a good option, because it is almost the only option. Many of the other ones (mountain climbing, hallucinogens, etc.) are just poor substitutes. Both of us had been through an ordeal, and I understood how and why it could happen. However I still didn't want to know, because it was simply not possible for him to throw me up against that elevator wall the same way. Not after seventeen years. That seemed to be what was required, but I could no more provide it for him than I could take back the mistake he made in medical school, make him satisfied with his life. His confession and apology were, surreptitiously, an accusation: I hadn't given him enough, held him firmly enough.

A s Dr. Katzenbach spoke, I had written her husband's name on my pad, in capital letters. Then thickened the letters. Then given them serifs. Then drawn a fat, cloud-shaped circle around the name and doodled around the circle until it was an elaborate series of decisive barbs, like a castle moat. The name was shackled inside the circle. I stared at his name while she talked, so that the letters began to break up, not make sense, the way the spelling of any word will when you look at it too long. Why did *Michael* have an *a-e?* Were any other words like that in English? Archaeology? Why wasn't it Mi-*keel*, then? I wondered if she called him Mike. Of course not; poets aren't Mikes. I tried to imagine how his name would sound in her steak-knife voice. At that moment she happened to say the word *call,* so the leap from *call* to *Michael* was not that large. The *l* at the end of the word was surprisingly soft, almost swallowed. More like *caw.* Not quite, but almost, *macaw.* I knew that unaspirated *l,* from my sales route.

"Are you from Pittsburgh?" I asked.

That stopped her. "Nearby. Why?"

"I recognize the accent."

She had been talking steadily, but now she paused. *I recognize the accent*: it was the second thing I had gotten out in this conversation, I realized, since I'd greeted the news of her helpless love for my husband with *that's quite all right*. What could she possibly think of me?

"If you don't want to hear this," she suggested testily, "I can stop."

Of course I didn't want to hear this. Wasn't that obvious? The words *of course I don't want to hear this* were not on the tip of my tongue; rather I was searching for them on the pad, as if I only had the strength to read them, not take them straight from my brain to my mouth. But she didn't give me time.

Ken had called her, she went on, after our son died. She had not spoken to Ken for years, though they'd kept track of each other's careers through friends of friends in medical school. That's how he knew she was in pediatric cardiology. He wanted to pick her brain. Had faxed her the autopsy. That was when the cause of death was still not absolutely clear, she reminded me: whether it was the accident itself, whether the jolt had caused the belt on the car seat to compress the carotid artery, or whether it was just a classic Anomalous Left Main Coronary Artery that happened to manifest itself during the accident.

"The thing about the Anomalous Left Main," she told me, "is that it doesn't present. Little kids don't know to complain, because they can't recognize chest pain. That's the problem. There's no heart murmur. So it's going to be just like an ordinary adult heart attack from exertion, but what is going to constitute exertion? Ken didn't think the force of the jolt, even with the shock of the air bag deploying and all the confusion, should have been enough to trigger it. But really all he needed from me was reassurance. That he shouldn't have figured it out. That had he known, he could have done something about it. Every doctor's worst nightmare—that you *missed something*.

"How could I not feel for him?" she went on. "I admit I got involved. There was one article in *The Annals of Thoracic Surgery* I faxed over to him. Another in *Zeitschrift für Kardiologie*. He called me, said he didn't know German. I translated the salient points. After a while I realized we were just talking. Asking each other stuff about our lives, and that was—you know. It's hard to make that happen. Your life just kind of—swallows you up. I don't want to make it seem like—well, Ken's every bit as wrapped up in the bullshit. The bullshit crushes you and you don't even know it's happening because officially you're the general. But inside—well, there is no 'inside.' There's no room for it. You just gird yourself for the battle. It's hard for outsiders to understand, which is why it is so refreshing, sometimes, to have a veteran."

The elevator scene I had conjured before, I thought, was preferable. Ken and Hillary pressed up against the wall of the elevator I did not enjoy, but Ken and Hillary whispering wet-eyed about their souls over my son's autopsy—this I could not abide.

I was showered, dressed. My shoes were even on. I did not hang up the phone; I simply put it down, carefully, and left the hotel.

The running shoes spring-loaded my steps, so that movement was easier than it had been barefoot, on the plush hotel carpeting. The running shoes were miracles of modern science—the high-tech equivalent of ruby slippers. But the shoes alone could not explain the energy I felt, the clarity. Nor could the nap, or the protein-rich breakfast. I felt single-minded and streamlined, the way nature shows portray hawks honing in on their prey.

Retraced in a kind of trance much of my path from the job with Zach and found myself at one of those come-hither megabookstores—cappuccino bar, lounging nooks, as many bells-and-whistles as a pinball arcade. Bright, inviting young people circulating through infinitudes of bright, inviting books. At least the illusion of options. We had these chains even in Ohio. Democracy's shining lie: that you can tread familiar ground and still be surprised as you turn a corner. Excitement without risk. Like everyone else, I enjoyed allowing the soothing evergreen and fake Britishy wood trim to work on me, although I had to stiffen, stifle some distaste, when I passed the self-help sections at which I had spent so much brave time for a while, trying to screw on a new mind-set toward tragedy as you would look up hotels in a tour guide or get clever curtain tips from decorating magazines.

Only on the escalator, calmly ascending, did I notice what I was clutching in my hand: the square of hotel notepad bearing my husband's lover's husband's name.

I went straight to the poetry section.

Found him. *No Love Lost.* A paperback with—how frustrating!—no dust-jacket photograph.

"For Gavin," the dedication read, in capital letters. Then underneath, smaller: "And for Hillary. Always."

In case I'd worried I had found the wrong Michael.

Did that mean for Gavin only sometimes?

I read standing, voraciously, in the aisle of the bookstore. I hadn't read any poetry since my undergraduate days, when I took far more English courses than your average math major. It had been years, though, so I should not have felt comfortable evaluating the poems of this man who was, according to the flap copy, a New Formalist. Yet I did not feel intimidated by the threat of sonnets or double sonnets.

I'd often heard about how schizophrenics, in certain hyped-up moments, get an adrenaline rush that allows them to bust the locks on their padded cells, hurl to the floor guards triple their size. I seem to have gotten the mental equivalent: my X-ray vision now applied to systems of thought as well as to pure emotions. Poetry was not much of a test, I grant. Would have been better to trot over to the science section and find out if I could follow, even remotely, something from physics. Or skim a car-repair manual, contemplate rebuilding my own transmission. But what I thought, with the poetry book in my hand and my legs striding Zeus-like atop the cloud of each running shoe, the shoes both soft and supportive, *al dente,* was: show me a man. And I'll swoop to his still center, no matter how fleet-footed the dodge of his rhetoric.

In Michael's case, I knew this much, at once. This man had not been faithful to his wife. You didn't have to be a pediatric cardio-thoracic surgeon to figure out that, in matters of the heart, Mr. Mike had been around, and judging by the publication date of the book, relatively recently, with poems like:

ADULTERY

As if on a workday, opening the door for the paper
you find instead, wrapped in plastic, a Vermeer.
One of how many, globally? Twenty? Rare
as it looks, the light so clear
caressing her face in the dark interior
you feel that you've already touched her
everywhere, often, yet you just got her
which you (no dolt) know for the thrill: not here
in real life, with fluorescent wife, inferior,
but in the lavish lair of simple desire.

Love is like art. Both need to be made.
But desire's just delivered, like the paper.

Desire becomes brittle, sour, old news,
while the painted lady remains fresh as dew,
as if Vermeer just this moment drew
the curtain to reveal the true
pleasures of the domestic. You were a fool
to think that's what you owned. Deluded.
She does not sit in her parlor longing for you:
even the richest donate their Vermeers to museums
where the wives become sluts, strutting their beauty
for all who wish to contemplate desire's paradox:

It's always clearer in the mind's eye.
Yet you always want to take it home, where you can really see.

(Why didn't "paradox" rhyme?)
(Or, in the following poem, "mouth"?)

MISSING A KISS

What mothers know that others don't:
want starts in the mouth.

The baby's sucking is ferocious
though he doesn't even know he is,
no less exists separate from the breast.
Hunger not a request
but his very essence.

A kiss is nothing if not oral.
We pretend to know this, but for all
our worldliness
we can't make sense
of that primal absence.

Can only take its pulse:
I am a big baby. I want you that much.

Kind of liked that one.

It was possible, of course, that these longings dated from his past. Possible, too, that Hillary herself was its object; maybe one or both of them had been married to others, or separated by distance, when they met. But I doubted it. Not if their oldest child was thirteen. One simply could not meditate, as he did in a poem called "The Scuba Diver," on the underside of the tongue of a spouse of fourteen-plus years as

> muscular, silver, iridescent
> like the belly of a glimpsed fish—

unless, perhaps, one was a poet. Unless one's vocation was to dwell on one's most minute impressions of a life lived. And why not? He was right, after all, about kissing. Built a case in several connected poems that what you lock into is the illusion that you have *stopped time,* constructed a barrier between yourself and death. You can't stay locked in a kiss, however passionate; soon the lover's mouth is like your own, carrying bad taste, decay, etc. (The only physical relationship that stays fresh, he claims, is that with a child, because the child's body keeps growing, changing, shutting you out.)

So I stood, and read, and had very mixed reactions. For the sonnet sequence on kissing I felt my old Victoria's Secret lust surfacing. (Sexy stuff. Mikey would need to take some lovers, if for no other reason than Research and Development, once married to Dr. Katzenbach. Unless she was a babe when she stripped off the lab coat, but, Ken aside, I doubted it.) Smugness about my own acuity because he was so close to how I'd imagined him. A tender father, a tender lover and husband, but maybe too proud of his accomplishment in the arena of life: the work brought a whiff of self-congratulation, as if every time he put a Band-Aid on a kid's cut, or noticed the sky was a nice blue, or stuck his prick in some poetess (his main or at least most recent mistress, I sensed, was a colleague), he had to run out and write a poem commemorating the experience. Though that might be an inevitable occupational hazard: maybe you can't dish up a poem the way you could pull together a pasta for a late-night dinner, from what's around, casually. You would have to be ceremonial, as if you'd just invented the sandwich.

No Love Lost. He was still seeing her, then, his poetess? Or just longed for her? Was she married too? Did she have kids? Did Hillary know? She didn't seem to know. Was she humiliated, when this book came out? How could she not be? I read his bio again, paying attention to where he taught. Poked around for Gavins with Irish last names—a poet too, I assumed—to see where *he* taught, lest he invited Mike to his place of employ and introduced him to a colleague. No luck.

Our poetess had brassy highlights in her hair. Her fingers were long and strong, with squarish nails. The nails had large white moons. She was a gardener. The nails therefore filled with dirt and so on. This is what Michael saw fit to reveal to me, his reader.

> To enter you
> I follow the mole through
> the night garden—

Cock as mole? I was ready for puns about moles as spies, but no, it was a totally straight-faced poem about sex so good it "shakes the foundations." This from the kind of sneaking-around husband that private detectives, I happened to know from a recent magazine article, nickname "The Shirt" (as opposed to "The Skirt") when they follow him to his assignations, snapping photos for the divorce court. *Gimme a break* I thought, and felt a surge of sympathy for Dr. Katzenbach, especially as I poked among the female poets, searching out Michael's squeeze.

Hillary was right! While she was saving lives, the poetesses were protecting their lettuce from rabbits! They all gardened, it appeared. To the last woman they could call each plant on the planet by its Latin name. (*Plant on the planet*: I, too, could play this game.) Gardened, cooked pies from scratch, soothed babies, and fucked like bunnies, all the while quoting St. Augustine. They all missed their mommies or whatever relative had died, hopefully in a colorful fashion, even if it was a second cousin. What was this, 1830? Hadn't any of these dames ever bought a white T-shirt at the Gap? Had a muffler fall off? Needed to pick up a prescription for an antibiotic?

They made me proud to be a mathematician.

The Irish men were just as bad. Same garbage—flowers, weather, oceans—except they fucked like ferrets and occasionally interrupted their accounts of their own virility with intonations about the IRA, Bosnia, or some other kind of political upheaval. Not believing their own rhetoric, that family mattered. Gotta get some bloodshed in there somewhere. As far as I was concerned, the Earth Mothery American poetesses and the bearded, bearish Irish poets deserved each other. Let them be partners in rhyme, screwing deep into the night in their fragrant gardens, competitively quoting luminaries to each other. Compared to the rest of these dopes, Michael, it appeared, was something of a crown prince. At least you could tell that he loved his kids, that they were more than props.

By this point I had been in the bookstore for most of the afternoon. I'd taken out many slim volumes that were now scattered around me as I sat cross-legged on the floor. The people who passed smiled at me warmly—was I not a charming poster girl for the allure of the megachain? "Only two topics," one of the poets quoted Yeats as having said, "can be of the least interest to a serious and studious mood: sex and the dead." For all their oozing and enthusing, these poets didn't know jack shit about death. Put all of them together with ice queen Katzenbach and her cohorts at their conventions ("Intraumatic Aortic Transsection: Diagnosis by Biplane Transesophageal Echocardiography") and you might—just might—come up with one whole, balanced human being.

Hillary and Michael deserved each other, should by all means stay married.

This was not fair, I realized, to either the charming couple or poets in general, but I didn't care. And I was very tired.

According to the "Also by" page, Michael had published two other collections of poems, neither available here. For purposes of completeness, I felt that I should check them out. Presumably Hillary would occupy more mental space in past volumes. Consulted with the overeducated, lilac-crew-cutted, nose-earringed toddler at the computer and discovered that yes, the books were in print and yes, they could be ordered for me, albeit from an obscure distributor, and would arrive in a mere seven to ten days.

That would be spiffy, if I had an address.

"I'm just in town for business," I said. The business of going bonkers.

"Well, we could UPS them to you. Even overnight, if you're in a hurry," he added, with a half-smile to indicate the idiocy of anyone being in a hurry for poetry. (Not as if it were a software operating manual.)

Nothing like trying to shop mail-order to make you confront the downside of homelessness.

"Or," he offered conspiratorially, "you could order them online, from amazon.com. Might be faster, actually."

Pay your employees minimum wage, you can't expect loyalty.

I bought Michael's one available book with part of my rapidly dwindling cash, though I'd already read it cover to cover and expected no new revelations. Out of a sense of courtesy to its author.

Had to take a taxi back to the hotel with the dregs of my cash. Saw that the phone was still off the hook. Thought: *good.* Threw myself facedown on the bed and willed a sleep that would wipe the afternoon clean, strip away all of it—Hillary and Ken, Hillary and Michael, Michael and the poetess, then the legions of poetesses, preaching a womanhood that was, I knew, a crock.

Jolted from dreams of poetesses in diaphanous dresses (poetesses playing harps, poetesses picking cotton) by thunder on the hotel door. Knocking so violent it wound, in the serpentine dream, into Nazis, coming to take people away.

Nefertiti! I should have complained to management days ago.

Or maybe it *was* management. But we'd settled the room charges already.

I could go to the ATM again, get more cash. I could do this. Only not just yet.

"Go away," I said, not loudly enough. "Can't you see the sign?" But in fact I had not managed to hang the PLEASE DO NOT DISTURB sign from the rearview mirror of the doorknob, because I could see it from the bed, on my side of the room. "Later!" I tried to say, more forcefully.

But after further knocking there was a rattle of keys and the door exploded to reveal two men.

They seemed gargantuan, but I was, of course, lying down, face still pressed into the bedspread.

Both were in suits. One reddish and red-haired, unhealthy-looking—eater of too much beef, drinker of too much beer—with a hotel name tag. The other black, young, very handsome, with a briefcase.

"Are you okay?" the reddish one asked, apologetically.

When I didn't answer fast enough he said "your phone" and pointed to the phone.

I swung myself upright.

Then he said, "Dr. Kramer was concerned. Your line has been busy all afternoon."

"I was out, actually."

Which they could have easily confirmed, since a maid had gotten in to clean. (Cleaned, but tactfully left my phone off the hook? That made no sense.)

"Well, we didn't know. The line was busy, then—I'm sorry. This is Dr. Taller."

Or something like *taller.*

The doctor nodded once, crisply.

I was dressed, luckily. "I'm really fine," I said.

"Mind if I?—" the doctor asked.

"Sure," I said. "It's probably a good idea."

"I'll leave you two then," the manager said, backing out of the room.

"Mind if *I?*" I smiled at the doctor, pointing to the bathroom.

"No, no," he said. Sonorous voice. Aware of it, too. A sense of great diplomacy and restraint in both the voice and his posture— an angry man acting calm. "Of course."

The bathroom gave me time to brush my hair in the mirror and contemplate the news that Kramer had called the health cops on me. Wouldn't want me to wind up like Norma Jean, though how I'd accomplish this was unclear (massive quantities of antacids? Send something out to be cleaned, tie my head in the bag? Electrocute myself in the tub, with the Four Seasons' blow-dryer?), when my whole reason for calling Kramer to begin with

had been to acquire meds, get calmly home. But I found that I
didn't mind. Was grateful, actually, appreciated his concern.

When I came out the doctor nodded at me again, beckoned me
over.

While I was gone he had begun to unpack his case on my little
table, from which breakfast had been cleared but not Zachary's
note, still propped on the bud vase with its one sad carnation.
How had I mistaken the black box for a briefcase? I sat docilely in
one of the twin armchairs and stared with admiration at all of the
briefcase's compartments, tidy as an airplane meal tray—slots for
stethoscopes and pumps, one-use needles wrapped in plastic.

"How are you feeling," he said.

"Tired."

Without wasting time on bedside manner the doctor gathered
some numbers. Stuck a thermometer in my mouth, took my
pressure, listened to my heart, flashed a light in my eyes, nose, and
throat. "Swallow." Felt my glands with two hands, grave as a
healer. "Any tenderness?" Whenever he touched me he looked
away, as if to both touch me and look at me simultaneously was
cheating.

An intern or resident, would be my guess; I would have
expected some retired family doctor. Usually I would try to draw
him out a bit, but I didn't have the energy. Besides I did not need
him to be too cordial. He was in my hotel room; I could smell the
vanilla in his aftershave. We were close enough.

"Last period?" he asked. Everyone sure was curious about my
menstrual cycles.

"Five, six weeks ago, give or take, this round at least. How soon
would the urine test pick up pregnancy?"

"You think you might be pregnant?"

"That might explain the fatigue, I guess."

He made a note. "Lots of other reasons for fatigue," he said. "Any weight gain or loss?"

"Not sure," I said. "I've been on the road. No scales in hotel rooms. Nothing significant, though."

"Your appetite?"

"Excellent."

"Sleeping?"

"Tons."

"More than usual?"

"Yes."

"Any pain?"

"You mean other than psychic?"

He didn't even crack a smile. "No," I said, chastened. "Just exhausted. Bone-weary. Think you could take some blood, check iron, run some thyroid numbers? Because I'm having some not-too-acceptable swings. From real energetic to flat wiped out. That suggests thyroid, right?"

He shook his head, no. "Do those tests back home, with your own doctor."

"But if I *need*—"

"Then go to the ER. Couple excellent ones within walking distance. I was only sent, really, to make sure you weren't dying or dead."

"As a courtesy," I said tartly.

He nodded, yes.

"And if I were?"

"Dying? Well," he said, "I'd get you to the ER."

"Couldn't you even do a pregnancy test?"

"Sure I could, but what would be the point? Why wouldn't you walk to the corner, buy a kit? Work just as well, on morning urine."

What *is* a doctor good for, anyhow. They might as well have sent the maid.

"Meanwhile, your doctor thought maybe you could use some Valium."

"Sure," I said, defeated.

He handed me a prescription for five-milligram Valium—I was unlikely to overdose on that number—and his card. He appeared to be a bona fide physician, in private practice.

Gregory Talliver. A married man, or a bachelor with a fake ring.

"This is, I trust, a sideline for you," I said.

"*Oh* yeah."

"Come here often? Interesting problems? Old guys having heart attacks atop their mistresses?"

He smiled. "Mostly stomach flus. A bad shrimp. A couple of bad drug reactions, from visiting rock stars. And a zit, once, from a famous opera singer doing a one-night gig with the Philadelphia Orchestra."

"A zit," I said.

"A big one, right at the tip of her nose," he offered, in her defense.

"Do your services appear on my hotel bill," I asked, "along with breakfast?"

"You got it. But I'll give you a bill, for insurance purposes." He was writing that up now, with gusto. Handed it to me.

Diagnosis? 780.7. "Fatigue."

" 'Fatigue,' " I said. "Less of a diagnosis than the global human condition."

He looked at me now, fully and with curiosity, for the first time. "You kind of seem okay," he declared. "Your 'doctor,' I think"—he said the word with only barely contained contempt for the psychological establishment—"overreacted somewhat."

I found myself comforted to hear him say so, although he had not really paid enough attention to warrant an opinion. But I suppose I had demonstrated mental health in the way most important to men: I'd shown an interest in his work.

This is not what I'd hoped for, from a doctor's visit. I hoped that within a day or so I would have a diagnosis. I would not study the phone's winking eye, but would sleep, or eat, or swim, and would be pleasantly surprised by a voice-mail message from this Dr. Talliver informing me that my thyroid levels were low, or high, so all I needed to do to be right as rain was take this tiny pill.

When will I see an effect, doctor, I could hear myself saying. *Oh, almost instantly. Certainly within twenty-four hours.*

Why, married to a doctor, would I think that?

And why, if I sought magic bullets, had I refused to even consider Prozac, which would have the added bonus of reducing, as side effect, my surges of inappropriate middle-aged lust?

Just to take the edge off, everyone on antidepressants had repeatedly assured me. I had given up telling these folks I didn't want the edge off. They took this to mean I was in some kind of retro Protestant denial. Or clinging to my pain, like some uncrossed-over ghost. You could watch their eyes follow the cue cards of these hypotheses in their brains, like rookie newscasters. Who knows. Maybe they were right. But I felt, strongly, that treating me for depression was like giving chemotherapy for a cardiac arrest.

Or like eating a handful of Amoxycillin, then getting screened for strep. Why obscure the edge? The edge *was* the condition.

I stood on the edge. It wasn't exactly high, or dark, or sharp, and I was not only not barefoot, but wore big, sturdy shoes. Lug soles. All the same, there was danger, of the most-accidents-happen-at-home variety. Not speeding on the highway but pulling out of the parking space at the grocery store. Highways most dangerous not in floods, but when just slightly wet.

The nature of my attempt to be vigilant, to exercise a certain kind of Zen mind-control and self-awareness, to not merely obscure the edge but to conquer it, was such that I thought if I *studied* the prescription for Valium—looked at the loops of Dr. Talliver's letters, watched myself walk to a pharmacy, get the prescription filled, master the childproof lid, maybe even ask for a paper-cone cup of water right there at the counter to wash one down—it should be as good as taking the drug. Similarly, if I thought warmly of my husband, I could, by a kind of telepathy, communicate to him that I was not angry, not really. I didn't imagine Ken so much as *gestate* him. He was very, very small, plus out of focus. But I was growing him in my brain—my own brain fetus.

Ken, I told and didn't tell him, on that edge of sleep upon which I spent so much time, I will be home soon. I am just going to finish my business here.

I am not sure exactly when it became clear to me that my business included Zachary's father. But the hotel room had Yellow Pages nestled in the end table with the Bible, and he was not hard to find. I assured myself that I would get an appointment with him, when I stressed that it was an emergency. His office was so close I could even walk.

Walking but not running through the city, clicking steadily on people I passed, I could use the new X-ray vision I wasn't even sure I had, until I imaged Zach's future, to see straight to strangers' souls. As a salesman I could always quickly calibrate someone's center of gravity from his walk—see how speed, caution, skittishness, or thrust are used as defenses, see where and how he was rooted, how he could be yanked free. I had lost this talent for a while, after the death; like a war survivor, I could hear only my own nightmare sirens. But then I'd discovered grief's trade secret: once you burrow that deep into yourself, you simply have a better nose for pain. Truth is, *hardly anyone is happy*. Not even the people with nothing wrong. They're all hunkered down in the bunker of self, in self's fragile failure.

Dan Kramer's take on all of this—for of course I'd tried to discuss it with him—had been something on the order of No Man Is an Island. On the contrary, I'd argued. Every man is. Yes yes, he had said, but. A cognitive therapist was our man Dan; he wanted to help me see the glass as half-full. Under this theory, pain could help me "grow." Right. Run over the dog and what do you have? A three-legged dog. Very elegant. "I'm not sure exactly what we're disagreeing about," Dan Kramer had said, rather petulantly. "Are we all essentially stranded in our own pain? *Sure.* Run over, beaten with a newspaper, caged at the SPCA. Pick your metaphor. But: we go on, no? On we go."

So on I went to test my skills on a man who truly *was* an island, a veritable fortress. Zachary's dad was going to be my tough nut to crack, the case that broke grief's back.

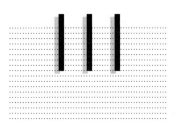

Another Michael. So hard not to divine messages from on high, but "how many are there, globally?" as the great adulterous poet Michael so rhymingly inquired. Couple million most like.

Except, hating the name's very commonness, he went, sportsmanlike, by his initials. Which happened to be M.D., so his name itself, given a specialty in medical malpractice, was an in-joke. As was the nickname on his nickname—he knew that younger colleagues called him "Empty."

Running on. The Hollow Man. The Lawyer.

Only one body part claimed his real name. His penis, I would later discover, he referred to as Mikey. This beautiful *ur*cock that could belong to Michaelangelo's David, if David were ever erect, he treated like a gap-toothed kid brother from a cereal commercial, or a finger puppet he could make to "talk," by jiggling the head: "Mikey'll be right back."

But first, he had to be willing to see me, and I couldn't even get an appointment with him.

"What can I help you with," a secretary asked on the phone, then lobbed me, with tones more sympathetically lilting upon learning of a child's death, to one of the great man's associates, a woman I suspected was sleeping with or had slept with him. The most lawyerly traces of possessiveness leaked through.

The pediatrician, I told her, had never taken a blood-gas reading.

"Which hospital?"

She dismissed me immediately when the hospital turned out to be in Ohio. They were not (of course) licensed to try cases there. They could probably recommend someone. And why would a pediatrician investigate blood enzyme levels anyhow, in a healthy child? And this was before I'd even brought up the accident, which would nix the deal for any self-respecting lawyer. Too complicated. The doctor, the manufacturer of the pisspoor car seat; the distracted housewife who, according to the police report, probably failed to turn in the direction of the skid, then slammed on her brakes; fate—no sole source could take the rap, pick up the check. Besides, what did we hope to gain? What solace could the cash infusion bring to such a prosperous couple?

"Truth is," the pediatrician had said, with inappropriate relish, "he could have died anytime, anywhere. He could have died running into your arms when you got home from work." Just one of those meaningless coincidences: car crash, heart attack, Elvis and me sharing a birthday. But the image had stuck: my son running into my arms, me replaying the tape slowly, frame by frame, as if it were Zapruder footage, searching for the gunmen in the grassy knoll.

Actually, I told the associate, Michael had been recommended to me by a friend of my husband's (don't worry, hon, I'm taken), and I would really appreciate getting his read on things while I was in town.

Well, he was at a settlement. Tomorrow he had a deposition. His schedule was very tight. With a little more notice, maybe . . .

This was not at all what I'd imagined. Bizarrely, I had not anticipated having to say even this much about the case itself. I'd seen myself appearing in my suit, briefcase in hand and laptop slung over my shoulder, imagined my leg swinging slightly, eye contact made, proceeding directly to the *real* solace. I assumed he would understand at once what I wanted, given his status as a Philadelphia lawyer and his reputation, gleaned from his ex-wife and son, as a womanizer. In fact the challenge for a woman in top form—the heat I'd been racing in, since meeting Zachary—would be to proceed directly to sex with no conversation at all, communicating in the universal language of Hormone. (Why wouldn't it work for extraterrestrials as well? I imagined a pornographic version of *Close Encounters of the Third Kind,* in which I, braless beneath labcoat, sexually fine-tuned enough to seduce Martians, sent out a Bach-like tone poem of estrogen, progesterone.)

"Any sense when I might be able to catch him?"

"He won't be back here," she assured me, "until late, if he gets back at all. I could have him call you, though."

But I would not be that easily discouraged.

By now my suit—in whisper-light summerweight wool, in one of those Armani gray-greens that give ambiguity a good name, but worn now for several consecutive weeks in summer—felt suddenly heavy, malformed, malodorous. I gave the Four Seasons a chance to demonstrate its ability to have suit and silk blouse cleaned while I was at the pool. I swam, napped, had a salad in my room, and then dressed to meet Michael Davidoff of Davidoff, Freed, Spelling and Associates with delicious care. Put my hands through the legs of my stockings slowly, to check for runs. Flossed my teeth. Even wet a piece of toilet paper and wiped away the line of muck that had collected on my shoes.

Arrived at his office with my briefcase and laptop (a less sleek look than I'd imagined, but I felt insecure leaving them at the hotel) at a little after seven at night, the time I'd deemed most likely for him to be at his desk alone, sighing and mopping up, with the less devoted drones having scuttled home.

Given my free hotel room scam, I was not concerned about gaining admittance to the building, about finessing the security guard. It should not be this easy, really. Women, too, can be disgruntled ex-mates, terrorists. But he wore just the look of indignant boredom of all security guards.

"I'm here for Mike Davidoff," I said.

"*Mike,*" he retorted, expressionless.

"Yes indeed, sir."

"Is he expecting you?"

"Nope." I leaned with elbows on his curved desk and did not whisper but leaned in, talking only to him, not that anyone else was around except, down a long hall, against a bank of elevators, a janitor propped up against a cleaning cart. "Not at all. I'm a surprise. I'm a present. I'm his dinner. The briefcase"—I held it up at desk-level, so he could see—"is merely a prop."

He grinned. "Oh yeah?"

"*Oh* yeah."

"Ought to be more of that going around," he said.

Definitely, I agreed. More surprise.

He told me I'd better sign in, then, and offered me the bad ball-point pen attached to the pad.

"Marie Antoinette?" I asked. "Madonna?"

"Whatever," he suggested.

I went with Hillary Katzenbach. "You have a nice night now," I said, he told me to do the same, and this felt, I swear, like real human contact.

The office was as one would expect. Heavy on the mahogany and pilasters. Leather-bound books, gold letters glinting on their spines, lined up behind the cut crystal of apothecary shelves: the high life, courtesy of Ralph Lauren. Lawyers! I tried to imagine an original one with a sense of humor—interior by Andy Warhol, all the bright-green upholstery sporting cartoony dollar signs. Probably people with bum knees from accidents, with ugly divorces or very high bail, are not in the mood to laugh at their problems. Doctors, of course, try to keep their interiors low-key, even dowdy. Patients do not like to feel that their illnesses are supporting interior designers. It's unclear why lawyers are allowed to flaunt their excess: is anyone cowed into thinking such rooms represent "old money," that they've been here for centuries, stable as the state?

Maybe just an old-fashioned power play. *We're rich. You're not.* The receptionist was gone for the day, but I had made a miscalculation: why did I think that at a mere seven in the evening the office would be drained of all activity generating billable hours, leaving Michael and me alone?

On the contrary, most of the lawyers were still here. The door from the lobby of the office was open and you could watch them spurt by like manic-depressive elves, ties tossed behind their backs, rattling sheaves of papers. To ask for him would ruin it, so I proceeded through the open doorway as if I belonged there. Did, almost, since I could evidently divine, with ornithological precision, in which direction I would find the biggest office with the best view. And his door was not closed, only ajar; in fact an elf was scuttling out, so intent on the papers before him that he didn't even register me. And then I was standing in front of the man himself, smiling.

"Michael," I said.

He did not "look up," because he seemed to have already been watching the doorway, expectant. He was very still. He smiled back but the smile was—well, beyond professional. Beyond, even, "false," because that entails an alternate composition, readable but dishonest. This face revealed, pointedly, absolutely nothing.

Figure, here, seconds only. Long enough for a "Hi," or a "You are?" or even a handshake, a raised eyebrow, some gesture of welcome or suspicion. From him, nothing. Nothing. I was even further put off guard because the face was so familiar, from Zachary. I had already slept with this man, is how it felt.

Claire the Loon.

What are you doing? I demanded of myself, a bit frantically.

I'm doing the father, the son, and the holy ghost.

Three, four seconds of him holding the poker face like a cat, paw raised, tail quivering, while my brain zoomed around having wildly dissociated thoughts like a nut-burying squirrel, squirrels being, of course, too stupid to remember where they buried the nuts, so all they do is bury them and dig up nuts some other poor idiot squirrel buried and now can't find. Several hundred expressions he might have seen, if he was paying attention, and he did seem to be paying attention.

"Your son Zachary sent me" is what finally came from my mouth.

Now his shoulders eked out the smallest *Ah, yes?*

"I'm a surprise," I said helplessly. "A present."

He considered this.

Our first meeting was, I realized, going exactly according to plan. Behind the desk, this attractive middle-aged man who never let anything happen to him, who "lived for his work" as they say and kept his heart squirreled away, studied me, deliberating about how to respond to a woman who announced she was a present but bore no singing telegram, jumped out of no cake wearing pasties; carried, in fact, a briefcase and sleek laptop; stood, now (for I had put the briefcase down, in our half a minute together), with hands clasped before her, the most secure and casual of supplicants. Was I not what all men wait for? Married, even: certainly he could see my diamond flashing against the subtle weave of my suit; after our tryst I would ease into the leather seat of my silver Legend and drive away.

Except I feared that I was deluded about my ability to control him, and the situation. Because his caution made me feel a twinge of desperation—as if I were already more in love with him than he would ever be with me. I had known him three minutes, and already I was acting like his jealous, needy wife! Hey, I reminded myself, you're a *salesman*. I met his stare, just slightly taunting. And in that short exchange I had won, for the nonce: I knew he was thinking, What the hell. *Just this once.*

"In fact," I said, "if you can spare the time, there's a case I'd like to talk over with you. You come highly recommended, of course."

I said this in such a way as to indicate that this was not at all what I wanted, but understood totally that it would be our cover, should anyone question us. The way I said it—firmly but without protesting too much—convinced him that I would be a reliable witness, should it come to that. And meanwhile he could be, to himself, thrillingly out of character.

He made, then, what must have been his first movement. He

had been holding a pen in his hand. Now he tamped it, deftly, against his desk—the gesture of an ex-smoker of nonfiltered cigarettes. Then he laughed. Here is the thing about his laugh, and remember, I had heard the ex-wife and son's grand clattering whoop: the father's laugh was completely soundless.

According to plan, his next move should have been to kiss me. The kiss would contain some calculated surprise. Hands not cupping cheeks but going straight for waist. Or no hands at all. Or the mouth would bite first, not lips but earlobe—I suspected this Michael would be rough—or no kiss, kissing dispensed with, stockings ripped down, etc. Why this idea not only didn't displease but actively excited me, how it was different from the slob in the Wilkes-Barre hotel room with his pink hand like a lobster claw pincering my nipple, I could not have said. Maybe the certainty that whatever move Michael Davidoff made would be studied. That I merely needed to be ready, to *avail myself* of him.

But in this regard, as with the initial greeting, he made me wait. He was not going to be so tacky as to inquire how I knew his son, or what I wanted from him. A gaze power-washed of everything but taunting expectation: *surprise me.* But I couldn't. I could straddle him, or burst into tears, or serve him papers, or say "You know how I met your son? He collided with me accidentally-on-purpose at a hotel swimming pool and within a quarter of an hour we were in bed; chip off the old block, no?" Whatever I did, I'd get the same *Ah, yes.* Behind that implacability, I knew, was a sadness so grand it was positively glacial. What did I need the tip of an Iceman for? What treasure did I hope to find buried in him, like dinosaur DNA in amber? Couldn't I just scale my own emotional mountains?

With such considerations, I actually managed to outwait him.

"Have you eaten dinner?" he asked.

"No," I lied.

His hands were folded on the desk, as if we were posing for a corporate photograph, of the type I had read are called Guys in Ties. He rotated his wrist to check the time, subtly. "Shall we?" he asked, and stood. Checked his watch *again.* An expensive sports-type watch—what a stupid contradiction in terms. The gesture made me remember that Fidel Castro used to wear two watches— one facing the inside of his wrist, one facing the outside, so he never had to turn his arm to know the time. Now he had given me the Achilles' heel, I could shoot, if I needed to. How you'd melt the mountain: with the emotional equivalent of jet lag. Throw the fucker off his circadian rhythm. His was a timing game, totally.

With this in mind I could smile at him serenely.

He was taller than I'd known, from seeing him seated. Taller than his son, and less densely muscled, with some auburn glinting in his coloration. The face chiseled and intelligent-looking. Of course all lawyers look smarter than they are, and know it—the other Achilles' heel. But because of the long legs, the lean and hungry look, Michael's face seemed intelligent the way a praying mantis's does. No matter how thoughtfully the head swivels, it is, after all, an insect.

When he reached me, he put one hand in his pocket, rattled change in a spasm. Then put that same hand lightly on my back, to steer me out. Standard old-fashioned "This way, lady" but the pressure felt thrillingly good.

Wordless in the elevator.

In the lobby, the security guard shared with me a leering eyebrow, a "toodle-oo" with lowered fingers. If it had been a romantic comedy, I could have winked as he tipped his cap. The cinematic dissociation under which I'd been functioning: as the lawyer again touched my back, positioning me in the revolving door, followed behind, caught up with me to steer me left, and loped alongside me, his hand just resting in the hollow where, a couple of inches lower, he'd be teasing my bladder, I saw us in a tracking shot from the kind of movie in which wary urban couples wend their way toward union against mirrored skyscrapers in a Toronto posing as Manhattan.

We were on Walnut Street, heading, I realized, toward the very restaurant that had made me puke, but going to another place, across the street. "You been here?" he asked.

"Don't live in the city," I said. "Just visiting."

"Ah," he said. "From?"

"Cleveland."

"You'll like it."

We got through the march to table, drink orders, drink arrival, the delivery of enormous menus, the ritual lascivious recital of specials, without exchanging any further information. If he had any curiosity or uneasiness about my identity—high-class hooker prepaid by son, as thanks for tuition? Divorced mom of one of his son's school chums?—he did not so indicate. His restraint was impressive, as was the room in which we had been seated.

The restaurant was a converted bank from the turn of the century, and we'd been shown to a halogen-lit banquette in the basement, in what had been the security-deposit vaults. Marble walls, marble floors, and vaults of Air Force seriousness. The brushed-steel walls of the vaults were over a foot thick, the doors operated by hinges more appropriate for fighter planes. A temple for the worship of Cash. Despite the cigarette smoke, it smelled good down here—the steely, oiled smell of manhood itself, and thus of history. Pistons, screws, joints. Hard to imagine a world in which this kind of hardware, so quaint-seeming and decorative now, would delude someone into feeling inviolable, but a wealthy fellow who visited his assets as one would visit a loved one in a mausoleum instead of putting it in the stock market would have been happy indeed, when all was said and done. If only it were still possible to feel safety in things, in the stolidity of the tangible world.

When I turned to Michael he was smiling, pleased with me. As if he knew exactly what thoughts I was having, and agreed. His restaurant choice an ironic commentary on our relationship's very evanescence—we would not amass anything together, but would merely alight in each other's accounts and move on, an electronic transfer.

I took my hand off the stem of the wineglass and gave it to him. "Claire Newbold."

He raised my hand, kissed it. The pressure, like the pressure of his hand on my back, exactly right. "Delighted."

Then just kept holding the hand, his thumb languidly stroking my thumb.

"Claire," he said, savoring.

Well, this could not go any better. Could not possibly. I let him work on my thumb. After a while of tracing my nail with his finger, his other hand appeared and he cupped my hand in both of his in a way that made me think of someone trying very carefully to light a match in high wind. In both of his hands, my hand felt candlelit, its pleasure private. He drew in my other hand, too, and held both of the hands at once, stroking first the prong that held my diamond in its setting and then the web or whatever it is called between my fingers, trying to make of that dumb, dispensable piece of flesh something trembling, tympanic. I felt this rather than saw it, because my eyes were closed. When they fluttered open he was watching me, and while the smile was the same set, suspicious one that was his lawyer's false face, his eyes were ignited, flickering. His eyes said, Yes, we are very impressive concentrating like this in the theme-park restaurant, among the clink of cutlery and chatter from the bar, but let us try to do this right.

"Okay," I said.

He laughed. This time a little noise got out before he throttled it. "Okay, then," he agreed, *patting* my hand—what? A patronizing good-dog pat, then he turned to face our waitress, who appeared to have arrived tableside.

"For the lady?" he asked me, totally professional and businesslike.

I had not even looked at the menu that had been under the orb of our joined hands. I told him to order for me. I was not hungry, of course. Not only had I eaten, but the business with my hand had made a different kind of hunger rise to my mouth, so that I wasn't sure I could wait through a whole meal to kiss him. He appeared to know this, because once the waitress had gone, taking with her the ludicrous annual reports of our menus, he put his hand to my mouth, finger out, at the angle you would to allow a parakeet to alight on it, and I bit, just a little, his finger. I was surprised by this—surprised he would be that open, in a restaurant so close to his place of employ. He seemed to be surprised himself. My teeth on the knuckle and tongue underneath, where it could feel something callused.

He twitched the finger just exactly enough to make of its bend a metonymy for other angles: for my raised knee, a sharp turn in a Pacific Coast Highway he would travel at night, cautiously; for a nipple, backlit, lapped. And for, of course, the tent of stretched fabric in his lap that my foot could find, under the tablecloth, if this were a tacky movie and the camera zoomed below to glimpse my pump slipping off, pointed toes probing. But this wasn't a movie. I don't think anyone would have even noticed us, the movement of his hand near my mouth was that small. The feeling wasn't at all lascivious: more cozy, like a kid who's supposed to be asleep making a tent of the bedcovers to read underneath, by flashlight.

When I opened my eyes his gaze had changed. It was moist and somewhat pained.

"Hard to imagine you"—I for some reason said or I guess actually semi-panted or moaned, letting him take his hand back—"with Margot."

That broke the spell, immediately. "You know my ex-wife?" he asked.

"Wouldn't say 'know.' Met, though. Had dinner with her and Zachary at Le Bec Fin, in fact, just a couple of nights ago."

At the name of the expensive restaurant he winced. The neat bourbon, or the promise of sex, had considerably loosened his poker face. If I concentrated, I could have watched a whole chronology of bad blood—3:00 AM weeping, custody hearings, alimony checks written with such deep hostility that one signature could have caused carpal tunnel syndrome—pass behind his eyes.

"And how do you know Zach?" he asked, in the same studiously casual voice.

"Bumped into him, literally, at the teensy Four Seasons swimming pool. Wound up talking a bit about medicine since my husband is a cardiothoracic surgeon."

"Ah. I take it your own marriage is currently undergoing some kind of interesting flux?"

"Marriages," I informed him, "are always undergoing some kind of interesting flux."

He considered that proposition. "If you're lucky. If not . . ."

"Not," I concurred. "This line of inquiry is less interesting, don't you think"—I said the word *interesting* with a shade of contempt that I knew he'd catch—"than the way we were proceeding heretofore?"

(This was me, I realized, imitating Zachary, imitating his father's imitation of his own litigator's style.)

"You liked that, did you?"

As answer I offered him my hands again, palms up.

He was prevented from taking them by the arrival of the appetizers, small portions on huge plates.

He had ordered me some kind of salad with unexpected grilled or marinated morsels nestled in the leaves. It was quite good and I ate it, although I was not hungry and also did not deem myself to need too much more roughage in one day. We did not talk at all. In his silence, I saw his son; we were sharing the same kind of companionable quietude that Zach and I had at Le Bec Fin, while Mom was in the bathroom. Someone watching us eat may have just assumed we were married, had nothing further to say. But it was a charged silence, not a dull one. Both of us ate and contemplated whether it would be possible to have excellent sex with a stranger, not in the fashion of *Last Tango in Paris,* with that edge of danger, hostility, but in a manner that was—chummy. Unthreatening. "Mutually rewarding," as a lawyer would say. Our scene was possible only because I was married, out-of-state, just passing through, clearly unavailable. That made me, I suppose, as safe as a woman gets; the danger was not deep, merely a kind of lubricant. Except any woman who not only consents to, but masterminds such a situation with a strange man must be inherently unstable, I'm sure he thought. Still, I had said the magic words, *cardiothoracic surgeon.* The assumption being that a woman does not leave a surgeon lightly. Even for a lawyer. Even for a lawyer who can provide the star-quality sex that I'm sure he thought—and it appeared he was not incorrect—I could anticipate.

We got a bottle of wine, very nice Pinot Noir, and our main courses. He'd ordered himself a steak and me a loin of pork in a crust, with some kind of berry glaze, accompanied by delicately fried zucchini blossoms and shaved potatoes the size of fingernail clippings. The kind of thing that sounds good on a menu but on plate and palate overacts somewhat. It was not the perfect choice for a second dinner but I was happy he had thought to order me this and not some fish that I would conceive as noble, because I perceived myself as always four pounds overweight. The kind of dieter who orders whatever's boiled or broiled—a hair shirt of an entrée—then rewards herself with extra bread slathered in sweet butter. And dessert. I was happy he took me for a drinker of blood-red wine, a lusty carnivore.

"What do you think?" he asked.

"Ambitious. But I kind of anticipated that, from the Keogh prospectus of the menu."

He laughed. "And what do you think of me?"

"I think you're not quite the man I thought you'd be."

"You mean, from talking to the fair Margot."

I nodded.

"Not Hitler, you mean?"

"Not even Warren Beatty."

He grinned, agreeing.

"Just a reasonably nice guy," I continued, "soul flattened a bit by life on the planet, life as an acquisitive American, who would like to fluff soul up a bit, doesn't quite know how. Likes the law, loves the law even, but tires of reputation, not entirely inaccurate, as sleazebag and would rather, therefore, be doing something else, preferably something more romantic than a glorified version of ambulance-chasing—write novels, maybe, like Grisham?"

"No, thanks," he said. "I'd rather be a scientist. Play with my little chemistry set. Cure AIDS. Identify cancer genes. Also," he confessed, "I play the cello."

"The *cello*?"

"Badly. And you?" He was warming to this now. "What was in that briefcase?"

"Christ," I said, startled. Realizing, now, as I looked frantically at my feet, that I had actually managed to leave the briefcase in his office. The laptop was with me—I had somehow slipped it off my shoulder after the walk here. But I'd forgotten my briefcase. Was not used, basically, to carrying both my briefcase and laptop out of their slots on my luggage cart, when I was in motion in a foreign port. As I had at the Four Seasons, at check-in, I experienced the threat of loss of my belongings as a deep and wrenching grief, as if I'd just regained consciousness at the war hospital to confront the stump of my leg. Or as if I'd saved the wrong things as I fled the house on fire. *Scatterbrain!* I scolded myself, to clear away the mounting panic.

"Well, we can get it," M.D. assured me. "It's safe at my office.

So: you. Traveling salesman of something lucrative—that case way too slim for samples. Lots of time, on the road, to discreetly satisfy your appetites. Especially now that your kids are older, less demanding. They're at—summer camp? Summer camp for the whole friggin' summer! 'Dear Mom and Dad. Joey put a frog in my trunk. It pooped. Dead cockroach floating in Bug Juice. Love, Junior.' Hey, you should be enjoying this freedom with your husband. When was the last time you were in Paris? But I bet he's *too busy*. . . ."

However my face had collapsed in reaction to this speech, the timing indicated to him that the offensive part was the last. The workaholic hubby with his predictable lunchtime liaisons. "Sorry," he said. I shook my head no and waited for the waitress to pour more from the bottle of wine, before I explained.

"One kid. Dead. I used to have a lot of fantasies about summer camp, actually. It's one thing I still can't bear, to listen to friends talk about their kids away at camp. The tenderness. The kind of— cheerful longing. Sometimes I used to do a little bit on myself, just pretend he *was* at summer camp, ruse of positive imaging. Not dead; just gone. I mean, if he was going to live in memory, as people always say I'm perfectly entitled to have him do, why can't the memory include a projection of the future? But I've moved on. Had to. Hated freezing him at twelve. Couldn't get him to stay in focus, voice changing, growing like crazy. Now I pretend he's off to college, just like your son. His adult form already in place but still becoming, still with all that excited sense of the unknown—just off my radar screen."

He dipped his head once, to say sorry.

We just studied each other for a while, and I watched a parade of thoughts flash past his face then get snatched away. Real pity for me. Some pornographic interest in the nature of the death, the when and how of it, whether it represents a litigable claim, an injustice—did the brakes function properly? Some disgust or shame at his own interest and some fatigue with it, too—who wants to be on professional duty with a woman he's about to bed? Some disappointment, because how is a woman in the grip of grief going to be fun to fuck, then some interest in rising to the challenge as he considered that perhaps my plan was to fuck my way *out* of grief, which would require a certain intensity of concentration and was news to him, too, somewhat off the beaten path of anger, depression, defeat, lust for retribution with which he worked daily. A memory that he needed to be working. Flash, both panicked and comforted, of the mountains of papers in a strategic map on his desk.

This is how he resolved the spate of conflicts: he stood, decisively. He whipped his wallet from his pocket and began piling bills on the table—fifty, fifty, twenties. I watched as each bill got slapped down: this was going to be a happy waitress. Then he slid in beside me on my side of the banquette, against the wall, so that one of his legs touched one of mine under the table. He put his arm around me, reached up as if he were going to stroke my hair but instead put the ball of his thumb on my second cervical vertebra and pressed down, hard, like some kind of acupuncturist.

"Claire," he mused.

Something about the way my name sounded in his voice—sharp, knubbly, skeletal—made me feel as if I were going to cry.

He said, "Shall we?"

Outside it seemed to have just gotten dark, as if sunset had waited for us. We were old enough to pass for long-married. Walking easily beside Michael, I saw that he was my husband's height and had pretty much my husband's body type, long and liquid. Still, he was not my husband. It appeared that we could stroll to his apartment, across historic Rittenhouse Square, which would be elegant, except for the panhandlers and deinstitutionalized schizophrenics, casualties of the failure of American health care. We could talk about that, probably.

Instead he asked, lightly, "What's the catch?"

He was looking at me sideways, probing, courteous. I tipped my head, to request amplification.

"Come on," he said. "A woman just shows up, offering sex—if I can be so bold as to assume that's what you meant by 'a present'—with no strings attached. Women don't do this. Not women like you."

"But men do? What are 'women' 'like me,' anyhow?"

"Who's taking the deposition here?" he asked, uncomfortably.

If you didn't count Zachary—and for some reason I didn't, quite (that seemed to be the point of Zach)—I had not touched a man not my husband for seventeen years. Nine or ten of them tied up with the child, before and during and after. Prior to that: Ken's residency. Ken getting into his practice. Three different jobs

for me, and three different houses (two rented), in three distinct
locales and climates: new checking account, new car registration,
new grocery store check-cashing courtesy card. Dinner parties for
Ken's current colleagues and their wives, women with whom I
couldn't possibly connect, although I had to look as if I were making an effort. If Ken and I divorced, my lawyer would make an
issue of this (*you helped put him through medical school!*), but I chose
the road. I should have been an army brat, I guess, or a diplomat's
daughter, though I'd spent a childhood in a stable family, in a sub-
urban split-level, and maybe that's exactly why I didn't want an
identity bound by place and things.

"I mean," he said. "Why me?"

The question was a fair one, really. But I couldn't answer it.
Instead I merely parted my lips, in a way that I hoped would indicate my helplessness before his irresistibility.

If this were a movie, he would not stop, before sex with a
stranger, to check his answering machine. But he did, as soon as
we got to his place. I excused myself to use the bathroom off the
hallway, to give him some privacy, but from there, even with the
fan on, I could hear the murmur of the messages playing: a
woman's voice, cajoling. Then a gruff return call—not to her.
Work-related. Get files from so-and-so. This made me feel highly
irritated with him. I hoped he planned to show me a good enough
time to justify whatever betrayal he was currently engaging in. "If
you're going to check E-mail and voice mail next, forget it," I
warned him, and he smiled, shook his head no, led me to the bedroom.

A bout first kissing this man, here is my conviction: that on my deathbed at, say, ninety-three, I will not have forgotten. Yet what will I be remembering? Only my own abandon.

No hallway groping. When we got to his bedroom he threw the keys and loose change in his pocket into the ceramic piece on his dresser that a designer had selected for this purpose, and watched me as I began to take off my clothes, not fast, not slow. There was a chair handy, to receive them. My suit fell in a crisp, lineny rhythm, as if the chair appreciated the hand of the fabric. I knelt on his bed. Then he began to undress too, watching me as I watched him.

I see myself, in memory, kneeling on his bed. The bed is not flat against the wall but, as a result of the interior designer's inspired burst, angled into a corner, and I am kneeling on the corner of the bed, too, so there is a kind of triangular motif, visually. I am sidelit, and feel it. Both exposed and private. Michael, jacket somehow removed but otherwise fully dressed, his shirt the same chemical blue as the city sky viewed from his high-rise window, stands yards away, symmetrically centered on the bed's corner: another triangle. Another: the distance between my yearning breasts and the well, below, to which all sensation flows. Yet another: the distance between those breasts and his hands, his hands and his mouth. All those Pythagorean equations that help the body sail.

Sex is a story you know the ending of. More or less the same story with the same ending, every time. Yet we want to keep hearing it, the way a child listens to a fairy tale, vigilant for variation. I knelt there in, I swear, a trembling suspense of not-knowing, waiting to see where and with what this man would alight on me.

This is what he did: kiss me, solely. No conjoining of hands or chests. If my eyes had been open, I could report how this was achieved. It must have entailed some canting forward on his part, using the bed as a brace. We were tongue-joined—tongue-and-groove. Blind and without history, I felt, and was, mouth only.

Not then but much later, retracing the scene, I would remember the other Michael's poem about breastfeeding babies, about the totality of the hunger and its relation to identity, and an equation would come to me that seemed to spell out, mathematically, the link between desire and deprivation:

$$Want = Want$$

Those words look how the kiss felt. Mouth. Mouth. A precise mirroring. The = was the "we." So by the time he—and this was his next movement, decisive enough to qualify as symphonic—put one hand, only, to one breast, as if to divine, by Braille, the relationship between nipple and mouth, then moved his mouth to the place his hand had just felt out first like a blind man's cane, to lip-read the language he had just invented, I was: well, I was way, way gone. Later there would be time to scold myself "What are you doing?" or remember to register some vestigial shame about the breast (which was not, any longer, in broad daylight, a young woman's), or come up with some distancing quip, like "You're quite the stud, for a Philadelphia lawyer." But for the moment I allowed myself the *Be here now, babe* that was the very point of sex with someone new.

Although he was not quite new. Son and father had, eerily, almost the same hands, the same teeth. The same earlobes, eyebrows, tongue; even, if one can be so crass as to mention it, virtually the same cock, in meat if not motion. (At some point it occurred to me that were it not for incest taboos, fathers and sons would be the scientific subjects of choice for Masters and Johnson, as twins, separated at birth, are for all controlled studies on biology and destiny.)

I would like to say that touch is simply touching. But I had not felt like this from sex with the son. With the son I had stood outside, watching. With Michael there was inside, only. There was, let's face it, a skill differential. The lawyer's sexual MO was highly unusual. The smallness of scale of his touch, the intensity of focus, on thumb or spinal column, may have been a trick, gleaned from an instructional G-spot video that he cribbed from as if it were an appellate brief. But it worked. It allowed me to fall into a well of my own sensation. Made the whole stretch of skin and time that was the act's narrative arc feel—not to put too fine a point on it—clitoral.

The word *love* itself clitoral, quickly swallowed by the vortex of its own sound. Love like a flock of birds *V*-ing into the horizon.

To say *I was inside the sex* is to immediately create a contradiction in terms. One of those Zen paradoxes, like "To think that I will not think of you is still to think of you. So I hereby vow not to think that I will not think of you." The second you say you are lost, you have located yourself linguistically. This is the problem with trying to talk about sex. We live, simultaneously, in language and in our bodies. Both impose limits. To complicate matters further, both words and acts exist in time, which is another limit, maybe the most stringent. Describing an orgasm takes far too long, and thus is false.

Only during sex can you have such thoughts without having them. My pleasure felt distinctly intelligent. I was aware of being driven back to something elemental about who I was and how I had gotten there; this included, even if it did not directly reference, my nursing son, the different yet related pleasure of watching his toes curl, his satiation intense but not tense. From outside, you would see only the soft-porn cliché of my leg around the lawyer's back, my foot arching and flexing. But no one watched. And Michael was not outside.

During orgasm you never see your own face, hear your own cry. You can't lose the self for long, though. Soon it all floods back. Dead son, philandering husband, thyroid problem (?), Hillary Katzenbach (!), court date, alimony payment, pretentious interior-design statement. Persistent car alarm. Then, bizarrely: hunger. How many times was I going to have to eat today? I tried to remember if the munchies were a symptom of early pregnancy, pre–morning sickness. No, I had probably just worked up an appetite. My body was a mess—a Rube Goldberg contraption, the bells of all needs clattering at once. But it was hard not to feel, as Michael left the bedroom and returned with a box of microwavable popcorn upon which Paul Newman grinned iconographically, then spooned up against me while I decided whether or not popcorn was, indeed, what I wanted, that in certain critical matters, my body still worked.

Well after midnight, Michael Davidoff, who planned to take a deposition by dawn's early light, played the cello for me, naked. While a nude flutist might achieve a certain Pan-like élan, a naked man sawing away at a cello can't help but look like a buffoon. Bach's suites, holy and funereal, require a tuxedo. The luscious wood of the instrument, its auburn glints the same tone as the chest hair it is covering. His bony-kneed, hairy legs sticking out on each side, ending in hairy feet: man and bulbous cello made a sort of stick-limbed Mr. Potato-Head. I watched from the couch, where I, too, was naked, inclined, breasts flopping, bowl of microwaved popcorn bull's-eyed on pubic triangle.

"I'm not very good," he confessed to me, from behind the cello. "But I stuck with it because of a girl who played the violin. Marion." Even now, he fondled the name a bit when he said it: his eternal Maid Marion. Every man had one in high school, including Ken.

"I was a real nerd in high school," he revealed, as if it would surprise me. It did not. Weren't all Casanovas nerds in high school? "On the Math Team, even."

"Me too," I said.

"Really?"

"Yes. Math team and literary magazine. Unusual combo."

"Ah. Reciting Plath by heart?"

"Yes. 'Daddy' and Joni Mitchell's 'Blue'—I felt really, really bad for her. How could James Taylor dump her? If Joni could get shat upon, who was safe? And penning my very own Depressed Ballads about how tough it was to get the car on Saturdays to go to the mall."

"Did you have real long hair back then?"

"Armpit-length, yes. In two braids that I wrapped in two circles over each of my ears, like ram's horns."

"Like Princess Leia in—what was that movie?"

The father, like the son, made cinematic allusions. I smiled. "Well, your son isn't a nerd, it appears."

"No. Because of the sports, I guess. I mean, I was around long enough for Little League. And even *in absentia* I was able to pull off a proper birds-and-bees speech, which my father never did."

"Now that I would have liked to hear."

He grinned. On the cello, he laconically sawed out a couple of bars of what might have been Hendrix's "Purple Haze." Then said, shaking his head as if slightly irritated by the recognition, "God, you're . . ."

"Thanks," I responded.

Really, we could have been dating. Why not? Other than the fact that I was already married. Plus there was the slight problem of the son. I tried to imagine us at dinner a couple of years from now, slightly drunk, telling our new joint friends about how we met. *She just stormed right in!* Could not imagine it, exactly. Nor could he, it appeared; as his hand stopped moving on the cello's strings, his face had closed back up, decisive as a Venus's flytrap. Just like that, I was not on his radar screen. And then the phone rang.

He did not pick it up, but the answering machine was right there, so as the caller left the message, we could both listen.

"So," a woman said. "What else is new."

It *was* the legal associate I'd spoken to, earlier in the day! I recognized the exasperated voice.

She paused. "Pick up," she said.

"Come on," she said. "You're not sleeping."

Then sighed, and hung up.

Michael looked at me, shrugged, as the answering machine noisily rewound.

I gave him a tight-lipped smile that indicated subdued sympathy. If *I* were dating you, the look said, I wouldn't let our roles slide into me whining for more, you pulling back. Do you need more of this, after Mar? But of course it was easy for me to say. I was going home. And knew better than to talk about any of this. Instead I said, "Got anything for me to drink?"

The cello-playing naked lawyer-stud emerged, in high spirits, from behind his instrument, to hold his other instrument, semi-wood, up toward me as if it were Bert or Ernie and asked, in goofy *Sesame Street* voice, "What can I get you, lady? Pepsi? Water? Prefer something more elegant: cognac?" And I heard myself say, "Cognac is pretty good with popcorn, actually, though you wouldn't think it. Notice I am saying this to you in my own voice. No talking clamshell vaginas, thank you very much."

He laughed, straddled me for a kiss. Proclaimed, "Salty." Proclaimed, into my very cavities, "In both senses of the word."

While M.D. fetches cognac for me, the following hallucinatorily clear word picture of a different MD.

Kenneth Leithauser, husband, in our kitchen. We have been disagreeing about something. Not exactly arguing; just discussing heatedly. He faces the sink, does not look at me. Scrubs in his own way, methodically. I hear him say:

That's a very, very if not circular, then at least convex, argument.

This line, only, in my husband's voice.

Very if not circular then at least convex.

Subject unclear.

The image so overwhelming that it knocked me out, brought back the cosmic fatigue in a rush, so that by the time Michael got back from wherever the liquor was kept, I was asleep.

He did not wake me, just fetched a blanket. By the time overbright dawn woke me, he had already been back to his office, to fetch the relevant papers and my briefcase. I had evidently slept right through his bleary-eyed workfest at the dining-room table. Rubbing stubble, groaning in his Calvin Klein undergarments, he looked stressed-out and manly—a living ad for middle-aged success.

"I am too old," he informed me, "way too old, for all-nighters. This is not good. If I screw up, it is your fault. Coffee?"

I nodded yes. My nakedness, under the blanket, had a morning-after rawness. He set the coffee down on the end table and lifted the blanket up and off me with an exaggerated *voilà*. Reached down with both hands to tweak my nipples as if they were clown noses. "Honk," he said.

"You're a real goofball, huh?"

"What can I say. You made me happy. How are you. How are *you*?"—nipples greeted, here, individually, each with its own mocking pantomime of a firm handshake. Then: "Whoa. Say what?"

I looked down. As we both watched, just one nipple pushed out a globule of murky fluid about the size and consistency of a drop of blood from a finger-prick test, which then dangled there, refusing to drop.

He flicked his forefinger quickly to catch the drop, tasted it. Put on a wine-taster's pondering face. "Not pasteurized, that's for sure, but definitely—hey."

I felt the milk arrive in the other breast. The nipple pushed it out in a fluttering spasm, like a fart.

"Cool," said Michael Davidoff, in imitation of his son. Then, concerned: "Is this regulation?"

"Don't know," I admitted. "Will have to investigate. Bathroom."

"Feel free to use toothbrush," he called after me, "figuring, germs already majorly mixed."

A physician's wife! A physician's wife who had not thought to mention as a symptom, when a doctor came to her hotel room, that her breasts were leaking, three years after burying a child who had not been nursing, anyway, for years before his death. Who had managed to suppress that detail—who even though she had, at the time symptom first happened, at the Four Seasons Hotel with Zachary, remembered the official term for the condition, could not remember it now, when she needed to, except that it had a sci-fi sound.

Milk this early, as a precursor of pregnancy? Unlikely, but in the bathroom that was my first, optimistic hypothesis. The second went to persistent, pathological grief brought to a head (if that is the proper expression for a nipple) by, perhaps, the shitball in Wilkes-Barre, the shock of his force to milk's source. Or, more likely yet, cancer. *That* was why I'd forgotten the name of the condition. Because I didn't want to confront my imminent mortality—knew without knowing, as women are said to intuit their husband's infidelities. Wasn't I supposed to think, now, *Good?* The bright side being that I could now rejoin my son in some backlit fourth dimension?

I tried to calm myself, took Michael up on the toothbrush. A physician's wife has the sense to say, reasonably, breathing deeply: *it's probably nothing.*

When I returned, wrapped in one of his towels, he offered breakfast—"many options, all frozen, frozen waffles, frozen bagels, Lean Cuisines if you want to start your day off with some fettuccine Alfredo," but convivial as the sentence was, his face was already elsewhere. "Gotta get moving," he said. "This is bad. If we lose I swear I will sue you. *You are responsible.*"

It was just after 6:00 AM.

The coffee, which I blew on although it was no longer that hot and sipped tentatively, tasted normal. As he showered I let the towel fall and did my daily check of reproductive status. (In the heat of the moment, as with the son, birth control had not been discussed. Frighteningly, the topic had not even surfaced in my brain.) Pregnant, about to get my period, neither—just going to skip this month's whole reproductive false-alarm call-and-response. About to die. No way to tell. I didn't feel bloated, though. In fact, I felt nicely scooped-out, taut. Of course good sex can do that, too.

I couldn't wait for Michael to leave, so I could get busy with my *Merck Manual.* Until then my best bet was to distract myself. When I could hear he was done shaving—he'd opened the door, just as my husband does and maybe all men, to let out the steam—I poured more coffee and went to curl up on his bed, to watch him dress. A lovely feeling, left from girlhood with fathers, to watch a man fortify himself with the armor of his workday and, on the other end, gratefully divest. Shoes tied taut as a corset. The Boy Scout seriousness of a man knotting a tie and, later, the swish of a tie knot unfurled, silky as hosiery. All men have their talismanic tricks for robing and disrobing, too, secret fetishes and eccentricities. My husband puts his pants on first, zips and buttons the pants, and only then puts on his shirt. Which requires unbuttoning, unzipping the pants he has just done up, to tuck in the shirt. I have often noted the inefficiency. *I just do it this way, okay?*

Ken often, anyhow, in scrubs. No zippers at all. Men in scrubs look about as sexy as mental patients.

The interior designer had spent some time militarily laying out Michael Davidoff's walk-in closet. Like his ex-wife, he was a clotheshorse. In his closet he got the manly lope of a carpenter, in tool belt. Each article of clothing he put on helped to construct his working self. He concentrated totally, oblivious to me.

The coffee was not going down so well. Father-or-son Davidoff spud abrewing, or acidic coffee on empty stomach after two dinners, excessive lettuce, overly energetic sex; popcorn, which takes, if memory served, a couple of decades per cup to digest. Or nerves, pure and simple.

"So, how long you around for?" Michael inquired of me, behind him in the mirror.

Mentally I retorted, *six months to live.* Bald and brittle, I would be grateful for my husband's forgiveness. What would chemotherapy do to the fetus? Maybe I could hang on seven, eight months. Ken weeping in his surgical mask, his finger stuck through the porthole of the incubator. What would it matter, then, that the baby wasn't his?

Then scolded myself, Just had an uneventful mammogram! Tumor-the-size-of-a-golfball, tumor-the-size-of-a-grapefruit highly, highly unlikely! Doctors do not permit themselves to spiral into worst-case scenarios. They take things calmly, step-by-step. Read the teeny-tiny print.

"I'm due home, really," I told Michael. "But I could try to finesse the weekend, if you'd like."

"I'd like, very much." He paused, cautiously. "Will have some finessing of my own to do, though."

I thought it best to let this one pass. "Do you mind if I stay a while?"

"Yes. Vacate the premises this second, in your towel."

Playfulness aside, he was already way gone, already composing himself to stride into lawyerdom. During our choreography about key and burglar alarm—"you don't need to answer the phone," he said, "the tape'll pick up, unless it's me, and you want to"—he checked his watch compulsively. If this is how he functioned on no sleep at all, it would be much harder than I'd originally thought to break his control. Might take torture. Or sex so good (and here a line from the other Michael came to me) that it shakes the foundations. No, no sexual earthquake. Because you can always just walk away, collect the insurance money. Lawyers, doctors—doctors don't need sleep, just take it wherever, whenever, like soldiers, or airline stewardesses: what would it be like to live with a normal man, who came home from work at a prescribed time, then stayed there? Reading, maybe, in an easy chair.

As if I were one to talk.

I would have liked to hibernate at Michael Davidoff's apartment without the specter of illness or death. Watch daytime talk shows, eat a Lean Cuisine, wash the fork. Make the bed, try a stranger's shampoo, scrub the mold off his shower curtain—as worthy a house guest as Snow White. Check out his portfolio of assets. Unearth the vibrator in the shoebox under the tennis racket. Or just nestle under his creamy quilt, so by the time he returned, exhausted, elated, from a long day of entrapping witnesses, I would be ready. We'd start with a premise of amicable efficiency, straightforward as rear entry, but would sink into it, pleased with our own abandon. Pizza delivery, dining naked, finer than the cozy cliché of girl in man's big shirt: I saw him curling up the slice vertically, so he could fit the end in his mouth, as he told me about the day's travails. I would not mind that he talked with his mouth full, cheese dripping. Sorry to hurt you (Michael to Legal Associate-cum-Lover), but we simply fell in love. Why is it that even when we should know better, all stories end with change, with fate? Because sex opens you up, if you're a woman. We can make a nest out of anything. We eye each twig and scrap of gum-wrapper tinsel for potential adaptive reuse.

How much does *The Merck Manual* weigh? Three pounds, four, despite the fact that the paper is Gideon tissue—thin, the type microscopic. Yet I had been walking around with this tome entombed in my briefcase for almost a decade, and why? Most of the products I sold I knew intimately. *Merck* provides, anyway, the most basic of summaries, flirting with out-of-date. Just enough information to induce paranoia. Relax in a hotel room with a guide to local yummy restaurants, a *People* magazine, and *Merck* for a nice chilly bedtime story: so many different things can go wrong.

Half an hour with *The Merck Manual* gave me my condition's name and outline. Galactorrhea, undercaptain of the Starship *Enterprise*. If production of "nonphysiologic" milk not result of "prolonged intensive suckling," could be (what couldn't?) stress. Condition exacerbated by antidepressants, Valium. "Must rule out hypothyroidism; increased TRH stimulates increased secretion of both TSH and PRL." Could indicate hormonal problem: excessive estrogen or, if in combination with amenorrhea—*no* menstruation! This had not even occurred to me! Much more likely in my case than pregnancy! That would explain the periods so light as to have seemed like the spotting of early pregnancy. For amenorrhea, one should—take thyroid level. Check "nutritional status": not starving Ethiopian, Olympic gymnast. Check for "psychological dysfunction—stress." That ought to settle it, in my case, except that one-third of women with complete suppression of menstruation have pituitary adenoma.

There it was: cancer.

Most microadenomal tumors not dangerous, I read! Most very small, slow-growing, or stable! Not neoplastic!

Almost all respond to drug treatment!

Not even open of business day and I had already gotten diagnosed, hysterical, cured.

Trying to stay calm, I ate one of Michael's cardboard-tasting frozen waffles, showered. Put myself back into the clothes from the day before. Nothing so quixotic-feeling as cloaking a clean body in dirty underwear. Then had only ten minutes to wait before I could get busy.

Dr. Talliver's business card was not in my briefcase, but on the bureau back at the hotel. He was, however, listed. I called his office, left a message that it was an emergency and that he should call me back at—but Michael Davidoff's phone number was not printed on the phone, as in the good old days. Nor was home phone listed. Nor did I think they were likely to give it to me at his office. But I was a clever girl. Called Bell Tel and got, after a series of volleys, the mechanism to obtain this information. #958, for future reference, gets you a computer, an emotionless crew member from The Good Ship *Galactorrhea*, reciting the phone number from which you just dialed. Called back Talliver, gave it to his secretary, as well as room number at Four Seasons.

Then called my OB-GYN in Cleveland. Told the secretary it was an emergency.

Friday is not the best day to get cancer. Friday is not the best day to do anything that involves The Helping Professions. Patients imagine the cruel doctors lolling about in golf carts. In fact the problem with weekends is the low-level folk—X-ray technicians, blood-test processors, even data-entry clerks who need to type in the insurance information in order to process the blood samples—whose Fridays start, generally, by lunch on Thursday. A Friday in summer, in August: forget it. I knew this. It is, of course, a little better in a town the size of Cleveland than in Manhattan, where all tissue samples from breast aspirations, from questionable mammograms, are taken on Friday mornings, so that women can wait until Monday afternoon, Tuesday morning, sometimes even later for results. A marathon straight fifty, sixty, seventy hours of not knowing whether you will continue being able to see your husband and children, of envisioning the cancer in you as a hairy fist or as greenish, long-toothed and slavering, something from *Alien*.

Could not, for the life of me, even remember where the pituitary gland was. Was not carrying a *Gray's Anatomy*.

Found Michael's dictionary, looked it up. While I was at it looked up *galactorrhea*, which had not made it into the *American Heritage*, but the etymology became obvious as I searched: galaxy. Milky way. All we know of heaven we learn at the breast.

9:20 AM.

The University of Pennsylvania's medical library was a short cab ride away. Even closer, my computer: I could hook into the on-line medical library at work, check out the latest research. But none of this would tell me a thing. I needed a blood workup, pronto, and I would sit right here until one was scheduled.

Nothing so awful as waiting to hear from doctors. I've sat through many casual conversations about what kind of death one prefers, hypothetically: instantaneous or delicately degenerative. As if one is given a choice. Everyone always picks heart attack over the slow, ugly ravaging. I wouldn't argue, even as someone who lost a child that way, in a lightning bolt. In neither scenario, though, do you *know*. That's the problem. The perfect death would be the one where you know in advance exactly when you will vanish in a flash. You could pick a date, say a Saturday in late May. A suitable engagement, then the ceremony.

Instead of going into a waiting-for-doctors fugue, I tried to feel, in Michael's apartment, like I was inhabiting that enervating point in a courtship in which nothing between you has been decided, but things aren't really fresh either. You wake up at his place and your own place—mail, fresh clothes, different lipstick color—beckons. This conceit made me feel almost nostalgic for my nice clean room at the Four Seasons. I went so far as to call the hotel, see if they could release my voice-mail messages, but they had no mechanism to do that by remote.

Why was I paying for a hotel, if I planned to stay with Michael? It only made me traceable. Did I, or did I not, want Ken to come? For Ken to make management open my door, find the bed unslept in, go to the police—all that seemed unnecessarily cruel. I really needed to call him, once I heard from the doctor, because I did not, of course, want the doctor to call and find the phone busy.

9:45.

Efforts to calm down with cable movies were equally ineffective. On one of Michael's premium channels, humorless Mafia hits, and on the other, a psychopath whose jollies were derived from burying victims alive. Being buried alive is no one's fantasy of the ideal death. I did not need to contemplate, currently, what I would do when I found myself awake in the inescapable dark of the coffin. The best I could come up with was to masturbate. Use up what was left of my oxygen with some heavy breathing, go out with a bang.

It was that train of thought that set me out to search for Michael's promised collection of pornographic movies. They were not, as Zachary had promised, prominently and proudly displayed. But they were not that hard to find, either. There were only a couple of the lesbo-fantasies that Zachary had foretold, but who knows, maybe Dad's tastes had evolved, for most of these (by no means a hundred, but more than several) were instructional numbers, focused on technique as if on golf swing. So I'd called that one right too; he'd studied both law and sex. I popped in *The Secrets of Tantric Love* and sat unmoved, in my suit, as a duo deep-kissed in close-ups that let you study their fillings, then made sensuous Love, to what sounded like elevator Muzak, so slowly that I had to roll my eyes, reach for the remote. Fast-forwarding through Tantric sex: now there was a mantra for our troubled times. (10:00.) The men all wore condoms. I didn't remember that, from porn-days of yore. A new couple was trotted out—I seemed to have flipped right past the last set's climax, if in fact Tantric sex permitted climax—featuring a bearded fellow who had a much stronger, more flexible back than any male with whom I had ever been personally associated, for he seemed to have no trouble standing, leaning backward at a forty-five-degree angle while hefting up a full-grown woman, and then rotating her whole body in dreamy circles, like some slo-mo rodeo roper, for about three or four years, during which, every so often, she moaned encouragingly.

10:15.

With her chirping as background I plugged in my computer, called up the file where I'd been keeping track of my menstrual periods such as they were, and neatly transcribed the numbers, so when my OB-GYN called and asked for them, I'd be ready for him.

When was your last period? *Depends on what you're calling a period.*

Like most women, I had fallen a little in love with my OB-GYN, after the delivery. Hard not to fall in love with a man brave enough to look into that gory mess. He had spoken to me musingly about the indignities of HMO bill-processing procedures while he stitched up my episiotomy, attentive to detail as a lace-tatter. He was short, like many GYNs—some almost Toulouse-

Lautrec height, scaled to practically stand eye-level between the stirrups. (The tall, strong guys, like my husband, are mostly orthopedic surgeons.) Short and sweet. He would not, I trusted, keep me waiting long on an emergency long-distance call, and I was right. I picked up on the first ring before *Tantric Love* was over, if it would ever be over. We got the small-talk quickly out of the way—yes, away on business, might be away for a while—and I filled him in on my preliminary diagnosis.

"Very good!" he said. "Been crammin' from your *Merck*?"

" 'Course."

"Any other symptoms?"

"Tired. I thought I might be pregnant, until I thought I might be amenhorreac."

We trotted through my computer-generated calendar of blood arrival. He was not satisfied with my bookkeeping. I had neglected to record length, so that it was hard to tell what was period, what was spotting. "Any nausea, breast tenderness?" he asked.

"Nope."

"Decreased libido?"

"Increased, if anything."

"Are you—hairier anywhere?"

"Pardon?"

"Any mustache, hair on your chest? Hirsute at all?"

I laughed. He was using the very adjective from *Merck*'s, to describe symptoms of Cushing's disease. "No," I said, "and my face isn't round, either."

He laughed back. Nothing like a good chuckle with your MD.

"Not to worry," he assured me. "The adenoma is a common problem. No biggie. Ten percent of the population, by some estimates, has it, if in fact that's what you have and given your commuting schedule, and all the other—well, it ain't necessarily so. Gotta run the numbers. Galactorrhea can occur spontaneously. If you and Ken have an athletic session of—I mean, if you have to *squeeze*, it's not necessarily symptomatic."

So the Wilkes-Barre pincher might, in fact, have caused onset.

"You know anyone around these parts?" I asked him. "Any school chums who would see me quick? I'd like to get a prolactin reading. Today, say."

"No hurry. Just call when you get home. Set you right up."

"Don't know *when* I'll be home and would like to know, actually. I mean my understanding is that the Bromocriptine—"

"Dostinex now," he corrected. "Big improvement since the Dostinex is twice a week versus twice a day on the other."

"My understanding is that it increases chances of fertility."

"Sure, but you're putting the cart before the horse."

"All I want is the blood test."

"Well, no one's gonna see you there over this. Not like it's serious. But it's a special test. You've got to have fasted the night before, no intercourse, no breast exam. And if the levels indicate—odds are it's nothing, Claire, but do you really want to have an MRI there, by yourself? And in Philly—well, for nonemergency, you'd probably wait two weeks there for an MRI."

I realized that an MRI by myself was exactly what I wanted, but it would be hard to explain this to him.

If I wanted something to do, he suggested, I could go buy myself a home pregnancy kit. That at least would settle that. Did I want to talk to Amy, make an appointment right away?

I dutifully made the appointment for the middle of the next week, but it was clear to me I would have to ascertain my condition before I went home. I would have been hard-pressed to explain why, but I did feel quite sure that I should know before I returned to Ken. To see a doctor here, I would have to lie. That shouldn't be much of a problem; I'd lied to everyone else. Meanwhile it was almost lunchtime, on a Friday. No way was anything happening today, even if Talliver magically returned my call and set me right up with a local OB-GYN, because my big night of love had evidently obviated my chances for a clean blood test. Nothing was happening until Monday, which meant that I would be encoffined into a whole weekend of uncertainty. A weekend like an MRI—that claustrophobic and scary.

F or a Monday morning blood test, I would have to make arrangements at once. But I had no doctor's name and was not about to proceed alphabetically through the GYNs in the Yellow Pages, despite the fact that any halfwit could oversee a blood test. So I went back to sleep and dreamed about traveling the quarter-mile to the Four Seasons, to check my messages and sleep in what I had begun to think of as my own bed.

In my dreams, Ken appeared to be waiting in the lobby, agitated. Thus I knew I was dreaming, because staking out a lobby was not Ken's style. There would be mail, though. Federal Express. A barely legible note on one of his freebie pads advertising new drugs: LOVE YOU

Just not quite enough to lavish on me a personal pronoun, or punctuation.

Asleep, I decided that if the Federal Express envelope from Kenneth Leithauser contains a note *not* scribbled on a drug company pad, and he managed to use the personal pronoun, *and* he filled out the FedEx form himself, in his own handwriting, rather than have his secretary type it and arrange pickup, I would go home today. Then a backup plan: even if there is no Federal Express envelope from Kenneth Leithauster, I will call him, put his mind at ease.

I'm surprised when he answers the phone at home, at lunchtime. He has somehow managed to have calls transferred from
the home phone to the cell phone. Answers from surgery. *Can you
hold on?* As through a conch, the *whoosh* of distant water. I imagine
the bloody thumbprint on the cell phone. Where did he put the
phone during surgery, on the tray with the instruments? Who is
minding the cracked-open ribs of the patient in question while
Ken says *Claire? That you?* I'd always loved the deep yet easy tim-
bre of Ken's voice. Asleep, I muscled into his voice as if hurling
my head into his neck, taking strength from the brute fact of marriage—years crosshatched and accreting like lath on a joist. *I miss
you!* Could say just that on the answering machine.

But I did not go to the hotel or call. I merely slept or half-slept,
with things coming at me in threes:

Galactorrhea
Amenorrhea
Pituitary Microadenoma

    Hillary
    Kenneth
    Michael

        Michael
        Zachary
        Margot

            Defective heart
            Defective car seat
            Shitty driver

Michael

Kenneth

Me—

a list that ended, somehow, in *summer camp,* my son (so tall!) the
only thing to emerge from the confusion whole and alone, except
that with his ponytail he also seemed to be Zachary, Michael
Davidoff and I his parents; and Hillary Katzenbach seemed to
have died in a car accident in Puerto Vallarta; and Hillary Katzenbach and Michael Davidoff seemed to have met (in a fender-
bender?) and married, leaving me to seek out the poet Michael to
console him, and fall in love with him, and help his raise his children, and allow him to express, in verse, the nature of my grief.

The hotel room at the Four Seasons now loomed totemic, like
the rental car parked in the Children's Hospital garage: a lost
thing, shadowy and incomplete. Presumably the room was still
being kept for me. I could touch base with the people at what I'd
begun to think of as The Desk, as if it were the CIA, or The Polit-
buro. My black suitcase was still in that room. Again I had to
demand of myself: who cared? Insurance would cover it, my
employer would replace it in a flash, and anyhow, I was a surgeon's wife. The only valuable thing in my life was my life. Even
if it was only sentimental value.

When Michael Davidoff returned from work, with several bags
of odiferous Thai take-out, I had been asleep all afternoon, and he
had been awake for almost two days. He was not sure, he
announced, that he could even stay awake through dinner, no less
for—and here he grinned, holding up the box from my recent
viewing pleasure—anything Tantric. But he planned to try, he
said. Fortify himself with some Pad Thai, give it his best shot. And

how, he wanted to know—he was still standing beside the bed, holding brown paper bags—were Elsie's famous leaky teats?

I sat up. "You don't happen to know a good OB-GYN in the city by any chance," I asked.

"Sure do," he said. "Don't move. Wait a minute."

I was foggy enough to think that, when he left the room, he would return with a doctor. But he was, in fact, just putting down the take-out bags. Then he approached to rip his down quilt off me.

I had known him only two days but this gesture—yanking back covers decisive as a toreador, or as a waiter wielding a fresh table-cloth—was already overfamiliar. And a poor fit for the delicacy of his sexual moves. Subtlety covering brashness, the brashness something about which he felt both pride and shame: therein, I suspected, lay his secret, such as it was. If we trotted through family genealogy, curriculum vitae, old flames, and old failures, I would understand.

He had in mind, presumably, the contrast of my naked, sleep-warmed flesh against his suit. Except I was in my suit too. I had never managed to get undressed. The suit just dry-cleaned, too. We both smiled at the idiocy of this. He bent to kiss, for some reason, in the vicinity of my belly button, at an angle that made his tie swish pubically, like some kind of French tickler.

I pushed him away. "No sex, I'm afraid," I explained. "Messes up the blood test I'm hoping to have soon. Like, tomorrow. Know a doctor you can pull strings with?"

"After dinner," he assured me.

"No food for me either. Got to fast."

He grinned. "Well, *this* promises to be a fun weekend," he said. "All-rightee. No sex. How 'bout if I just—"

But I grabbed his hand. "This has to be the part where we, retrospectively, 'get to know each other.' "

He did a lawyer's gesture of doleful acquiescence. But I could tell he was too tired to be as disappointed as he thought he should act. In fact, I could tell he was as puzzled about why I was there as I was myself.

Michael had in mind for me for the blood test, he told me as he ate, a Dr. Sharon Rieff, who sometimes testified for him in cases involving unnecessary or botched surgery, and complications during delivery. He had known her for years, well enough, it seems, to beep her on a Friday night to arrange an impromptu look-see for a friend. "Ohio," he said, smiling at me reassuringly. "Yeah. I know. But." From tone alone, from just those lines, I could tell that Michael and the doctor had once been lovers or maybe were still, although their relationship seemed awfully tension-free for people currently entangled.

No food, no sex, Dr. Sharon Rieff reminded me. "No other drugs, obviously. Furthermore, since M.D. will undoubtedly ask, nothing *sexlike.* By which I mean, if you've got symptoms of galactorrhea, give the breasts a rest."

That established, it was time for Michael and me to chat. Where were we from? Where did we go to college? Did we have brothers and sisters? How did I get into medical sales? Where did Ken and I meet? How did I feel about Jewish men, how did Michael feel about shiksas like me? Why had he never remarried? Was he seeing anyone seriously? How old were we, our first times? How many times, total, in our lives? How many times married?

Staggering, the number of things you'd need to know to make even a superficial profile. Easier to think I knew something without all that, merely from observing the speculative way he squiggled the remains of his shrimp tails and bean sprouts around on his plate. All of personality encoded in the gesture.

He was too tired for much inquiry, although I did manage to get out of him that he and Dr. Rieff "had a thing, once." She was not the current object of affection, about whom he was properly circumspect. I watched him eat, then watched him sleep. Hard to think it was totally meaningless, as ships that pass in the night, that we had managed to get ourselves, for our one weekend together, on such radically different schedules. I watched the clock, watched bad TV, and slept a bit, fitfully. All of my energy was focused now on the gleaming needle that would bring me answers.

I f you ever want to know where you stand as an American, try gaining admittance to a hospital the computers of which do not already have a record of you. An imprint of my Blue Cross card, a xerox of my driver's license—I was a citizen. A confirmation call from Dr. Rieff to the reception desk allowed my tall, white, entitled-looking escort to take me right to Labor and Delivery, where the surprisingly young Sharon ("Shar!" Michael exclaimed, grabbing her face and steadying it so he could kiss her loudly on the cheek, a kiss avuncular for public display only) sat among the chattering nurses and residents, doing record-keeping with a big stack of patient files.

I had not anticipated Labor and Delivery. I had expected an anonymous cubicle in her office. But Dr. Rieff was on call and had told us to meet her right there, at the big steel table in the center of the hub of cubicles, where she was making herself take up the least amount of room, not getting in the way of the nurses, not being distracted in the least by the mingled screams and moans of the women behind the doors.

I had not been in Labor and Delivery since my own. Had not been there before that except once, for the hospital tour, during which I obsessed about the absolute necessity of being placed in one of the two spacious, pastel new Birthing Suites, just like hotel rooms except for the state-of-the-art equipment. When push came to shove, however, I was not first come, first served. The Birthing Suites were occupied, so I was wheeled from one of the minuscule, decrepit cubicles, mung or glue visible underneath the peeling wallpaper, to the old delivery room. The pain wiped out the disappointment. Who invented the myth that women forget the pain of delivery? "What's it like" we had all asked about contractions, during the classes. Like King Kong picking you up in his fist and squeezing you, so you are both possessed by the pain and curiously outside it, watching yourself, tiny and distant, in pain's palm. The thing is that, unlike most pain, it doesn't linger. No aftermath. The contractions just stop, as if it has snowed twenty inches and suddenly sun out, snow melted, not even a trace of salt on the concrete.

Dr. Sharon Rieff stood to thrust out her hand. Short, like my OB-GYN. Big, big wedding rock. She asked a nurse if there was a spare room, told Michael he could get some coffee and come back in twenty minutes. "Got a gown for her?" she asked the nurse, and before I knew it, my legs were dangling over the edge of the gurney (hospital fluorescents make even recently shaven legs look bristly, blue, lifeless, the limbs of an unidentified person washed up from the river) and the little lady was squeezing my nipples. Hard.

"There we go," she said. "And this started when?"

I was very hungry. The frozen waffle would have been my last food and that was the morning before. Through the wall, the woman in the cubicle next to me, in the early stages of labor, let out an exploratory wail. A male voice muttered encouragement while Dr. Rieff felt my glands, asked some more questions, had me lie down, screwed in the cold speculum, reached into me with that face OB-GYNs make: staring into space, as if imagining your insides on an overhead projector.

"Seem pregnant?" I asked.

"Not obviously. Why? Feel pregnant?"

"Sure tired enough."

She smiled. "What we'll do," she said, as she rummaged in drawers for needles and bottles, wearing the universal expression of doctors repressing irritation when they're performing a task that ought to be performed by an underling, "is run the blood-work, give you a call if it's clear, get the results to your doctor in—"

"Ohio. So," I asked, as she got my vein to pop. "What's increased libido a symptom of?"

At the very second the needle entered, the woman through the wall screamed. My doctor laughed, either because of the synchronicity or my question. Probably the latter, for she said, "Michael. It's a sign of Michael. Lust is not a warning sign of many diseases, except maybe mental ones. Exactly the opposite, in fact, so if you're hot-to-trot, odds are you don't have a thyroid problem. Or The Adenoma for that matter."

Same as my doctor—that *the*.

When I looked up from watching my blood fill the vial, she was checking me out with full-throttle curiosity. She'd registered *my* wedding band and my home state; she wondered what I was doing with Michael. But she didn't have to wonder hard, because she thought she already knew. What she was confirming, with pleased surprise, was her own indifference to Michael's amorous activities. Whatever they had done, whenever, was "in the past," not ragged and jangling but snug as a bug in a rug. As my blood ran out she was checking the safety of her own marriage, her own life—surreptitiously, as you adjust your bathing suit when you come out of the pool. She seemed like a decent sort (OB-GYNs often are), and I knew I could say a sentence or two about my son, gain from her a sympathy that might momentarily soothe, might also gain her cooperation and haste for the task at hand. But I would not do so. Had spoken plenty to Kramer about the way that I "held" the pain, but those who would argue for "letting it out" did not understand grief's most essential feature: the pain is exactly the opposite of a contraction. Not clearly outlined and temporary, but permanent. Best you can hope for is pain management. Or distraction. Sleep with this person or that.

Dr. Sharon Rieff had finished with my blood and now, I realized, had her thumb to my wrist, checking my pulse. "Are you okay?" she asked. "You look really—"

I was pale and breathing hard, in Labor and Delivery, cold in my blue gown, listening to another woman shriek through a wall. I shook my head: fine. And then Michael knocked on the door and entered, with a show of bashful restraint, exactly as a doctor would, having given you time to get your clothes off. The doctor and I both gazed up at him, tall and glowing in the doorway. I felt preposterously happy to see him. Felt, in fact, like I was in one of those movies where the woman goes into labor while her husband is out of town and he rushes back, gets there just in time. His face, gauging me, so full of tenderness and respect that you'd think he *was* my husband, even if he had no idea who I was or what he was doing with me—which makes him, I suppose, like most husbands. Toward Michael I felt—still feel—a profound gratitude, an utterly unironic appreciation for the kindness of strangers.

"Michael," I said. *"Feed me."*

He did. We were then free to make love. Creditably. Languid, biting—my memory of that sex dissolves into shards. He saw to it that I opened up, exploded, like a tulip in time-lapse. But this session felt like it was superimposed over the original, better print. I could remember, as from long ago, the weight of his first touch on each place he touched now. The memory was edenic, was of loss. Our sex had been lush and sudden, like an action painting or a flamed French sauce. All of this—all of this was just *monkeying-with*.

I should have either left, or planned to stay. But this, the Weekend of Love like an unmoored houseboat: this was awkward.

By Saturday, before dinner, my whole life felt like a car dangling over a cliff in an action-adventure film. Close-up on the spinning wheels in mud. Close-up on the tree trunk on which the car's weight rests, slowly cracking.

He had to go grocery shopping. Would cook dinner, he said, if I didn't mind something simple. Did I want to come, or stay and rest? I chose, gingerly, the latter, which was, of course, a choice of some significance. Because I could have sat beside him in his car, bantered about his consumer choices in the store. This being Michael—a man so reserved he made my husband look like Heathcliff—even his asking me to accompany him *meant* something, was fraught with the implication that I could stay, or at least flirt with the idea of staying, if I wanted. That we had, however unlikely it seemed, a future together.

So I felt bad to say no, flat-out. Felt I had to tell him: "You know how some people are afraid to drive, after a car accident? My thing has been, since then, grocery stores. *Hate* them. Really have to drag myself. Family life, in its full glory. Aisles of diapers, Jell-O, sugary cereals. The yowling infants in the carts."

He smiled. "This is a more elegant emporium, though. Mesclun, gourmet take-out—little stuffed-quail kind of things."

"Right," I said. "Baby vegetables. Baby squash, baby eggplant, baby corn. Baby, baby, baby. Fiddlehead ferns . . ."

Before he left he brought me a glass of white wine. I did not move from the bed while he was gone, even to go to the bathroom. Just sat up enough to sip, the wineglass resting coolly on my stomach. That I had had sex—that I had done, ever, *anything*— amazed me. But Michael would come back with more food (his job in life, vis-à-vis me, seemed to be to provide sustenance), and I would get through the weekend, and by Monday Dr. Rieff would give me some kind of hint of whether or not I was going to live, or dive straight off the cliff.

Coffee, bagels, Sunday *New York Times*. Michael has the Business Section. I study the wedding announcements as I do every week, reading past the scam of journalistic objectivity—daughter of, son of, alma mater, job—to see what kind of fault lines are most likely to swallow up bliss. Truly, marriage is a glass house on a cliff in Malibu, with a view, but no earthquake insurance. There is always a balance of tales threatening dramatic tension (Dad and Mom both remarried, Dad to bimbo, Mom to minister who will perform ceremony) with wholesome-yet-successful kids from stable families (Jill will teach kindergarten while Jack says "Sure I want to make partner, but it's family that matters"). Who knows, maybe he will even mean it. Or think he does.

Some weeks, seems like every person getting married is an investment counselor.

Then the pull story, in which people with unusual careers (maker of kooky hats, gold-leafer of illuminated manuscripts) meet cute and engage in cagey courtship, not yet aware of what is clear to all their interesting friends, that they are "made for each other." Laughing at each other's jokes as they help the homeless.

Michael wants to summarize for me an article on the fiscal politics of neurobiological research. While we sip our coffee, some labcoat with a grant fiddles with Neuropeptide Y, the neurotransmitter for both hunger and reproduction. Someday you can take your pill, get pregnant without having sextuplets. Lose twenty, thirty pounds while you're at it. Then there's Oxytocin, the chemical for fidelity. The unfaithful, it appears, don't have enough of it. Take a supplement, save your marriage.

" 'Course it will obtain," Michael says, "that the Y and the Oxytocin don't mix too good. Like alcohol and Tylenol—people with, say, high blood pressure will be dropping like flies."

"And that's where you come in," I offer.

He nods, almost smirking. "Woman desperate to get pregnant to save her marriage keels over at the wheel of a car, kills Young Ma and babe just out for a stroll, just crossing the street. Who pays off the bereaved dad?"

I stare at him—fondly, I'd thought. He wears a terry-cloth bathrobe very much like my husband's and maybe like all men's, with a belt too thick to properly knot and sleeves that bell, stupidly, midforearm, so they threaten to droop into food, knock over coffee cups. Who thought this up? Is it some kind of cruel joke on Samurai getups? A very bad mismatch of fabric and cut, like fur diapers. And why a terry-cloth robe, anyhow, in August. For him to be comfortable, his AC must be up way too high.

"God, I'm sorry," he said.

It took me a second to figure out why he would apologize. Michael in a bathrobe, I in my newly acquired underwear and one of his white T-shirts, washed and folded, clearly, by some Chinese laundry, because it had deep creases going down from the V-neck, like a pressed dress shirt: the differential in our degree of coverage had made me shiver. But he'd taken my hugging myself as vestigial grief triggered by his tactless remark. Here we were snuggling over the paper—pretending that the world was a known quantity, a land we'd gotten the lay of, that furthermore we were known to each other, as lovers and/or pals, when in fact we were missing each other, mostly. Mostly mysteries. Not that we weren't doing pretty well, for people who had only just met. But any miscommunication, like the one we'd just had, could pull away the trampoline, topple the whole illusion of buoyant ease. Comfort and danger: so hard to get the balances right. Because it's not as if I *knew* my husband. Rather I knew him so well I couldn't see him anymore. I knew him the way I know myself. All of our years together—they weren't money in the bank. They were cash in a mattress that could burn. Our years together were age, age itself: an indignation.

No way to summarize this to Michael or even to myself. It was already gone. I just shook my head.

"The problem is," he said, "you do so well. You wouldn't even know. I've got clients who—like you said yesterday—could never drive again. Could never sit behind the wheel of a car. One woman, her settlement included a driver and a limousine. Permanently. Limo to go anywhere, even to the grocery store."

I nodded, sympathetically.

"How many kids in your state died that year?" he asked. "Do you know?"

I did. I told him. "Twenty-eight."

"Did you figure your odds?"

"I did. And the odds of the ALMCA."

"The huh?"

Anomalous Left Main Coronary Artery. A congenital heart disease occurring in one of every 300,000 children. Three-ish in a million. Symptoms similar to, but not identical to, those of myocarditis or dilated cardiomyopathy. Symptoms generally present before two years old, which put my son in right past the bell of the bell curve, unlike, say, that seventeen-, eighteen-year-old rookie who keeled over at the tail end of a slam dunk. They figured it was drugs like the last one, but no, bum heart. Figure the odds for that mother's son—NBA draft pick, then dropping dead on the court. Or the odds of ALMCA kicking in during a car accident, that unglamorous taker of lives—car accidents, I happened to know, accounted for 37 percent of the annual deaths of children under the age of nineteen, followed only by firearms.

I gave Michael the basic outline of the cause of death. Then was quiet. He made a face that encouraged me to explain what I was thinking.

I was remembering how, when my son was tiny, I snuck into his room every night to watch him breathe. To fall asleep he humped his back and tucked his hands under his pelvis—a swimmer's move, as if he were diving into unconsciousness—and that is how I always found him. His mouth turned sideward to sip air. Asleep, still, he was stretched out to his whole shocking length, so you could study his eyelashes and the soles of his feet. His back smooth as a dolphin's. There was a surprising little curve where his back met his armpits ("armpits" seems a misnomer, in a person that size), and every time I saw that I would smile, as if my mouth were meeting that curve, imitating the musculature.

For those seconds I would just drink him up. And every night I'd think (if you could call it thought, because everything with a baby happens in breathless bytes) how deep, how almost sinful is the pleasure of the nightly pilgrimage to bedside. You know that as you're watching. So while it's a pure pleasure, it's also strangely self-conscious. After the flush of the gaze itself you think, I am here, watching the baby sleep, and I fear I won't be able to remember how good this feels.

And you're right. You won't. Even if the child lives, as they almost all do, you can't get back the baby. You have just these couple of sweet years and a heap of things too tiny to remember: the way you hold a very small baby on your forearm, its head in your palm, its butt in the crook of your elbow, amazed that you can be so blithe with a creature so fragile.

You sneak in, listen to them breathe. You can barely believe they can *keep* breathing, without your vigilance. But then you get over that. They drive their bikes to the pool, your car to the prom. Most of them do not wind up wrapped around trees.

Ironically, both I and the woman who hit me had been driving Volvos. This was before the advent of side air bags. Given the ALMCA, it was not at all certain that side air bags would have made any difference. Illogically, but understandably I think, I would never drive a Volvo again. I inherited Ken's Acura and let him buy himself a proper surgeon's Mercedes.

This was longer than I could bear, even still, to think about cars. I squeezed my eyes shut to clear away the images.

"If you're lucky," I summarized for Michael, "you'll be a grandparent someday soon. Hold a baby again."

"I never much liked babies. Probably I'll like 'em even less when they prove I'm old enough to be a grandparent."

Picture of Ken, who was terrific with babies, holding a bundle of brand-new grandchild, then the flash reminding me that *the thing between* him and the grandchild was gone. Not fair to even call this a "flash." Certainly not flash*back*. Once the grief was oceanic but now it was, mostly, an absence. Lack on a level almost molecular. Infinite absence because, as per Zeno's paradox, if you cut "it" in half, then in half again, in half again, it's still—there. There as absence.

"You ever try one of those griever's groups?" Michael asked. "They've helped a lot of my clients. Shouldn't work, but it does. Misery loves company—like AA."

As he said the sentence something interesting happened. Ken, holding the baby—the image melded with the line from memory from the other day, *a very if not circular then at least convex argument,* so that I was looking at Ken in, say, a soap bubble, floating, very far away. But suddenly I wanted to see him whole and in the flesh. Wanted, in focus, his hands around that baby, and it wasn't the baby I was viewing but the hands themselves: the fingers bony, big-knuckled, pale from overscrubbing, from all that time spent in rubber gloves.

Suddenly I missed him, ferociously.

"A lot of deaths," Michael was telling me, "are so *stupid.* Did you hear about that teenage girl couple of years ago? They couldn't peel her off the bottom of the whirlpool. They couldn't find the shut-off switch. Friend of mine did some work on a class-action suit on that and now the whirlpools come with all sorts of warnings, and everyone laughs. But she drowned in three feet of water, in a whirlpool. *Stupid.*"

"Actually," I told Michael, "I've got to use your phone."

And he nodded in a way that seemed to me knowing, almost proud, as if he had manufactured the reunion. Which in a sense, I believe, he had.

B ut Ken wasn't home. My own voice on the answering machine invited me to leave a message. Paged him but, when asked to enter the phone number, realized I yet again did not have one, on the bedroom cordless. Had to hang up, call into the other room to ask Michael, dial again. Was about to enter the number before I realized that leaving Michael's phone number for my husband was not a phenomenally good idea.

Eleven AM on a Sunday: racketball with a pal? Reading the paper over cappuccino and crumb cake at a Barnes and Noble, looking up over his glasses every so often to explore the women he was now free to pursue? No. Not at a museum, not with a "friend." Not having forget-your-troubles communion with the lawn: we pay people to do that. On call, probably.

How far out of my life would I need to be cast before I couldn't be reeled back to the predictable orbit? The Sunday paper in the damp grass. Ken's lax hand on the steering wheel, patch of hair below each knuckle. Groan of garage door lifting.

Ken's smile. To a stranger it might look sarcastic. The teeth on the top, on one side, overlap where the orthodontist screwed up, and he still smiles like a teenager, to hide that, or even before that to hide the braces; as he smiles he hunches, too, a tall man's shy self-effacement, as if any happiness needs to be hunkered down in. How far out of my life before the thought of those overlapping teeth engaged my tongue?

This far. Like a child I wanted him now, this second.

It's not as if Ken had found a handy nurse to suck him off in a broom closet! He had chosen a grown-up, married physician he had known in college, with whom he had been discussing his confused guilt over his son's death. Maybe even admitting his anger at his blank-eyed zombie-bride. No question I'd merely been going through the motions. Who could blame me? Why Ken, of course. That's what a spouse is for.

And Hillary—she'd fallen in love with him. As why shouldn't she. Because he was *nice,* especially for an MD. Probably nicer than her husband. Tenderness is what she lacked in her life, despite the poet sawing away at the swelling violin strings of their family moments. Ken was gruff and crusty, but that made the tenderness more moving. She had cut him open like a grilled steak, let the blood run out.

This was not a productive line of inquiry. Hillary I could think ill of 'til the cows came home, but I promised myself to do my husband the service of not oversimplifying him. Not making him transparent, an anatomy-lesson model of a man. Some woman had wanted him so much that she choked up, still, at the thought of him. Unlike death, desire is complicated. As I had now seen, personally. From the glass-ceiling, glass-floored house in which I currently tiptoed, barefoot, I would not cast stones.

Because if Ken demanded what I was doing here, with Michael, I would not be able to answer. Would dislike having my motivation flattened to "payback" when I could not even answer to myself.

I sat on the edge of Michael Davidoff's bed and put my hands so they covered my whole face, like a hockey player's caged mask. Through my fingers I allowed myself to peer at, admit what I wanted. When I got back to the hotel I wanted to find my husband leaning forward on a couch in the lobby, his dark eyes full of longing and forgiveness. Veins pulsing in his hands and forehead. I wanted to have the kind of sex one can have, with one's husband, only in hotels. On Monday I wanted him to hold my hand lightly in the OB-GYN's office as we discussed the treatment of the microadenoma. Then I wanted him to take me home. On the plane, our elbows sharing the armrest, Ken in his sky-blue work-shirt, which he never wears to work so it does not smell like the hospital. Just clean, free Ken-smell.

Eventually Michael came in and leaned against the doorjamb. "You okay?"

Through my fingers, he elided into his son at the pool, reporting that we'd almost been found out by his mother. For an ominous second I flirted with the idea of telling Michael about Zachary, then decided that was not my job, and anyhow what would I say? That episode would have to be written off. Hillary Katzenbach and The Other Michael, after all, not to mention all those tittering couples at the hotel, engaged in similar activities *without* grief and life-threatening illness. It was only sex.

Later I might have time to feel guilty that I did not bother to care how Michael felt when I announced that I had to return, at once, to the hotel. He volunteered to walk me there. I declined. We had a short conversation about how long I'd be in town, when I might return, how and when I would contact, or be contacted by, Dr. Sharon Rieff.

It occurred to me that I hadn't done Michael Davidoff any favors. This weekend wouldn't help him cozy up to his lady lawyer. He would see her for another nine months, a year, during which she would more and more often—postcoitally, say, aiming for a tone that wasn't too strident—go over the game plan of Their Future Together. In her early to midthirties, not even sure if she wanted to make partner or quit and raise the kids that Michael, I knew, would never agree to have. Any woman with an ounce of sense could see that. He wasn't interested! That, finally, was probably why he had agreed to sleep with me. Because now he could confess it to the lawyer and soon she would go the way of Sharon Rieff, angrily longing for him. With any luck, they would eventually manage to stay friends.

The sensible thing for Michael, of course, would be to find a self-sufficient divorcée about my age, preferably with an established career of her own, her kids grown and gone. But he would not do that. Not after Mar. She'd crippled him as surely as he'd crippled her. He'd stick with the perky thirty-two-year-olds. When challenged on this, he would use as proof that he *would* consider an equal, should the right one present herself: Me.

The houseguest who had the sense not to overstay her welcome.

I caught myself dismissing him. Had managed, in the seconds this scenario presented itself, to even find him ugly. His coloration not auburn but a drunkard's outright red. His posture pompous—self-satisfaction coming off him like a *smell*. Strong as coconut tanning lotion. Come on, I scolded myself, anything could happen to him. With the amount he works he might stall his midlife crisis, his face-off with the cosmic emptiness, but he would get there eventually. Even if health problems had to force him there. And *then* he would have a real relationship. But no: at fifty-three, he would capitulate and finally marry one of those thirty-year-olds. A plain, cheerful, uncomplicated one—a dental hygienist. And to no one's surprise, because isn't this story as trite as any other, he would then have children, whom he might, in his dotage, even enjoy. Zachary's son calling his granddad's son uncle, as they dig for worms together in the yard.

And who was I to say that wasn't the marriage he was meant for? That everything else—me included—was what would help him get there?

Michael Davidoff took my face in both hands and planted on me a kiss with all the trappings of deep feeling, as skilled as any movie star's. I missed my husband far too much to process it. But I knew I would remember it, even inhabit it, in memory. The way the bride and groom are always absent at their own wedding but reconstruct it, later, from the pictures.

My walk back to the hotel was a gauntlet of street people. Trembling and Tourettey, cajoling and cursing, like extras from a Bosch painting. They were staking out their assigned panhandling spots, not planted as a personal warning to me, although a surprising number were dirty-haired, dentally challenged females. *Once upon a time, I was a very successful career woman. And my husband was a surgeon . . .*

In my previous life, I kept all my loose change in the front pocket of my purse, and would bestow it on the unfortunates along my route until the change ran out. For all I knew, that change was now all I had. It had been days since I had attempted to ascertain my fortunes. Michael had kept me as you'd keep a child. I had not attempted to withdraw more cash from an ATM since the Victoria's Secret shopping day. Instinctively, I'd been afraid to: did not want to have to resent my husband if he had further cut me off from my own money; did not know what the balances were in our joint accounts; had no idea whether Ken had managed to pay bills, my job in the marital division of labor (as most things were that did not directly involve slicing people open, and, actually, the residents did even that for him, devoted little sous-chefs); had not, obviously, run Quicken, or done any on-line banking; was existing as surely as those streetpeople on the resources on hand, albeit with a much cozier safety net.

But I realized, as I entered the hotel, that I had not even managed yet to ascertain how my room had finally been secured, after the initial difficulty. Clearly it *had* been secured. Room service had been sent to me, and a house doctor. Still, I determined that I would take care of any potential problems now, and got on line at the desk.

At my feet, waiting for his mother, who was settling up her bill ahead of me in line, was a child about the age that Evan would have been. The boy had spread out a fistful of coins on the rug and was presiding over them, gleefully counting out loud. So thrilled with his mastery of the bounty, so full of hope about more to come! Adults can't feel this kind of pleasure in money, even juggling frequent-flyer miles for upgrades. For a moment I allowed myself to dwell on his hands, their unstudied voluptuousness. But now his mother was hurrying him along. "Come on, you can count in the cab." *But I'm almost done!* The coins, carefully sorted by size, scooped up. Kid indignant.

This whole scene stabbed me like new sutures. I got control of myself just as my eyes fuzzed, so that the coins glinted watery, as if through wishing-well water.

"Ma'am?"

Mother and child stormed off in a ragged Cubist cloud of belongings—brass straps on her fine luggage; his transparent Gameboy, electronic guts thrillingly open to view. My turn at the desk. My file retrieved.

The clerk squinted at the saga of my file. He even looked up to take my measure, suspiciously, as an immigration official might. "You have house doctor charges here," he informed me.

"Right."

"It appears," the clerk reported, "that the first night was paid cash, and then we didn't have a credit-card imprint, and there was—and then we got one."

"From whom?"

"You, I assume."

" 'Fraid not."

He investigated further, then delivered this news: "The manager approved taking a plate number over the phone."

"From whom?"

"It wouldn't necessarily say. Wait. Here—Dr. Daniel Kramer."

My kind, efficient therapist had given his very own credit-card number to secure in my behalf an undisturbed stay? Unbelievable. Especially given the amount of the charges—the Four Seasons is hardly cheap.

Waste of money, though presumably accommodations at a private mental hospital are far pricier.

This clerk, considerably more agreeable than the last, said that it would be no problem to transfer the charges to my own plate instead. They wouldn't need a plate; just the number and expiration date would get them an approval code.

Not a single message awaited me in the room. Not Ken. Not even Kramer, ascertaining that I was still alive.

I plugged in my computer, eager. No E-mail. No personal, no professional—zip. But it was the weekend.

I counted my money. Almost $100. Enough to get to the airport, although not enough to pay for a ticket home.

If I were to die like this—just shrivel up, vanish—it would have been more dignified, and certainly more lively, to do it as a road movie. If all I was going to do was screw strangers, might as well vary the backdrops (St. Louis's Golden Arch, the Golden Gate Bridge) rather than just peel off my gray-green suit (not much of a costume drama, either) on the same old bed, same old bathroom.

I sat on the exact place on the bed where I'd sat at Michael's, hating myself, and called Ken again.

"Mea culpa, okay?" I said, hating the nasal sound of my voice. Then the trump card: "Should have, by tomorrow, workup results on pituitary microadenoma. If I don't answer, I'm at the pool."

Suddenly I felt as full of pep and possibility as a caged guinea pig.

It's these rooms! I thought, alarmed, as you will notice, halfway through a long flight, how stuffy the plane is. Put your palm, hopeful, to the air nozzle above you—nothing. *Go home,* Ignatia had commanded in Pittsburgh. *Air no good here.* She was right, even if it had taken me—what? A month?—to long for the comforts of home, where the windows actually opened.

Only then did I realize I had not seen a pool for almost a week. Had not even *remembered* swimming. In my hurry to return to the hotel, to receive Ken's call, I had not even thought to ask Michael if he belonged to a health club. Of course he would! He would go three times a week for comfort and kinship as people used to go to church! Was probably there now, at this very second.

My bathing suit was hanging by one strap over the shower head where I had left it, stiff and crusty, so redolent of chlorine despite the washing that it was hard to believe the fabric was not being reconfigured on a molecular level.

As I tried to swim at the Four Seasons pool under the eye of the same bored guard, among the squeals of splashing children, my life felt reduced to absurdity. Stern in my goggles and bathing cap, I was a deep-sea diver in the rain collecting in a pothole. The only way this could pass for a real pool was in the amount of chlorine used—just as well, if diapered infants are going to piss therein. Real pool, real life: could not clear my brain of the thought that I had neither. Each lap I fantasized that if I did another lap, stretched out the time I was away from the room, the message button would be blinking when I returned. Undulating light like an earring in a bellydancer's navel.

Each lap, pushing off: *Ken!*

But he had not called.

Waiting to hear from the Doctor, then the Doctor. Waiting for phones to ring. Waiting for periods to come or waiting, conversely, for pregnancy. Women wait. Waiting for calls, from men or children, women are *on* call, like doctors. The red eye of the message light, the feminine pink flush of the positive pregnancy test. All my life I had been pecking at expectation like a laboratory pigeon.

What choice did I have, though? For a while after Evan died, I had carried around a Zen book. It was the only thing that comforted me, that seemed to make any sense. But then I decided I didn't have enough strength for that kind of peaceful passivity, that it was too much to ask of myself, and settled back into itchy desire, disappointment.

Back in the room I flipped on CNN to their bizarre anchor—why was her hair so long? Was this sophomore year in college? And why was she always smirking? Why did she always look as if, the minute the camera was no longer trained on her face, she would burst into merriment? Did she not understand that the news was serious business?

"A twenty-eight-year-old woman was electrocuted today," she said—this was in Baltimore, at a hotel, hardly fleabag but a reputable chain I had often used myself—"when she used her key card to admit herself to her room. She had been coming from the hotel's swimming pool." There had been no other electrical problems, and nothing was obvious.

They were investigating.

I heard this sitting wet-haired, in my bathing suit, on the bed, the key card still in my hand.

A current strong enough to kill had come through a wall and traveled up an innocuous square of plastic to a damp hand. It did not quite seem possible, although the anchor's face registered her usual restrained amusement, no more or less. Her eyes flashing occasionally ("Where am I?"). They did not show a picture of the dead woman. I sat through a whole other cycle of third-world strife and sex scandal to hear it again, at the quarter hour, the anchor meeting my eye as if to challenge: "It will be hard for you not to take this as a message, although the message is awfully dumb. 'There is danger everywhere'? 'Live each moment as if it is your last'?"

No new information was provided. The same three, four sentences, unsatisfying as a lap across a hotel pool. I tried the real, top-of-the-hour CNN show to see if hotel electrocution was explored in more detail there, but it was not even mentioned.

Thus I used up almost an hour and only thought on twenty or thirty occasions that Ken had not yet called. Only imagined a baker's dozen of scenarios of how I would pick up the phone, what I would say, what he would say, and what did it matter anyway because we would still have to play out the hand of the marriage in real time, not CNN time or time as it exists in the kind of novels with plots, in which events intervene that determine fate.

Not that there wasn't fate. But it only brought death. And death was not a story. Only the end of a story. The rest of us just wait—has-beens and wanna-bes, like Tiny Tim in his hotel room in Minneapolis, dyeing his hair and plotting his comeback.

By now my bathing suit and hair were dry. I stared at the phone like a child, willing it to ring, and it did.

"Ken?"

Ken: "Hey."

"Hey."

Then the electric silence I'd imagined. A current in which we could each imagine the other alive in time on the other end. In my head his tentative *hey* was an elevator door decisively opening, as on old episodes of *Star Trek*: at first, nothing, but then Ken's DNA recombining itself so that he appeared, whole and arms folded in front of him in his clean green scrubs or no, since this was just in my head, why not naked, the dark hair on his chest swirling in a pattern like the whorl of stars in a Van Gogh sky. In my head I just buried my head in his chest, wordless.

Ken gave me time to do this. Then said: "Sweet."

As if *sweetheart* would be too much, which it would have been, he was exactly right.

He let me drink that. Then asked, "Should I come?"

I said, "Come."

Then added, *Please.*

Aware, because I was right on the brink of the relieved tears that I knew I was going to allow myself—on the brink of them the way, before coming, a woman is on the brink of that, watching pleasure move toward you in reliable rings like those made by a skipped stone—that what I wanted to do was say his name, and I did. And in *Ken* I heard *Evan,* that same soft *e*; aware too of the long *e* in *sweet* and *please* as some kind of contrast, dramatic as yin and yang, out of which was going to come: ease. Not the beginning of things or the end, but the fine, full middle.

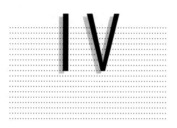

here was nothing wrong with me.

Well, there was something wrong with me. But not much.

I had slept like a baby. Dr. Sharon Rieff called first thing in the morning, brisk and cheerful, before I had even had time to wonder how long I could survive before hearing from her. Thyroid within normal range. The prolactin reading was only a little off. She recited the numbers as if I would know exactly what they meant, but I did not—only that the two sets of numbers were slightly out of balance.

Nothing alarming. Nothing, even, that would require treatment. She would let me be, personally. She would send the test results to my doctor in Cleveland for him to evaluate, but odds are he would simply want to keep an eye on things.

At first I felt not relief, but disappointment. The pituitary microadenoma would have been an explanation. Micro was the right size, and furthermore it was not in my head. A pea for the princess. So much for an immediate, containable cure for fertility problems and whatever else was still going to ail me, once I got over my delight at being restored to my life.

"You don't think," I asked Dr. Rieff, "that it'd be a good idea to try some kind of dosage of the Dostinex?"

There was really no indication of a microadenoma from those

numbers, she said, not enough to even warrant doing an MRI, although, again, I could talk over treatment with my doctor. The galactorrhea—might be related to the elevated prolactin, but might not.

"Could easily be triggered by stress," she said. "Or if there has been any dramatic change in your sex life—I mean the way your breasts are touched . . ."

This was my opening, it appeared, to shoot the shit about Michael Davidoff, girl-to-girl. Before morning coffee, before I had even brushed my teeth. But gratitude for her excellent service aside, I felt I had done my weekly share of dissecting shared men with female physicians. The night before, I had packed, laying out my clothes for the day, that gray suit I knew I would never be able to wear again once I got home, and in the process flipped through the book of The Other Michael's poems before putting it in the suitcase; two pages were stuck together, or rather not properly separated by the printing press, and when I unsealed them carefully with a fingernail there was a poem about—swimming. Poolside, Michael watched his prepubescent daughter swim. Brand-new nipples in Speedo. The girl in her bathing cap slick and friendly as a seal, etc. Nothing out of the ordinary, but the coincidence, especially after the fried swimmer from Baltimore, was hard not to take to heart. From my bed, with the phone pressed to my ear, I could see the glint of the book's pool-blue cover on the top of the open suitcase and the two Michaels mentally pressed themselves together, their edges blurred, as did the two crisp female physicians, at the end of which was an impression of—a nipple. Everything narrowing to the point of that need. Even without one of those exaggerated, conical Madonna bras, a breast like a natural exclamation point, the nipple capping its own amazement with the whole damn business.

Precisely this kind of thought, a couple of days ago, had made me feel like a Looney Tune. Now I just watched the train of thought bob off. It only took a couple of seconds. Interesting how very short a silence can officially be, with someone you don't know.

"No," I said. "To tell you the truth, though, I wish you had a little more of an answer for me. Something—clearer."

She laughed. "Hey, if you read the literature, physicians can't even agree on how best to treat a *yeast infection.*"

"That's encouraging," I said.

"Well, here's an upbeat way to think about it. You appear to be, as they say, 'in touch with your body.' You can read all the signs, how everything interacts. You'd be amazed how few patients—well, you even try to get a clear account of *symptoms.*"

I knew all about this complaint, from my husband. Most of his patients can't even tell their hearts from their stomachs.

"But you had some intuitive sense," she went on, "of how everything came together. So all I can say is: trust it. Like listening to the sounds of a car's engine. Know that doesn't sound very scientific. But—you get a woman sometimes who, months before a bad mammogram, has knocked out coffee, begun to eat tons of tofu. Like her body *knows.* Or chocolate—I mean it does, in fact, have documented antidepressant qualities. Releases the same endorphins as strenuous exercise."

My shrink was a dietitian. This OB-GYN appeared to be a dietitian, too. "So what's the tune-up for this old car?" I asked.

She laughed again. "Sex always helps," she said. "Take Old Betsy for a spin, floor it."

Yet another opening. I declined, yet again, to take the bait. Told her how much I appreciated her help.

"So are you staying at Michael's," she asked, "or the hotel?"

Persistent!

Thanked her again, told her where to send the test results. Would call her, actually, with a fax number.

After Dr. Rieff and I were done, I took Michael's book from my suitcase. It fell open to the swimming poem, which had been secret, hidden; now it seemed I could not flip through the volume without this poem being thrust in my face. I studied it for clues, as if it were the Bible, or the *I Ching*. Here is what I felt: nothing. I leaned into it, as if into the vibration of a tuning fork, and heard: nothing.

Blank slate! The man was a stranger to me!

And there, just like that, was my *Twilight Zone* coin landed on its side again. Restored, just like that, to ordinary not-knowing.

I was right about one thing, though. My husband had, indeed, been on call Sunday morning. He had business at the hospital this morning, too, but then he would come for me, even though that made no sense, really, although maybe it did, because how exactly I would pay for a ticket and get home myself, with no credit-card plate, was unclear.

On this score, some good news: Ken had not been so crassly controlling a husband as to attempt to entrap me by flagging my credit card. The Fraud Department had called me, rather insistently, at home, to make sure some recent charges were mine—in my early days on the lam, I'd paid for some plane tickets myself, rather than going through the company travel agency as I did when I planned better, and manic travel charges apparently cause alarm. Ken had returned their call, concerned, said he wasn't sure how or when I could be reached. When they wouldn't speak to him, since he was not a cardholder, he armed his secretary with my birthday and mother's maiden name, as I'd guessed, and thus they'd tracked my whereabouts during the frantic message period—at least until the plate number was changed and the new card reissued, at the fraud folks' suggestion. Ken assumed I had other cards at the ready. And would have gladly given me all relevant details, or FedExed the new plate to me, if I had deigned to speak to him. Why they hadn't called me at work remains a mystery—I would have gotten the voice mail. But they didn't, probably because Ken's girl had worked so fast.

I almost told Ken, then, about the hotel scam. Decided to pass. Enough of this first, romantic phone call had already been devoted to bookkeeping.

Logistically, we were left only with the question of whether or not I should keep the hotel room until Ken's arrival. Or get a different hotel room. The latter option had occurred to me. I was already packed and ready to go. My mind had snagged, somewhat, on this complexity. Given how little use I'd gotten out of the hotel room thus far (how long had the rental car sat in the garage of The Children's Hospital?), it was really no tragedy to keep the room for the extra day, see if it would be of use. Not a big deal, either—save the embarrassment—to check out, give my one bag, briefcase, and computer to the porter, check back in if that was deemed necessary.

Fact is, I had no idea what Ken would have in mind. Would he think, if it was necessary for him to come and fetch me, that I'd be a shaky, frail Frances Farmer whom he would need to steer by the elbow instead of the floozy who was ready for wild, marriage-affirming Reunion Sex followed by (or preceded by) a nice restaurant, a stroll to the Rodin Museum to see the bronze nudes?

He could be furious.

I had to keep reminding myself of this possibility, even likelihood. I had been gone for a month. Soon August would be over. From friends with living kids, I knew how endless those last days of August were, before school started, as bad as the wait for labor. Labor Day: it never lined up quite right with the calendar. Always seemed to come an awkward number of days before the end of August, or jut out too far into September. Tired as you are of summer, itchy as you are to get to fall, it also seems like: *already*? Wistfully, the way parents talk as their children head to college.

At home, the grass would be mowed, and green. Ken would have managed to turn on the sprinkler. The maid had a key; the kitchen would gleam. Ken is not the kind of man who cannot manage to put the glass he has just used into the dishwasher. In the den, with its paint colors I'd personally selected, amid much grave indecision about yellowish vs. reddish beiges, at whatever point in my life I had cared about such things, the latest volume of *The New England Journal of Medicine* might still be open by his reading chair.

I tried to imagine him single, in a bachelor pad. Could not. A failure of imagination. Of course he would not have to make any effort to "meet women." They would virtually carom into him in hospital hallways. We would have to sell the house. Could not think about this either, although I had no special attachment to it.

Nothing wrong with the house. There was the matter of Evan's room, of course. Parents of dead kids know that there is no way to circumvent the problem of the room as memorial. Leave the stuffed animals on the shelf and you make a sick shrine. Box the toys, reconvert however temporarily into "study" or "guest room," and you pretend to bury the past. Fact is, the room stays there, stolid, foursquare, box only. The box stays in the ground. Even buying a new house doesn't help, because the new house simply does not have *that* room, and who is anyone fooling. Not living in a house? An apartment somewhere foreign, where you have no connections, none of your own things? I'd considered it. Ken's work made that impossible (he could maybe endure a month outside the structure of the schedule that kept him sane, and how could I begrudge him that?), but I imagined a villa somewhere like Tuscany, room after high-ceilinged, plaster-cracking room just empty, the furniture draped with dusty sheets. Wild, hilly garden to poke around in or not.

The line came to me sometimes, petulant, *You deserve that.* Why hadn't Ken suggested it? Is The Vacation not an obvious salve? But then I would pull back. It would not have helped. Well, the tropical foliage of Puerto Vallarta did help Ken. Opened him right up. I held myself back from the trace of bitterness: no scenery would help us now. More critical to keep alive in my head the fantasy of many rooms, just as keeping alive the fantasy of sleeping with a stranger—you could do it, you still had it in you—had proven more fulfilling than the act itself. It was the time *before* the sex, the decision itself, that I'd remember. Sex was sex as a room was a room. Both buried in the box of your head, which is finally all you're married to, pay mortgage on.

For the foreseeable future I would not be divorced, or dead. In the square bed, in the square room, I felt, if not exactly squared away, at least not crazy.

Not pregnant, either. This I discovered in the bathroom. The spot of blood was discreet, dime-sized. The shiver of disappointment, emptiness I felt was automatic. Maybe spotting only, I permitted myself to wishfully think before I caught myself. This dot, dark as type on the new white underwear, was decisive and this was preferable, obviously. A true period that ended whatever sentence I'd been running on in. Too much gunk had built up on the mental walls. My extramarital sex had functioned like a D & C, wiping the slate clean. When my husband and I made love now we could do so, for the first time in a long time, in a context outside of procreation. Not that love doesn't come, always, with the shadow of loss. But at least the thing I'd almost lost could now be the man himself. He certainly deserved at least that much.

When we did make love I would not have forgotten, even if I didn't consciously refer to it, his shock, then his smile, when I stood up to go to the bathroom the day after the delivery and the blood gushed out of me. *Christ,* he said, standing outside the bathroom door, *it looks like you clubbed a seal to death in there.* And he had been to medical school. But he was still surprised, and alarmed, because it was my blood. Doesn't matter that the child is dead. He watched the child emerge from me. Sex is different after that. Even if what was required of us now was that we clear the birth canal of birth—no longer think of that space as The Baby's Room—there would always be the ghost. The little haunting. Not to mention the others who had left their fingerprints on the walls—Hillary, the Davidoff guys.

But that was who we were. And as such was good. Because it meant we knew each other, which included knowing what haunted us. So when Ken told me during the phone call, endearingly nervous, in the way of making conversation, about a TV show he'd watched the night before, that had disturbed his sleep—a plane crash over the Amazon, a seventeen-year-old girl who stayed alive by herself for nine days, picking maggots out of her wounds with her bent engagement ring—I could say, "I guess *she* knows the trouble we seen," and he could laugh, knowing just what I meant. And when I told him about the electrocuted swimmer, the story would have a bite, a solidity. Like buying a car owned by the proverbial little old lady from Pasadena, who hands over meticulous repair records. Here, as per Sharon Rieff's metaphor, was our marital tune-up, our lube and new filters.

I had no Tampax. I would need to buy them in the overpriced hotel shop. Found myself wondering how much breakfast in the hotel dining room would be, whether I should spring for both Tampax and food, thinking about my money the way you think about disposing of the foreign currency you have left, in a foreign airport, down to the very last strangely oversized penny. But then I remembered that I could charge the breakfast to the room, and this made me ecstatic. A hearty breakfast—the *bounty* of it! All I could eat! And Ken coming too, any minute.

Patience. What is the point of middle age, if you haven't learned to wait?

After breakfast and the newspapers (the *Times* confirmed the electrocuted woman in Baltimore, but provided no new information; I would probably have to track down the *Baltimore Sun,* I realized, for a follow-up), I left a message at the desk and walked to the park across the street, where I sat on a bench, close enough to the fountain that a breeze—a breeze in summer always feels like a gift—tickled the water to my face, wafting the smell of fresh mulch from the bed of geraniums behind which, on the grass, a couple necked.

They were grown-ups, not kids, uniformed in full workday regalia, he knotted and belted, she sausaged into pantyhose. They didn't care. They would go back to work with grass stains for this kiss. Her pointy pumps were not kicked off but lined up neatly beside the invisible magic carpet of the kiss that contained them, carried them away. She wore pink linen. The sun glinted on the wrinkles in the dress. What kind of fool wears light-colored linen to fuck in grass before lunchtime, I thought, but then I realized how good it was to see them, to remember kisses that simply had to be had that instant. Nothing in the world but the smooth moistness of lip. Time itself suspended. This was not a casual relationship; they would marry, these two, but they weren't sure of it yet, and that was precisely what made it lovely. His hand hovered over her back, as if to touch her would simply be too much sensation to endure.

I realized that I was staring. It was lovely. Don't put your hand down, I thought. Wait. When that hand lands on her back she should be able to come, just from the slightest pressure of your hand on the linen. This kiss will be a memory planted right down in the soil of her that will bloom, annually, every time she smells summer earth.

And that second they obeyed me. They pulled apart, they just stared at each other, and I felt a smile flushing my face as I thought, if I truly practiced what I preach *I* could come from this, from the idea of it: patience! Restraint! Then I almost laughed out loud at myself, a horny middle-aged woman of dubious sanity, with no money, alone in a city.

I had left *The Merck Manual* in the end-table drawer, with the Bible. This felt pleasingly ceremonial, even though, as a gesture, it did not mean much (would have to buy a new one, anyway, in a month or so).

"Zachary!" I heard, and turned sharply.

"Zachary, you stop right there. Zach!"

Not Zach Davidoff. A child, twoish, racing toward the fountain. The mother behind, hot, cross, laden with stroller and the diaper bag bulging with diapers and wipes, the bottle and plastic bag of Cheerios, the extra pacifier, the immense weight of motherhood—"Young man, you stop this instant! I said no! You stop *now!*"

The weight of the diaper bag was tipping the stroller with its inadequate plastic wheels as she tried to reach him. I got up too. I ran. I got to them just as the kid deftly hurled himself over the edge of the fountain, laughing as his mother just stood and screamed, her hands held away from her body and shaking—exactly the posture, exactly the scream of that famous Vietnam photo, the nude and napalmed child running away from the mayhem.

They always warn you, as if you don't have enough to worry about, that babies can drown in even an inch of water. But the child was fine. Delighted. I reached the fountain and scooped him up while the mother screamed. Clothes, shoes wet but his laughter liquid as I grabbed him, hitched him aloft to the screaming mother and she took him, keening his name.

In the seconds in which the soaked child squirmed from my arms to hers the background behind us blurred into a sea of primary colors with red predominating, like the cheering audience in the stands for a bullfight, but as she took him from me the focus deepened so that I saw that the lovers behind the geraniums now sat up, alert, watching us. Enjoying the theater, the happy ending. Smiling, their hands lightly joined. I felt the arc of my now-wet arms and knew that I was the link that joined the lovers to the mother, sex to parenthood; with a lungful of pride and confidence I saw that I understood something primal I would never have dug down to the loam of, had I not been forced. But here it was, and it was not fragile, not mummified, did not have to be preserved carefully wrapped under special lights. It could be held aloft like the laughing baby, it could take the sun and the breeze, it was strong.

"My God," the woman said. "How could he be so *fast*?"

"They're fast," I said.

"Oh thank you," she said and, with the baby between us— reaching now for the fountain, whining his unquenchable need to repeat the scene—she hugged me. "Thanks!"

We made a baby sandwich, then grinned as we pulled quickly apart, and she, realizing she'd gotten my shirt wet, grimaced in apology.

"You're going to have to put him back in," I said, "or he won't give you any peace."

She sighed, agreeing. "God only knows what's in that water."

"Well, he's not going to drink gallons of it."

"I was just at the museum this morning, looking at the mummies," she said. The coincidence of both of us having mummies on the brain was not lost to me. "Do you know what most of them died of, in ancient Egypt?" I shook my head, smiling. "Stomach bugs," she told me. "Twenty-four-hour GI jobs."

"Antibiotics," I said. "You don't think about 'em."

"Right. Forget the wheel. Forget electricity. Penicillin is the cornerstone of our civilization. Thanks so much. I—"

"I know," I said.

The baby screamed, reached, yanked her. She rolled her eyes.

"I know it's hard," I said, "but try to enjoy it."

"Yeah, yeah. It'll all be over soon enough, everybody keeps telling me. But when you're stuck in the middle of it, it feels—"

"Yes, but when you feel trapped like that you can always take a deep breath, close your eyes, put your face to the sun. Sort of step out of it, get your bearings."

She gave me a full-throated laugh. "And who are you exactly, the Dalai Lama?"

"Just someone who has been there, done that."

Throughout this exchange she had been steadying the stroller with her knee, trying to hold the child's legs straight and still enough to remove his shoes, her eyes and head darting to avoid his swipes and punches, to hear me over his remonstrances. I remembered, as I thought I wouldn't, how it felt to be that manacled. But I also remembered—as I watched her turn one miniature basketball shoe upside down and attempt to drain the water out of it, with an expression of defeat, then automatically, unconsciously, lovingly squeezing the pale foot—how sexy babies are.

"When are you due?" I asked.

Her surprise was so strong, she almost spurted it. "I would hate to think I'm showing. I am, like, two weeks into this thing, tops."

I had no idea, actually, why I'd asked. Pregnancy must indeed bestow that nimbus attributed to it, a kind of fairy dust that glimmers around the outlines of the breasts and hips for anyone attuned to such things, as I was. I had watched so carefully for the signs in myself, for so many years. Now what I felt growing in me was possibility itself. Hope.

The woman was now staring at me, curious. "How about you?" she asked. "How old are yours?"

I caught myself about to tell the comfortable lie of the kid in college, that Brown University freshman on the tennis or swim team so familiar he could have been real. The lie, I realized, was over. I could never use it again. But "dead" did not seem appropriate either; for a pregnant stranger, it was almost hostile. Yet I had to say something. Once again, the inescapability of the Empty Bedroom.

But the right thing suddenly came to me. I held up my thumb and forefinger like a Hindu deity to squeeze the pollen-sized speck that was my future, and she turned to me with the silent congratulations of her generous smile.

That was a lie, too. But a better one.

"I am definitely too old for this," she said, as she airlifted the child by his armpits back into the fountain. "Not just over the hill.

I can't even see the hill from here. I am *so tired*," she said. "Hey, are you hungry? I could go for a hot dog. Just the prescribed healthy food for a pregnant person."

Because her son was in no way ready to leave the fountain, I volunteered to fetch the hot dog for her, from a vending cart across the street. She was extremely grateful. We talked for a half hour or so about the things women talk about. Exchanged war stories about labor and delivery; discussed the havoc that children wreak on marriage and career (she was yet another lawyer, which even I, with my mind obsessed with synchronicity, did not make anything of). The conversation might have irritated me back home. I had little patience for domestic blow-by-blows, had never managed to get much from playground friendships. But because we would not see each other again and knew it, the simple daili-ness of our exchange touched me.

When she left, I realized the lovers had left as well, while I wasn't paying attention. I found myself staring at the grass where they'd been, expecting some kind of a memorial, like a slant of afternoon light. Did not see it. Still, I felt as if I had closed some-thing.

Ken was going to be with me so soon I could hardly stand it. For a second I felt all of my newfound calm deserting me. Where should I be when he arrived? I'd checked out of the hotel room after all, repaying my shrink in the process. Sitting in the lobby seemed desperate. What I wanted to do was wait here, by the fountain. I wanted to be at ease, and at some point look in the direction of the hotel and see him coming toward me. A trick of timing. It was stupidly romantic, meaningless as mutual orgasm or Rockettes kicking or the synchronized swimming in Busby Berkeley films, but that was what I wanted. I'd told them at the desk that if my husband came to say I was in the park, but what if the desk staff had changed over? I did not want Ken to have to sit in the lobby, waiting for me. I did not want him to merely be told that I'd checked out. That would not please him at all. That would not be fair. I should have left a note, I thought, then attempted to calm myself down by remembering the woman in pink linen, the hand hovering on her back. There was *no suspense* anymore, after all. He was coming. He would be here soon.

Still my brain was chattering *Go back, stay here.*

Could not make up my mind. *Go back, stay here.*

For a while I sat with my eyes trained toward the hotel, but then I forced myself to look away. Patience, I thought.

When I next allowed myself to look, there he was, just as I had hoped. He had spotted me. Nothing but relieved welcome in his smile. And the very blue shirt I had predicted, sleeves rolled up, arms swinging as he came toward me with his long, loose stride but also the tension of his waiting, his holding back. Not until he was closer did he say, slightly breathless from the trip and the heat, from the sheer satisfaction of finding me exactly where I was supposed to be, *Claire.*

ACKNOWLEDGMENTS

The author would like to thank the following people for their valiant help as diagnosticians of the imaginary: Ellen Feld, MD; Signe Lundberg, PhD; Allen Oseroff, MD; and Victor Zachian, MD. Thanks as well to members of the security staffs at the Four Seasons Hotel in Philadelphia and the Westin William Penn Hotel in Pittsburgh, who have asked to remain anonymous. Lastly, my gratitude to Jeanne Tift and Daniel Menaker at Random House.

ABOUT THE AUTHOR

LISA ZEIDNER is the author of three novels and two poetry collections—one, *Pocket Sundial*, won the Brittingham Prize. Her stories, essays, and reviews have appeared in many publications, including *GQ* and *The New York Times*. She is a professor at Rutgers University and lives in Haddonfield, NJ, with her husband and son.

ABOUT THE TYPE

This book was set in Bembo, a typeface based on an old-style Roman face that was used for Cardinal Bembo's tract *De Aetna* in 1495. Bembo was cut by Francisco Griffo in the early sixteenth century. The Lanston Monotype Company of Philadelphia brought the well-proportioned letterforms of Bembo to the United States in the 1930s.